Bra[ndi creates] ... acte[rs that will] ...

—CECELIA DOWDY
AUTHOR OF CHESAPEAKE WEDDINGS

you ... and hold you fast. Brandi Boddie has written a book that is compelling and heart tugging. I didn't want it to end.

—MARY CONNEALY
AUTHOR OF THE KINCAID BRIDES SERIES

Not afraid to tackle sensitive subjects, Brandi Boddie weaves an intriguing romance around fascinating characters. In *The Preacher's Wife* Ms. Boddie drew me into the story of 1870s' social prejudice in a small Kansas town. The more I read, the more caught up in the lives of these brave settlers I became. Truly a rewarding read.

—Donita K. Paul
Best-selling author of the Dragon Keeper Chronicles and Chronicles of Chiril

The PREACHER'S Wife

The PREACHER'S Wife

Brides of Assurance

BOOK ONE

BRANDI BODDIE

REALMS

Most CHARISMA HOUSE BOOK GROUP products are available at special quantity discounts for bulk purchase for sales promotions, premiums, fund-raising, and educational needs. For details, write Charisma House Book Group, 600 Rinehart Road, Lake Mary, Florida 32746, or telephone (407) 333-0600.

THE PREACHER'S WIFE by Brandi Boddie
Published by Realms
Charisma Media/Charisma House Book Group
600 Rinehart Road
Lake Mary, Florida 32746
www.charismahouse.com

Unless otherwise noted, all Scripture quotations are from the King James Version of the Bible.

The characters in this book are fictitious unless they are historical figures explicitly named. Otherwise, any resemblance to actual people, whether living or dead, is coincidental.

Cover design by Bill Johnson

Visit the author's website at http://brandiboddie.blogspot.com/.

Library of Congress Cataloging-in-Publication Data:

Boddie, Brandi.
  The preacher's wife / Brandi Boddie.
      p. cm. -- (Brides of Assurance ; bk. 1)
    ISBN 978-1-61638-843-0 (trade paper) -- ISBN 978-1-61638-844-7 (e-book)
    1. Rural clergy--Fiction. 2. Widowers--Fiction. 3. Women dancers--Fiction. 4. Bars (Drinking establishments)--Fiction. 5. Frontier and pioneer life--Fiction. 6. Kansas--Fiction. I. Title.
    PS3602.O32564P74 2012
    813'.6--dc22
                                        2012025536

First edition

13 14 15 16 17 — 987654321
Printed in the United States of America

To James,

whose love and encouragement served to make this long-held dream a reality.

I'm blessed to call you my husband.

Acknowledgments

I'D LIKE TO thank my agent, Kimberly Shumate of Living Word Literary Agency, for taking a chance on this first-time writer. Your expertise and support have been invaluable.

I'd also like to thank the members of ACFW's Colorado Springs chapter of Worship Write Witness for welcoming me into their community when I first moved to Colorado. This journey would have been lonely without you.

Thanks to my editor, Lori Vanden Bosch, for her knowledge and time spent getting my writing into top form.

Thank you to the entire Charisma House team and authors for welcoming and supporting me throughout the entire process.

And a big expression of gratitude and praise to God, who made the desire of my heart come to be.

Chapter 1

July 1870, Kansas Plains

WHAT DID *I get myself into?* Rowe Winford carried his three large valises from the passenger train to the station wait area. He had arrived in Claywalk, Kansas, sooner than he expected. Then again, he had been daydreaming the entire trip, from the carriage ride in Richmond, Virginia, all the way west on the tracks of the Missouri-Kansas-Texas Railroad.

So this was to be his new home, away from the war reformations, away from the bittersweet memories of his late wife, Josephine, and their stillborn son. The land seemed to engulf every living thing in its wide-ranging vastness. He felt like a tiny speck upon the face of the green, rolling earth.

"Over here, sir." A tall, lean man in rugged canvas trousers, work shirt, and Stetson hat waved him over to the other side of the wait area. A small schooner and horse awaited him.

"Welcome to Kansas, Rev'ren." The man's white teeth flashed in his tanned face as he grinned. "We wouldn't have expected you this early if you hadn't sent that letter. I'm Dustin Sterling." He stuck out his hand. "My friends call me Dusty. David Charlton sent me to come get you and take you to our lil' town of Assurance down the road."

Rowe shook his hand. It was rough with calluses. He

guessed him to be a horseman or rancher of sorts. "It's a pleasure to meet you, Dusty. My name is Rowe Winford, but how did you know I was the new minister?"

He pointed to Rowe's overcoat and gray trousers. "Clothes don't get that fancy in these parts. I knew you must be one of them city preachers back East."

"Richmond."

"Yep, I was right." He picked up Rowe's valises and hoisted them into the schooner. "Well, you'll get used to this place soon enough, if you have the mind to."

Dusty drove him away from the train station. The trip toward the "lil' town of Assurance down the road" turned out to be more along the lines of sixty minutes. Rowe passed the time taking in the nearly treeless plains and the endless open sky. To his left and right he found himself surrounded in a sea of green grass.

"We just got rain last night, after a dry spell." Dusty chatted amiably along the way about the land. "You have to watch out for the July wind."

"Wind? There's barely a breeze out." As the words escaped Rowe's lips, a sudden gust blew in his face. He grabbed hold of his hat before it flew from his head. "Where did that come from?" He coughed as the wind forced air down his throat.

Dusty chuckled. "Some say the devil's in the wind. That's how come it knocks you off your feet."

"Well, as long as we can keep him in the wind and out of town, things should be alright."

The wiry man cast him a wry glance. "'Fraid you might be getting here too late then, Rev'ren'. The devil's come and set up shop in Assurance. And, sadly, business is sure boomin'."

"What do you mean?"

Dusty shook his head. "There's a saloon run by a businessman named Jason Garth. He can get a man to part with his wallet faster than a rattler strikes your heel. His girls help, with their short skirts and paid services."

"You mean prostitution."

Dusty shrugged. "I went to the dancehall before it got bad the last year or so. I haven't been lately, but you'll hear things. You'll get your fill of gossip in Assurance."

Rowe thought about the people who hired him. "What about the church? Haven't they tried to put a stop to what the saloon is doing?"

"They grumble mostly. Folks here believe they shouldn't sully their hands with the things of the world. Much easier to judge from a distance, I suspect, but I'm just a hired worker."

"Aren't you also a town citizen?"

He shook his head. "I'm all the way from San Antone. David Charlton hired me to tend his cattle, but I used to drive longhorns up here to the railroad."

"Well, it sounds like the people of the church don't want to confront corruption."

The cowboy gave him another look. "Maybe that's why they hired you."

Rowe chewed on the inside of his jaw. His first position as head of a church. An apathetic one, from what Dusty implied. He could prove himself by going after the saloon and its seedy practices, but what would be harder, doing that or convincing the church to get their hands dirty along with him?

"Get thee clothed, heathen woman!" A man yelled down at her from the raised dais of the town square. "Thou art the scourge of this fine land, with your harlot's garments!" He shook his fists.

"I'm not a harlot. I'm just a saloon and dancehall girl." Words she had repeated all too often.

Marissa Pierce recognized the man as a traveling speaker, clutching his worn Bible to his chest. She hurried along the edge of the main road toward the bank, doing her best to hide her face from the disapproving looks from several of Assurance's finest and upstanding populace.

They would be right to judge me if I was an evening lady, she thought. *I wish they knew the truth.*

She walked faster, adjusting her headpiece in a self-conscious attempt to push down the high feathers. Jason Garth, proprietor of the town's only saloon, sent her out on a last-minute errand while she was getting dressed for the weekly Wednesday Night Revue. The money had to be deposited in the bank before it closed today, he stressed. Well, he could have let her know that earlier, before she changed into the tawdry costume!

More than a few men eyed her in her knee-length ruffled skirt and soft-soled dance boots peeking out from her coat. She knew a number of them as patrons. Those walking with wives, mothers, or another respectable woman had the presence of mind to avert their gazes.

"Have you no shame, lady of the night?" The orator cried in the profession's flowery prose.

"More than you'll ever know," she muttered.

Marissa kept her back straight and face forward, tightly gripping the leather money satchel that held the saloon's ill-begotten earnings. Would that she could put a stop to the corruption and leave the shady establishment today, but soon she would be away from it all. Her saloon contract with Jason was about to end, and she had some money saved for room and board.

She considered her investment in a small share of the general goods store in Claywalk that was up for sale. If she received all the money due her, it would be enough to live off of until she found employment in the nearby town.

A rush of excitement surged through her as she contemplated a new life elsewhere. She would be free, in a respectable position where no one knew of her horrible past.

Marissa slowed her steps as a schooner rolled down the street. A dark-suited man seated atop peered about curiously, shielding his eyes from the afternoon sun.

"That must be our new preacher." Linda Walsh, the town's young seamstress, walked up beside Marissa. Always eager for conversation, Linda would speak to anyone who stopped to listen, as Marissa had learned since coming back to Assurance a couple years ago. "We weren't expecting him for another two weeks. I wonder what made him take off from home so fast."

Marissa groaned at the thought of meeting another preacher. Every preacher she came across had turned her away once they discovered her profession.

She watched the small schooner pull up to the local inn. She recognized the driver Dusty Sterling seated beside the other man. Dusty hopped down and tethered the horses. The man in black stepped onto the dusty curb. His recently polished boots gleamed.

"Fancy one, he is," Linda continued. "I hear he comes from a city somewhere in Virginia."

"Where did you hear that?"

"It was in the paper a month ago. Our advertisement for a new preacher was answered from a man back East."

Marissa focused again on what was in front of her. The traveler indeed looked foreign to the prairie. Not a hint of travel dust stuck to his long, black frock coat and four-in-hand necktie, probably changed into just before departing the train. His gray pants were new and expertly tailored. He removed his hat briefly to wipe his brow, and Marissa saw the dark, wavy hair cropped close to his head.

"He doesn't have a wife or children with him. Such a

5

shame." Linda clucked her tongue. "He's a handsome fellow, for certain."

Marissa agreed with her on that. He must have stood over six feet tall, with broad shoulders and a powerful build. The man's profile was strong and rigid, his square jaw and straight nose a true delight for the eyes. Assurance's former preacher, Reverend Thomas, did not look like this.

"Would having a wife and children make him a better preacher?"

Linda tossed her a look. "That's got nothing to do with it. One ought to be settled down at a certain age, wouldn't you say so? Instead of running wild with the barmen?"

Marissa absorbed the sting of emotional pain. Anything she said in response would not sway Linda or anyone else's notion that she was just a beer-serving streetwalker. She put on a polite stoic face. "I'm sure the ladies of this town will clamor for his attention. Will you excuse me, Miss Linda? I should be going."

She left the seamstress just as Dusty carried the new preacher's valises inside the inn. The preacher moved to follow then stopped short, pausing for Marissa to walk past. Marissa saw his blue eyes widen and take in her entire form, from the feathered hat on her head to the dainty-heeled boots on her feet. By his expression she didn't know whether he admired or disapproved.

His lips settled into a firm line of what looked to be distaste, and she got her answer.

The preacher hadn't been there for an hour and already she drew out his scorn. Marissa returned the stare until her image of him blurred with beckoning tears.

He jolted from his perusal. His low, straight brows flicked. "Good day to you, ma'am." He amiably tipped his hat to her.

She paused, not used to being addressed in that fashion. Kindness was in his greeting, not the sarcasm she normally heard from others. Marissa tilted her head to get a clear look at him. His eyes were friendly, calm deep pools. The rest of his face, with its strong, angular lines, remained cordial.

"Good day," she replied, hoarse. Awkwardness seized her person. Marissa hastily continued on her way to the bank.

Rowe stared after the brightly costumed woman, not noticing Dusty come from the inn until he stood in front of him, blocking the view.

"Your cabin by the lake is still bein' cleared. The Charltons will pay for your stay here since they don't have room at the farmhouse."

"That's kind of them, Dusty. Who is that saloon woman? I hoped she didn't think me impertinent for stepping in her path."

Dusty squinted in the distance. "Oh, Arrow Missy? She's a dancer down at Jason's."

Dancer. That explained the light-stepping gait. "Why do you call her that?"

"She's got a sharp tongue and even sharper aim with the drinks. That is, before I stopped going there." Dusty scratched his chin.

"I think I upset her. She looked sad." Rowe studied her shrinking form as she went inside the bank. She was a lovely young woman, tall and raven-haired. Her features carried an exotic lilt. He guessed her to be in her early twenties.

If he wasn't the one who caused her to be upset, then what made the tears brim in her eyes?

"You carrying that last bag in, or you want me to do it?"

Rowe picked up his valise. "I've got it, Dusty." He went inside the inn, glancing one more time in the direction of the bank, his mind still on the melancholy woman with the dancing boots.

Chapter 2

TWELVE CASES OF whiskey containing nine bottles apiece. Add four cases of bourbon, and we have one hundred and forty-four bottles in total." Jason Garth, owner of Jason's Saloon and Dancehall, stacked the ledger books on the table. His long face stretched into a smile as he pushed several lank strands of prematurely graying brown hair off his forehead. "It's going to be a very good week, wouldn't you say, darlin'?"

Marissa dragged her heel under the table, watching him take out a pencil and record the respective amounts. Last night had been a good night for the saloon. Tonight would also likely be a winner. Men were sure to come out in droves for the Revue this evening, eager to spend their hard-earned money from the production of crops, livestock, and merchant goods on strong drink. Their money went to the saloon girls too if they persuaded the men to dance or buy them a libation.

"Yes," she replied, her enthusiasm for the work long gone. "We earned double the amount we usually make in one evening."

Jason smiled slyly. "Triple, actually. You were right about reducing the drink prices for large crowds so they could buy more. With that head for business, I might put you in charge of the bar counter soon." His pale green eyes glinted. "What do you say to that?"

"The last time you put me behind the counter you charged customers more than the actual price of drinks. May I lower the prices?"

"No, there's a profit to be made. You can't give away liquor wholesale."

"That's not what I'm saying. Give them a reasonable price. I feel like we're cheating them."

He chortled. "Maybe I was wrong about you havin' a head for business. Listen, if you want to be a partner in this, you have to do it the way I taught you."

Marissa listened to the saloon girls outside in the hall, giggling and chatting with each other as they prepared for another evening of entertainment. Some of the ladies made a profit both on and off the floor from the male townsfolk, having no qualms about getting money in any way possible. She flatly refused the latter method. Jason had tried to make her into a "painted cat" with one horrendous experience that she wanted nothing to do with ever again.

Even now she had to hold her emotions in check, lest she relive the pain and revulsion.

"Our 'partnership,' Jason, never existed. My contract is soon to expire. I'm going to leave here and open my own business."

He laughed. "Selling what? The wares you have now make you a lot of money."

She stiffened in the wooden chair. "You know I don't sell my 'wares,' nor have I ever. I serve ale behind the counter and keep conversation with the customers. I dance—"

"Exactly. You have a standing-up position. If all my gals were paid just to be looked at and not touched, like you, they wouldn't complain. You've got a good thing goin' here." He reached over the table and grabbed her arms. The table dug into her stomach as he pulled her close. "You will never be more than a saloon girl in this town," he said quietly, a hint of menace in his tone. "With me, you can at least make it a profitable business."

"I can make my own profit, without ill means." She shook

free of his grasp, adjusted her costume, and walked out of Jason's office.

An hour later Marissa found herself holding on to her dance partner for dear life as he lifted her clean off her feet. Railroad worker Keith McCauley yipped and hoorayed as he moved to the music. "You havin' fun, Arrow Missy?" he yelled over the piano and the other dancers.

It couldn't be called dancing. His movements jerked and whirled far out of time with the piano keys and hurdy-gurdy strains. She scraped the toe of her boot on the sawdust-covered floor as she came down from her ascent.

The song ended, thankfully, and Keith released her from his whirling dervish. She grabbed hold onto the nearest sturdy object, a wooden banister in the corner.

"How about a drink?" She led him to the bar once she regained her equilibrium. "I could use one."

He caught her by the bodice ruffle. "You sure can. You're practically about to stumble over."

She grudgingly settled into the saloon's usual money-making routine as she took her place on one of the empty stools.

"Give us two of your best ales," Keith ordered the clerk behind the counter.

Marissa tried to swallow her guilt at her part in fooling him. Unbeknownst to the man, her drink was never made with alcohol but with weak tea. His drink contained the real potency. She kept him in conversation as the clerk poured. "How's that rail work coming along?"

"Real good. We just laid four miles of track goin' further into Indian Territory."

"Keep that up and you'll cover that area in no time."

The mugs were placed in front of them. She took a sip of her "ale," frowning at the blandness of it.

"Too strong for you, honey?" Keith took two swigs from his mug.

"No." For all the gallons of the weak brewed tea she had to drink every night, the least the bartenders could do was put sugar in it. But Jason was a cheapskate. At that minute he was still in his office, poring over his ledger books, accounting for every fraudulently earned penny.

Were all men either mean-spirited or controlling like him, she wondered, or stupid enough to be taken advantage of, like his patrons?

The image of the handsome preacher she saw in town that afternoon flashed in her mind. It was odd that she thought of him at that instant. He probably was not mean or gullible, but he was a preacher, and preachers didn't associate with her kind.

Although something about him struck her as being different. He showed her a modicum of respect by not seizing the opportunity to condemn her in front of the town like the traveling orator had done.

She put her foot down. If she wanted respect from others, it was time she showed respect for herself.

"That's it." Marissa set her mug on the counter, splashing tea across it. "I can't do this anymore. Keith, you're being cheated. My ale isn't real. It's tea."

The clerk heard her outburst over the piano tune and whirled around. "You're drunk, Marissa. Of course your drink is real. I poured it for you myself."

She steeled herself against his challenging glare. "No, Pete, I'm not drunk. I'm perfectly aware of how we're all making men pay their right arms for weak tea and colored water." She turned to her dance partner. "Did you hear what I said, Keith?"

Keith gazed at her with lovestruck eyes, heavy from the

five brandies he consumed beforehand. "Now you're not thinkin' o' jumpin' on that train to Indian Territory and leavin' me, are you? I'd sure miss that pretty face. Your whiskey-colored eyes..."

"Whiskey-colored eyes?" Marissa wanted to tear the mug from his hand and tell him again that he was being cheated out of his hard-earned wages. She had the urge to jump on the counter and yell it out to the whole saloon, but Pete hovered inches away, ready to drag her by the hair if she spoke any further.

"You better shut your mouth if you don't want me telling Jason what you said. He'll drown you in what you're drinking." Pete seized her mug and topped it with more tea. "Now get the gentleman beside you to take you for another dance once he's finished with his ale."

Keith grinned, lopsided, and ordered her another drink in advance for the second round of dancing.

Marissa lifted her mug. The watery tea did nothing to wash the bitter taste that filled her mouth.

The racing wind continued to blow on into the evening as Rowe lay flat on the small hotel bed, hands behind his head as he stared up at the ceiling. What was he to do on his first night in his new town? It was still early, and he had already had supper in the dining room downstairs.

He touched a picture of his family that rested on the nightstand. He shouldn't have taken it out of his valise, yet the image comforted him. His parents and three brothers stood in the foreground, while he and his wife, Josephine, were seated on the small couch. Her face exuded contentment. She had told him the morning before the photograph was taken that she was carrying their first child.

He let out a long, wearied sigh. Did the photograph truly

bring comfort, or remind him of a home he could never go to again?

Josephine was gone. His parents were aging, and his brothers all had lives of their own on the family's tobacco farm. There was no place for him there as a lone twenty-eight-year-old man.

He jumped to his feet before that familiar longing started to sink into his skin, rendering him unable to do anything except fall into self-pity. He had to move on. Somehow.

"God, You've provided me with a new life in a different part of the country. Help me to make the most of it by serving You." Rowe prayed quickly against the crippling thoughts.

He had to do something to take his mind off the pain. Rowe left the hotel and strolled down the wide dirt road that served as Assurance's main thoroughfare. The extent of the town's development was two rows of shops that ran parallel to the main square.

Rowe heard an old piano's *tink-link-a-link* from somewhere. He walked farther and found the source of the music coming from a saloon. The wooden sign above the structure shouted JASON'S SALOON AND DANCEHALL in big red and white letters.

He remembered the woman he bumped into that afternoon. "Arrow Missy" worked there.

"Come on in, fancy feller." A saloon clerk in a slightly worn coat invited him from the doorway. "Jason ain't got a charge to take a look at the ladies."

"Thank you, but I'd rather not." Instinct told him to pass by, but she was inside that place. She intrigued him. He got an unexplained burst of excitement at the chance of seeing her again.

"You sure you can't be persuaded by a cool drink and a pretty woman, sir?"

No woman in that questionable place could make him

forget his principles. He simply needed to make his amends to the young lady and leave. But what if someone saw him go in? What would the citizens think of their new preacher entering a saloon, on his first day in town, no less? It would be nigh impossible to explain that his intentions did not involve imbibing or paying for the company of immoral women.

Rowe hovered near the entrance. His feet seemed to be blocked by an invisible barricade. Scanning the dancehall through the open doorway, he saw bright skirts whirling about stocking-clad legs and men's hats flying in the air. He had to go in and apologize to the young woman. There was no admission price, as the clerk mentioned. The proprietor Jason would be just as pleased if he ordered any type of drink, so long as he paid for it. Emboldened by his reasoning, Rowe gave a nod to the clerk. "I'll come in."

"That's more like it." The clerk made way for him. Rowe dashed in before his confidence had a chance to wane.

Immediately his nostrils were assaulted with the mingling scent of smoke, sweat, beer, and damp sawdust. He brushed by some unwashed cattlemen at the gambling table. He could tell their occupation not just from the clothes they wore but also from the smell emanating from them.

He kept on until he sighted her at the bar, below the hanging brass lamps. She stood behind the counter, serving drinks to a group of four men on the stools. She was smiling, but she didn't look particularly happy.

He seated himself on a stool next to the men. They tossed curious glances his way. Rowe figured it was due to his clothes and unfamiliar face. He nodded a greeting, and they shifted their attention back on the woman.

"I'll have another rye, Missy," said one.

"Coming right up, Bill. You, sir, what'll you—?" She spun without seeing Rowe's face but broke off midsentence once she did.

"I—" He couldn't speak either. She wore the full costume he'd seen before, only no long coat was there to conceal it. He turned his eyes away from the lacy bodice and folds of material draped artfully about her form. *You know being a preacher doesn't let you forget you're a man. But don't be rude.* "Good evening." He managed a smile. "I'll have coffee, please."

She wiped her hands on her apron and proceeded to pour Bill his drink before setting a small cup and coffeepot in front of Rowe. "I find it odd that you would come to this establishment, sir." Her full lips pressed together as she poured steaming coffee into the cup. One hand rested on her hip, accentuated by the full pouf of her skirt.

"I knew it's where you would be." He smelled a faint lavender scent on her, a much appreciated respite from the other questionable odors about the room.

She raised her smooth black eyebrows in question. "Why are you looking for me?"

He wrapped his fingers around the warm cup and watched the steam rise from it in curlicues. "We ran into each other in town today."

"You stared at me because of my costume. I remember, Reverend."

He sat up taller, surprised by her knowledge of his identity. Others at the bar heard her and turned. He looked down at his coffee. "My apologies for offending you. The costume is, uh, colorful."

She handed the coffeepot to one of the ladies serving tables. "You can say revealing. That's what it is. It's meant to get attention."

She cut through his awkwardness like a steel lancet. *Arrow Missy, assuredly!*

"My name is Rowe Winford. And you are?" He held out his hand.

"Arrow Missy is what I'm called." She stared at his outstretched fingers, as though deciding if she should grasp them. Her long, elegant hand disappeared in his wide palm.

"I've heard of your stage name, but your Christian name?" He spoke kindly, as gently as possible. Her skin was soft and smooth beneath his fingers. Silk.

She softened her tone. "Marissa Pierce. I guess my reputation as a saloon girl precedes me." She withdrew her hand and stepped lightly to the right, her agile grace evident in that small movement.

"That, and the origin of your name, although I've heard nothing too bad." He teased, and he hoped she took it as such.

Marissa huffed. "Ha! In this town? I don't believe you, even if you are a preacher man." She nodded to his mug. "How's your coffee?"

He inhaled the fresh roast and took a sip of the strong, hot brew. "Perfect. Pitch-black the way I like it. So you don't prefer the town of Assurance?"

"No." She dropped her voice. "This is not the life I intend to maintain for the rest of my days."

"Are you from somewhere else?"

"I was born here, but I left with my mother and father to live in St. Louis. We lived in Missouri for nine years until I had to come back to this town. I liked Assurance when I was a child. Now..." She looked off at some faraway object, her eyes hooding mysteriously. "I guess it's not a place where I can thrive."

Marissa revealed much, but Rowe understood little of what she actually referred to. If she didn't want to be in Assurance, why did she stay? He considered the possibility of her having a family or a sickly parent that required her financial support. "Does your family live here with you?"

"My mother died three years ago. My father is off somewhere on a riverboat, trying to pay his gambling debts, as far as I know." She pursed her lips and gave a small shake of her head, saying no more.

"You said this town isn't a place where you can thrive. What do you think you need?"

"You do ask a lot of questions." She watched him with her light brown eyes, seemingly perplexed. "You are the strangest preacher man I've ever seen."

"Why?"

She threw out her hands. "Look where you are and to whom you're speaking!"

Rowe kept his composure in the face of her outburst. "This isn't my first time in a public house. I've had to retrieve many a missing husband or wayward son. I'd be a very ineffective minister if I kept my conversations strictly within a church."

Marissa mopped the counter where it was wet from sweating glasses and spilled drinks. "Well, don't start a sermon in here. You'll get run out quicker than you can bow your head."

"Don't worry. It wasn't my intention."

"What was your intention, if I may ask?"

Her eyes reflected an inner sadness beneath their bold gaze. The hurt ran deep, he sensed, because her sad countenance never left completely.

"Missy!" Another patron summoned her. "Let me buy you a drink."

Marissa shifted her body, hands on hips. "You know I don't drink while I'm serving customers, John."

The man shot a Seated Liberty Dollar down the bar counter. She promptly stopped the coin between her fingers.

"Make it a double Wild Rogue, hon. Only the best for you."

She took a bottle from under the counter and poured herself a double shot. "To your generosity." She gulped it back in one swallow.

Rowe raised his eyebrow.

She leaned over the counter when the patrons weren't looking. "It's just weak tea," she whispered.

He blinked, more astonished. "But that man just paid a silver dollar." He kept his voice low so the other patrons wouldn't be privy to their conversation. "I know some tavern keepers charge high prices, but that is far beyond reasonable."

She nodded her head in a show of remorse. "I know and I'm sorry, Reverend. I hate cheating them out of their money too. Jason's built his business on deceit. I want to make it known, but he'll get me if I tell them."

The proprietor's blatant dishonesty bothered him, but he said nothing. He didn't want Marissa to get in trouble with her employer on his account. Something had to be done about it in the very near future, though.

"Marissa." Another woman came behind the counter. Her voice was husky, and she was a bit older, judging by the fine lines around her eyes and mouth. "Jason wants to see you upstairs in his office."

Marissa's face shadowed. "Take over the counter for me, then." She removed her apron. "Best of luck with your work, Reverend Winford. Good meeting you."

He paid her, including tip. "You as well, Miss Pierce."

She collected the money. Nearly all the men in her path turned to catch a glimpse of her long legs moving beneath her knee-length skirt.

Rowe finished his coffee as she retreated upstairs, leaving him to wonder exactly what manner of business the proprietor called her to. Marissa wanted to get out of this place. How could he help?

Marissa entered Jason's office, where he surrounded himself in a fortress of account papers, receipts, and pencils. A filled ashtray decorated the corner of his desk with a smoking stub of a cigar hanging from the edge of the glass.

"You needed to see me?"

He thrust the open ledger book in her face. "Do this month's figures look right to you?"

She glanced at the numbers on the page. "I'm not the best at arithmetic, but they look right to me."

He groaned. "Then I'm short this month. I'm going to have to take it out of everyone's pay."

She recoiled. "No! My contract is ending, and I need the money."

"So do I, and I have a lot more financial responsibility than you."

Her pulse sped. The tight bodice made it hard for her to catch a breath. "You can't renege on what we agreed to. You had us all cheat for you to get your money, and yet you still don't have enough?"

"Watch your mouth when you speak to me. Did you forget that I own the saloon? You're only here because I made a promise to your ma upon her death that I'd look after you. If she hadn't keeled over before her contract expired, I'd have left you a long time ago to pick up scraps along some riverboat dock."

Marissa bit her lower lip. Her voice wavered when she spoke. "Jason, please. I've spent years earning that money for when I would be able to step out on my own accord. I can't lose it all just as I'm about to leave."

He peered at her, narrowing his eyes. "What's this I hear about you servin' coffee to a preacher tonight?"

She stiffened. "The new preacher arrived in town today and wanted something other than a libation."

"A better question, then, is why he would come to a saloon, of all places, for coffee. What's he look like?"

"Tall, dark hair, clean shaven." She withheld her opinion of the striking dark blue of his eyes, or his reassuring smile and how it put her at ease.

Jason was able to read her thoughts, anyway. "You think he's handsome."

"Absolutely not. I only saw him as a paying customer." A feeling deep in Marissa's gut let her know that she was denying the truth. Warmth spread in her chest when she thought of Rowe's calm and gentle words spoken to her in the face of the saloon's harshness.

"Go back to work," Jason ordered. "I don't want to do it, but I'm taking three-quarters of everyone's earnings tonight."

Marissa wanted to break something. He was lying again. She clenched her fists and marched downstairs.

She had to go to Claywalk tomorrow to look for work and check on the general store investment. Her exit from Assurance could be in place as soon as she was able to leave the saloon. Then, when it was safe to do so, she would expose Jason's practices.

"Your friend's gone," Simone said at the bottom of the steps. "He left right after you went upstairs."

Marissa felt a twinge of disappointment. She barely knew the man, yet he left an indelible impression on her.

"Don't cater to him again if he comes back," Simone continued. "He'll make you lose your other customers. Let another girl tend him."

Rowe's former seat was occupied by Keith McCauley. He waved her over for another dance.

Marissa sighed. "This poor man is just handing Jason his wallet tonight." She resigned herself to another stumbling round of the Varsovienne. She wouldn't charge Keith for this one.

Chapter 3

THE VERY NEXT morning, as soon as Marissa saw that the day's supply of liquor, drinking glasses, and money for the register were ready at the counter, she left for Claywalk.

"Where are you off to, dressed so highfalutin?" Jason caught her as she got to the door. He folded his lean-muscled arms in suspicion.

Marissa tugged on her gloves then adjusted the brim of her hat. Although her eventual departure from the saloon was no secret, she didn't wish to stir up conflict with him by telling of her plans to find new work. "I have several errands that I need to tend to. I'll return before the early patrons arrive."

"What errands in Assurance require you to be in a frock fit for Sunday?" He raked his eyes over her. "With that on you could almost convince me you were high bred and not quarter-Indian."

Smoothing a portion of hair at the nape of her neck, she replied, "I'm not trying to fool anyone. I just want to look respectable as I tend to my business. Please, Jason," Marissa entreated as she backed away from his approach. "Let me leave to return in time for work."

She froze as his hand caught the back of her neck, his fingers probing though the wispy strands not concealed by her hat.

"Hair this black won't fool anyone who's been around the tribes. And those round, soft lips." The rough skin of his tobacco-stained thumb scraped the sensitive pink of her mouth. "You remember when I kissed you, don't you, Missy?"

Terrible memories sprung to the surface. Of his hungry mouth—with its hard stubble, scratched and bit—leaving her with the sour taste of stale bourbon. Her muffled cries for him to stop as the fabric ripped from her dress, her limbs clad in tattered stockings kicking and thrashing beneath the heavy weight thrown upon them.

"Yeah, you remember." He lowered his mouth a hair's breadth away.

The pain and humiliation consumed her all over again until her knees buckled, making her teeter on her feet.

"Jason." Simone came from the dancehall, broom in hand from where she had swept. "Let Marissa get some air. She's looking pale."

Jason opened the space between them again. Marissa grabbed the back of a chair as light-headedness claimed her.

"Your eyes are going bad, Simone. Missy's as tawny-colored as she ever was."

Marissa touched her face. It was clammy and tingled from where her blood drained. Jason and Simone sounded like they were speaking in a tunnel.

"It's stuffy in here. The fresh air outside will do her some good. Isn't that what you need, Marissa, to go outside?"

Marissa nodded as her senses slowly returned to normal.

"Get back in time for tonight." Jason slunk back to the counter. Pete and the other clerks hurriedly returned to work so he wouldn't know they stopped to watch the incident.

Simone propped the broom against one of the gambling tables. "You alright?" She laid her hand against Marissa's forehead. "You can't go fainting in here. He'll think you're putting on, and he gets real mad."

Marissa offered her a weak but grateful smile. "I won't faint. Thank you."

Simone nodded with a compassion that most people rarely witnessed from the steely-faced woman. "Best go before he comes back."

Marissa made for the doors, pushing them open to the hot sun outside. There was never a time she felt happier to be out in the heat.

Timothy Lyle, one of the liverymen's sons, worked alone at the stables that day. She found him mucking the floor and greeted him good morning.

"I need someone to take me to Claywalk. Are there any drivers?"

"I'll take you, ma'am, when my pa gets back from the house. Be about an hour."

Marissa opened her brocade purse. "I'll pay an extra two dollars if you can take me now. I've got to be back before evening."

Timothy tied the reins of a horse to the livery post. "Stay here until I get another worker to come watch the stable." He ran off across the street.

A little over an hour later Marissa stood in one of Claywalk's two general stores. The time it had taken her to calm down from Jason's lewd advances only served as a prelude to another upsetting incident of a different sort. "What do you mean, the store's been bought and sold? I made a deposit weeks ago, as did your other investors."

The store owner shrugged his shoulders helplessly. "The store took out a loan from a banker in Topeka before we were having financial troubles. He put a lien on the property when we couldn't pay on the loan and claimed a right to the store. Sorry, Miss. Nothing we can do."

Marissa shook her head, incredulous. This news wasn't worth the five dollars she paid to hire a driver to take her down the road. "Why did you advertise the store as being up for sale when there was a lien attached?"

"The store was up for sale. That was our attempt to get an outside investor to put up enough money to pay off the loan and buy the business before the bank could get to it."

"You didn't specify that in your advertisement. You stated that you were accepting payments for the sale of the store and that they could be sent in installments. I sent you three of them."

"Yeah," the owner said cautiously. It was apparent that he did not expect to be questioned to this degree about the acquisition of his business, especially by a woman. He scratched his arm. "My business partner and I thought that with enough money from the installments, either from many folks or one investor, that we would be able to pay everything off. We were gonna give the one investor all rights of ownership to the store, or we would divide the rights among multiple investors, should that be the case. As we've been foreclosed on yesterday, none of our goals were met."

Marissa folded her arms across her chest. "What about our money, then? Do we, the investors, get it back?"

"I'm afraid not, ma'am. All the money we received from our advertisement went into paying off some of our lesser debts. We really didn't expect this to happen. Times are hard, you know."

"This scheme of yours to repay your debts sounds illegal. I'm questioning whether the banker in Topeka knows about it."

"If you want to pursue us by law because you think you're owed money, get in line behind everyone else. We've got claims to settle that are worth far more than the fifteen dollars you put in every month or two." In a dismissive gesture he picked up a carton holding sacks of sugar and carried it into the storeroom.

"Thieves," Marissa uttered.

The man's shadow grew smaller until it disappeared from sight. Picking up her skirt hem, she marched back to the coach.

"Where to now, Miss Pierce?" Timothy jumped down from his box seat and opened the door, but she declined his help in stepping inside.

"Back home. This trip has proven to be a waste of time."

"Sorry to hear that." The red-headed young man closed the door. "Do you want somethin' to eat before we head out?"

"I'm not hungry, Timothy, but I'll wait for you to get a meal before we leave."

"I had some corn hash while you were in the store. Thanks all the same, though."

Marissa's coach left Claywalk at two in the afternoon. Pulling the curtains to the windows, she had no further interest in seeing the town that would have been her new home had things turned out the way she planned.

It made no sense to find a boardinghouse in Claywalk, either. None of the merchants were hiring. The town had three saloons, but she didn't want to inquire in them. That was the life she was trying to get away from, not go back to.

She tucked more of her skirt and bustle beneath her for extra padding on the hard wooden seat of the jostling coach. Didn't God want her to leave the saloon and be a proper woman? Why was He letting this happen when He could see she was trying to better herself?

Seems as though I can never escape this.

You can if you want to. A still, small voice whispered a reply in her mind.

Marissa disregarded it as wishful thinking, an attempt to cheer herself when her plans had gone awry. She had to think of another plan, and soon, because her contract with Jason was set to expire in a little over two weeks, with a lesser amount of money than she had expected to receive. The streets would be her new home if she didn't act fast.

An hour passed, and the coach drew to a halt in front of Assurance's town square, next to Linda's seamstress shop. Tired from the physical and emotional strain of the trip, Marissa allowed Timothy to help her down from the platform.

"Well, well," an artificial, girlish voice called out. "Look who's ridin' around town, unescorted."

Sophie Charlton, daughter of the town's wealthiest resident, David Charlton, came out of the shop. Linda followed her, as well as Sophie's close companion Margaret Rheins, another member of the town's small group of eligible young ladies.

"Thank you, Timothy." Marissa handed the young man some coins.

"Much obliged, ma'am." He tipped his hat and hopped back onto the coach, driving off.

Sophie waited for the dust to settle before approaching. Her steps were quick as she treaded lightly in her silk brocade gown, the soft blue color bringing out her eyes and complementing her shiny, gold ringlets. Her face had the look of a baby doll, but it held nothing innocent or sweet.

"Good afternoon, Marissa." Sophie smiled with her mouth. Her eyes were cold. "Looks like you've been traveling. You're positively covered with dust."

"Do look at her, Sophie. Her hair has blown out of her hat," Margaret added with a smirk and giggled. Her voice contained hints of the English accent of her immigrant parents.

Linda giggled too, glad to be welcomed into the fray.

Marissa addressed their leader. "Good afternoon, Sophie. I'm in a hurry and can't stay to talk."

Sophie laughed, much higher and shriller than the other

young women. "Whatever for? Do you have customers waiting?"

Marissa steadied herself, something inside pleading with her to remain still. This did not warrant a confrontation. "I needn't remind you that your father is a genteel farmer. He'd think us foolish if he heard us now."

"The only thing my father thinks is foolish is a girl like you wasting her life away in a den of iniquity."

"Sophie, that's enough," Marissa countered. "You're doing nothing to show yourself a woman above juvenile reproach."

Sophie and her cohorts all glowered. Linda taunted, "You dance the hurdy-gurdy. What do you know about gentility and proper womanhood, anyhow?"

"Marissa doesn't know." Sophie put in. "She's just a common, ungracious, mixed-breed Comanche with a prostitute for a mother."

Marissa huffed. "My mother was no prostitute. How dare you speak poorly about a woman in her grave?"

The wealthy young debutante beamed at her reaction. "If she was not a lady of the night, why did she leave you in the charge of Mr. Garth when she died?"

"Don't talk about things that you know nothing about."

"Then school me. Why did she give you to Mr. Garth, and why are you still with him as a grown woman?"

They sounded like cruel school-age girls taunting one of their peers. Marissa berated herself for taking part in the juvenility. She was twenty years old, too old to listen to any of it. Their words stung, but what did she stand to gain from defending herself against their pettiness? They wouldn't believe that it was her contract that held her at the saloon past the age of majority. Besides, there were bigger things to worry about, one of them being homelessness if she didn't find employment.

Without further answer Marissa took her leave of Sophie

and the other young women and strode the rest of the way to the saloon.

Afternoon sunlight highlighted the dust particles trapped between the grooves of the heavy oak cabin door. Rowe winced at the loud, high-pitched creak it made when he pushed it open. "Remind me to get some oil for those hinges. And a locksmith."

Dusty came in after him and looked behind the door. "That's what this bar and latch is for."

"Then I'd have to leave it unlocked when I go outside. That's not very secure."

"Oh, you don't need to worry. We don't have that kind of trouble here like in the big cities."

Rowe set his crate of canned goods and meat from the general store down and studied the cabin's interior. It had two floors. A small staircase led to the second floor, complete with two bedrooms. The main floor contained a common area and a hearth for the old GM Iron Column stove left behind. The adjoining room was much smaller with one window.

"Spacious and bare," he remarked.

"Our old preacher used to keep his study there before he and his family left for the Dakotas." Dusty indicated the smaller room. "He had a family of six."

Rowe nodded, taking everything in. "Many people once lived here. It's just me now." A flash of loneliness took a stab at his heart.

The farmhand's mouth curved into a rakish smile. "Not if the town pretties have anything to say about it."

"You'll get no competition from me, Dusty. I've got a congregation to think about."

It was Rowe's intention to keep himself busy within

the church and by making repairs in his home so that he wouldn't give in to memories of Josephine and the child that never was. Shelves needed to be built, the door hinges lubricated, and the fence outside required mending. A second trip to the general store for building tools was necessary.

"Speakin' of town pretties, here comes the best filly right now." Dusty left the windowsill and tore outside.

Rowe heard a girl's high-pitched giggle close by. Curious as to Dusty's sudden departure, he peered out the window to see the cause.

A petite young lady with a glorious golden crown of curls rode sidesaddle up the path leading to the Charlton farm. Beside her rode another girl, not dressed as extravagantly as her companion, but also in fine clothes. The two women chattered like baby birds, oblivious to anyone or anything taking place outside their conversation. Rowe could hear everything through the thin glass.

"I saw him at the general store today, Linda. He is simply marvelous!" The golden-haired one gushed.

"Did you introduce yourself?" Linda asked.

"He was too hurried to see me and left before I could say anything. But I'm going to introduce myself to him this Sunday and congratulate him on his first sermon here."

Rowe's brow quirked at the flattering reference. He double-checked to make sure they couldn't see him from his vantage point.

"My, my, Miss Sophie, you've got the whole thing planned, don't you?"

Both women turned their heads to Dusty. Sophie wrinkled her delicate little nose. "You're just jealous, Dusty, because I don't pay you the same mind."

"Oh, that don't bother me none." He leaned nonchalantly against the side of the cabin. "You're just practicing those sweet charms so you can use 'em on me."

She gave him a pinched look, much like one would if offered buffalo chips for a snack. "The only thing I'd use on you is a good switch to send you on out of here."

"You can't do that because your pa rather likes my work on his farm."

Sophie snorted, managing to make even that guttural noise the daintiest of sounds. "Daddy doesn't know how vile and uncouth you truly are."

He blew her a kiss. "Such pretty words to get my heart stirrin'."

Sophie's apricot complexion turned crimson as she fumed. "Let's go on up to the house, Linda. Away from the *hired help*." Her voluminous skirt and petticoats ruffled in the wind as she took the reins to her horse and resumed the trip. The horse was her animal extension, as it appeared to sashay up the hill. Linda followed on her mount.

Dusty chuckled. "She'll come around."

"You think so?" Rowe raised the window and stuck his head out, giving the farmhand a start. "She seemed very unwavering to me."

"Aw, you know how those Louisiana gals are. How much of that did you hear, anyway?"

"Most of it, but I'll put a good word in for you if Miss Sophie approaches this Sunday."

"No worries, Rev'ren." Looking a bit chagrined, Dusty turned the topic around. "Did you send for your furniture?"

"I don't have any. I sold everything before leaving."

"Why did you go do that for?"

"It would have been an extra load to ship." Rowe instinctively glanced at his valise. The photograph was enough to remind him of his old life, of what could never be again. He needed no other physical items from his old dwelling.

Dusty shrugged. "I 'spose you can always buy some in

town. The Sunday school teacher Miss Kensey'll lend you a table and bed frame until you get your own."

"I would appreciate that. The people here are very helpful."

"They're real eager to have the church filled again after so long." He secured his hat firmly atop his head. "I have to head back to the farm. See you Sunday. Bye, Rev'ren."

"Bye, Dusty. And thanks." Rowe gave up on getting the man to call him by his first name. Though easygoing in nature, respect and propriety were ingrained in the cheerful farmhand.

The quietness of the cabin turned Rowe's thoughts. Perhaps it would be filled with joy and laughter a few years from now, God willing. Then guilt rode his back as he remembered his wedding vows to be true to Josephine. How could he imagine taking another wife when he was responsible for the death of his first? Already he betrayed her memory simply by admiring the beauty of another woman. What would Josephine have thought of his tête-à-tête with Marissa? Or his brothers? They would have frowned on his behavior and said he was dallying with a midnight lady.

Rowe circled the room, thinking. He had ministered to prostitutes before, and Marissa appeared to share little in common with them except for her place of employment. At the saloon she concentrated on serving drinks to her customers rather than responding to their amorous advances.

If she was a prostitute, then she wasn't pleased about it. What if he could help her leave the business? If she was just a saloon girl slugging drinks each night, he had to uncover why she felt compelled to stay.

He sat down on his largest trunk, a makeshift chair for the next day or so, and contemplated which of the canned goods would be the source of his supper.

Chapter 4

S UNDAY MORNING BROUGHT with it beautiful weather with calm breezes. Standing outside under the shade tree near his cabin, Rowe could almost believe he was back in Virginia.

He saddled his new horse and rode to church. The forested landscape thinned the closer he got to town. His leg brushed against his favorite Bible, nestled in the saddlebag. Thanks to several church members, he knew his way to the building and where the pastor's office was located inside. In the three days since his arrival, his home had been the site of unexpected yet pleasant visits. On Friday Miss Kensey and her mother stopped by with a delicious pot pie made with stewed vegetables and roast beef. On Saturday three members of the choir came to welcome him.

Rowe was glad to be initiated so warmly into their midst. In Richmond people had their pick of churches and ministers. The congregation at his old church, where he worked as an associate under the pastor, saw him as little more than a clerk to put announcements into the weekly bulletin. Not so in Assurance. Already townspeople were eager to receive him as their new church leader.

"Morning, Reverend." A gray-mustachioed man called to him from one of the three wagons lined up in front of the modest church. The building's white steeple and cross sat proudly atop the newly shingled roof.

Rowe waved. "You're here early. I don't think even Miss Kensey is here to teach the children yet."

"My daughter is inside waiting for her. I'm the organist,

Albert Pate. You met my wife yesterday. She leads the choir. We're usually here before the congregation to practice."

Rowe swung his horse around to the wagon and shook Albert's hand. "Glad to meet you. Is there anything I should know about the church before I deliver my first sermon?"

The organist thought. "A few folks dropped out since Reverend Thomas left. The preachers in between weren't too good. Most folks don't like it when you keep them past midday hour. That's probably the same where you're from, isn't it?"

"I'll get everyone out in time for the noonday meal." Rowe dwelled on the organist's comment about the church's decrease in attendance. Hopefully there would be a fair turnout this morning.

"You'll have to end the sermon early because some of the church wives put together a welcome dinner for you. They thought it'd be a good way to show how glad we are to receive you."

"I'm honored." Genuinely surprised, Rowe relaxed the tension on his horse's reins. He had attended celebrations and dinners with his seminary colleagues in Richmond, but never as the guest of honor.

His first sermon had to be a very good one.

"I have to prepare for this morning, Mr. Pate. Will you excuse me?"

Rowe went around the small, oak-timbered church and unsaddled his horse. From what he remembered of his tour of the building yesterday, the quickest route to the pastor's study was located near the back entrance. He dropped the satchel containing his Bible twice before he was able to unlock the door. *I'll knock the entire altar over if I don't get myself settled.*

Eventually he found his way to the study, where he put his

robe on over his suit, only to pull the draping garment off. It was much too early to get dressed for service.

Rowe knocked his Bible over again when a knock came from the door.

"Yes, come in."

Miss Kensey pushed through the door. "Good morning, Reverend Winford." Her gaze traveled to the fallen Bible, and she formed a puzzled frown. "I wanted to know if you could come meet the children before their lesson."

"Yes. Yes, of course." Setting the Bible on the desk, he followed her out to the Sunday school room.

Miss Kensey taught an informative Bible lesson that not only gave the children instruction on right living but also entertained all in the class, including Rowe, who stayed for the entire lesson. By the time he left the children's room, the sanctuary was starting to fill. Albert Pate started on the organ as Rowe dashed into his office before anyone could see him.

"Oh, no." He hadn't gone over the sermon yet today. Rowe flipped pages in his Bible until he uncovered his notes. *A Reminder About Deceitfulness.* Rowe had spent his time since his saloon visit preparing the sermon. He trusted that God's Word concerning fairness would call to mind any questionable practices the clerks and merchants of the town allowed. Jason Garth likely would not be in attendance, but other townspeople could hear the message.

Marissa's face formed in his mind as his thoughts turned toward the saloon. What would persuade her to come to church?

The choir began to sing. As Rowe scanned his rushed handwriting of sermon notes, he realized the question would have to wait until after the service.

Why did Jason always insist on doing inventory on her days off? Marissa spent the entire Sunday morning hunched over ledgers and helping the workers get the whiskey on the shelf and the ale on tap. Now she could spend the rest of the day in peace at the lake.

When she was a child, her grandparents and mother took her there to play. Smiling to herself, she remembered splashing along the water's edge and trying to catch minnows in her little hands. Closing her eyes, she tasted the picnic lunch of biscuits, chicken, and strawberry pie that her mother always made. While she ate, her grandmother often told her stories from the Bible that centered on water, such as Jonah and the whale, or how Moses parted the Red Sea, and how Jesus walked on water. Marissa didn't know if it was the lake itself or the memories of once having a place in someone's heart that kept her coming back.

She passed the church, where the congregation was letting out. It wasn't a large group, but people filled the doorway as they said parting words to their new preacher. He shook hands with them, speaking briefly to each. Marissa's stomach tightened as she saw how his wide back filled out his coat to taper at his waist. His suit and fine gauge frock coat were much better for the dry summer heat than the heavy, dark wool he wore earlier. If he was still unused to the heat, he gave no indication. The sun shone on his rich brown hair as he smiled, laughed, and chatted happily with the congregation.

Realizing that she had stopped walking, Marissa pulled the wide brim of her hat down closer to her face and carried on. A man and his family came down the church steps. He put a protective arm on both his wife and two daughters as they passed by her. Perhaps the man thought that the very sight of her would cause the women of his life to lose all of their propriety and go the way that she did. If she were raising her family in the church, she might react the same way. Still, the man was teaching his family to prejudge. Her mother told her that Christians weren't supposed to be that way.

"Excuse me, Miss Pierce." Reverend Winford called her name from a short distance as he descended the steps. "Allow me to have a brief word with you."

Marissa felt the derisive stares of the congregation, sensed their curiosity as to why their preacher would stop to speak to her. Why did he have to do this? Didn't he have more than enough people to tend to in his congregation?

She had to give him her full attention because he stood at arm's length. He wore that pleasant look again, the one she first saw on his face last week. Kindness emanated from his eyes.

"I looked for you in church." It wasn't an expression that he put on for others to see, but his actual demeanor.

The soft wind carried his clean, woodsy scent to her nose. "I don't attend church," she admitted slowly. "I haven't gone in some years."

"Today I gave a sermon about being dishonest with money. Maybe someone will inform your employer of what he or she heard."

Her eyes shot up. "You shouldn't have done that, Reverend."

"Please call me Rowe. Why shouldn't I reveal what the saloon establishment is doing if men are being taken advantage of? You said you wanted to make it known too, but you can't because you're employed there."

Marissa turned her head to the church. The remaining congregation watched them with rapt interest and bewilderment. Her hat brim brushed the tops of Rowe's suit lapels as she drew closer to him. "Jason is many things, but he is not an imbecile. He'll know that I told you about that drink scheme. You're getting me into trouble."

He bent down to peer beneath her hat. "I had a duty to share the indiscretion because Mr. Garth is robbing the town. I have to say it, Miss Pierce. You are doing the same. Your hand and those of the other employees are the first to take money away."

Reeling from the terrible truth of his accusation, guilt and shame hit her like bricks. "I'm not a saint, Reverend. I have to see to my survival just as much as I do the rights of the saloon patrons. My work is only until I can do better." She sighed heavily. "Simone was right to warn me. I don't know why I said anything at all to you."

He appeared unwounded by her admission. "Maybe it was laid upon your conscience."

"Don't preach to me. I've heard everything you have to say."

"Marissa—"

"I may work in a saloon, sir, but that does not grant you the right to use my first name without permission." She wanted him to be just as flustered as she was.

Rowe gave a polite nod instead. "My apologies again, Miss Pierce. I do hope you see that I'm not your adversary."

Marissa became grateful for her wide-brimmed hat. It blocked much more than the hot sun.

"Oh, Reverend!"

Sophie Charlton suddenly appeared, floating down the steps with her two brothers and younger sister in tow. She placed herself between Rowe and Marissa as though Marissa weren't there. Touching the preacher's arm, she steered him away. "Everyone in the church is waiting on you so they can eat."

Without pausing for his response, Sophie kept on. "My name is Sophie Charlton, and these here are my siblings David Jr., Bernard, and Rosemarie. I wanted to congratulate

you on a wonderful first sermon today. Your preaching spoke
to me and lifted me right on up."

Rowe looked back and forth from Marissa to Sophie.
"Thank you, Miss Charlton. It's a pleasure to meet you and
your family."

Sophie continued her chatter, folding her hands and
preening about. "My father will be back in town tomorrow.
I'd be pleased to introduce you. Would you honor my family
with your presence at supper, say, on Wednesday?"

"I usually prepare my sermon for the week on Wednesday."

The persistent and emboldened Sophie would not take no
for an answer. Her curls bobbed beneath her lace bonnet as
she tilted her head and batted her sky blue eyes once in an
imitation of childlike innocence. "But my father would be
simply delighted if you could make it." Her New Orleans
drawl became more breathy with insistence. "Simply
delighted."

Marissa scrunched her nose at the contrived display. The
oldest, harshest-looking saloon girl could put on a better
show of virtuousness than that, and make a man believe it.
To her astonishment, Rowe gave in.

"Alright," he said. "I wouldn't want to disappoint good
people such as you and your family. What time should I be
at your home?"

Sophie beamed. "We lay supper on the table at seven."

"Seven it is. Oh, and Miss Pierce, we will speak again soon,
I hope."

Marissa overlooked Sophie's territorial glare and sidestepped her, the Charlton siblings, and Rowe. "Good afternoon, Reverend."

Walking alone once more, she pushed away the odd feelings that tugged at her. If she was irate at the reverend for
drawing more bad attention to her and the saloon, why did

41

she care that Sophie had her eye on him? A woman with Miss Charlton's standing was a good match for a preacher. As much as Marissa wanted to convince herself, the thought left her unsettled within.

At the lake she caught up to Dusty Sterling, returning to the Charlton farm after church service. They hadn't spoken since he danced with her two years ago at the saloon. He was one of the few gentlemen she did not have to remind to keep his hands at her waist.

"Hello, Dusty."

She was unsure if he knew her anymore, but his hazel eyes lit up. "Miss Marissa, I haven't talked to you since I was on that one cattle drive from Texas."

"Yes, you drove them here to be shipped on the railroad to Missouri."

"And stayed ever since." He grinned broadly, pleased that she remembered. "You sure look mighty pretty in that dress."

"Thank you." She tucked her hands in the pockets of her airy cotton frock. "I see you just came from church."

The brown waistcoat he wore over a clean white shirt matched his trousers. His polished boots sparkled. "Yep. Quite a sermon the new rev'ren delivered."

"He came into the saloon for a cup of coffee the night he arrived and got today's sermon out of it."

"Is that so?" Dusty's mouth twitched. "In that case I'd say he's taken a shine to you already. Not a tough act for a lady like you."

Dusty Sterling was always the flirt. Marissa smiled at the compliment. "I think Rowe is taking a stand against the saloon in order to establish himself as a good preacher."

"Using first names now, I see." Dusty nodded as though he possessed knowledge far beyond her understanding to reveal just yet. He needed to be stopped from going down the path he was about to tread.

"No, Dusty, don't start assuming things. That's what too many people in this town do, and then trouble starts."

"I didn't say anything, Miss Marissa." His wide grin was just as charming and mischievous as a little boy's. Her disapproving look tickled him so much he barely suppressed his mirth.

"I know what you're thinking, and nothing's going to come of it. For one, preachers and saloon girls don't mix well. Two, I've no time for courting because I'm leaving Assurance as soon as my contract with Jason runs out."

All the humor in his face dissipated. "Why are you leavin'?"

Stooping down to pick up a blade of dried grass, she twirled it between her fingers. "There's no life for me in this place. I don't want to always be seen as Arrow Missy or worse." A shudder went through her as she thought of the names given to women who worked in saloons, whether their work therein was scrupulous or not—painted cat, soiled dove, shady lady. Those names stuck to a woman for the rest of her life.

"Think it over, Miss Marissa," Dusty pleaded. "Assurance has enough trades so you can change your way of living if it ain't suiting you."

"Not with Jason's wildcat temper and not with everyone remembering where I came from."

"This town's got liars, cheats, and gossips, but there's some real good folks here too." He puffed out his chest. "Like good ol' Dusty here."

She laughed. "I don't know how you reconcile your attitude with the humility of attending church. You're something else."

"Yeah, if only Miss Sophie could see that."

Even he wasn't immune to the ways of Assurance's resident Southern belle, Marissa thought wryly. "If Sophie can't see the good in you, well, she's still got that Louisiana cotton stuck in her eyes."

Dusty laughed. "Guess that's a good way of sayin' it. And I'll keep goin' after her till one of us gets tired. But please think hard about what you're gonna do."

He tipped his hat to her and went away to the Charlton farm on the other side of the lake.

Marissa found a secluded spot in the low shade to view the water. After a few minutes she closed her eyes and listened to the sounds of nature. A bird chirped. Water lapped against the bank. The trees seemed to whisper to one another. For moments she felt peace.

People like you can't be helped.

The wind slapped her ears. She opened her eyes with a start.

Wind ripped atop the lake, destroying its calm surface. The sun fled behind a cloud and left the earth below in a pallid, drab hue. Even small signs of life in the area were gone.

The bird no longer chirped.

An odd mixture of dread and hopelessness came over Marissa, its source unknown. Goose bumps formed on her arms before she rose and headed back into town.

Chapter 5

I T WAS SO good of you to join us this evening, Reverend," Mr. Charlton declared.

Rowe sat at the head of the table, overwhelmed by the amount of food on his plate. Seven platters of beans, chicken, baked ham, rolls, and potatoes decorated the space in front of him.

Rosemarie, the youngest child, filled his glass with more iced tea so that it threatened to topple over the brim.

"Given this food, I would say the pleasure is all mine." He speared a slice of ham with his fork and tasted the juicy, honey-sweetened meat.

The Charltons were a well-to-do family, but he didn't think they would go to all of the trouble to showcase it just for him. They sat on upholstered chairs. The dining table was covered by a silk and lace tablecloth. The china was French heirloom. If a butler greeted him at the door, he would have sworn he visited a Virginia country plantation.

Mr. Charlton smiled over his glass. "You have my daughter to thank for that. She does the cooking since my wife's been visiting family in Louisiana. Sophie made sure that the ham baked this morning, the beans stewed at the right temperature, and the rolls came from the oven hot and fresh by the time you knocked on the door."

Sophie inclined her head demurely. "Why, Daddy, our guest doesn't want to hear how I slaved over the fire."

He went on, goaded by the batting of her golden eyelashes. "This little lady went so far as to choose our Sunday best for dinner attire, even though it's Wednesday."

"Daddy," she gasped, but still obviously delighted in the attention being given her hard work. "I only want the reverend to see us at our best."

"You have a wonderful family, Mr. Charlton," Rowe said. "A charming daughter and her bright younger siblings. Our Sunday school teacher tells me that Bernard and Rosemarie do well."

"And what about you, Reverend?" Sophie began to cut her slice of ham into ladylike morsels. "Do you have family back home in Richmond?"

The potato he was chewing quickly lost its savory herbed flavor. "Not anymore. They left the city after the war and moved into the southern part of Virginia to raise tobacco. It was my father's original profession before he married my mother."

"So farming is in your blood, then, eh?" Mr. Charlton leaned forward, indicating interest.

"Yes. My great-grandfather started planting the little tobacco field that grew into what is now the Winford farm. All the generations maintained it."

"Your father didn't farm?"

"My father wanted to pursue studies at university, so he left the country behind for the city. He met my mother, Francine Rowe, in Richmond. They married, and I was born a year later."

"Are you their only child?" Sophie asked.

"I have three younger brothers. All of them have gone back to farming. I'm sure my great-grandfather is beaming down from heaven at their accomplishments in reviving the crop."

"What made you choose to go into the ministry?" Mr. Charlton spooned some more beans on his plate. "You look like a strong enough fellow to drive a plow."

"God called me to the ministry about seven years ago, when I was a soldier in the Confederacy. Seeing the violence, the politics of land possession and slavery...I couldn't be a man who stood for those causes." He bit into a chicken leg. "I couldn't go to the family farm because it bore the history of those things."

"Well, I can assure you, *my* family treated the workers on our plantation with the utmost fairness and decency." Sophie sipped from her glass. "Some of the workers were freed and simply worked our land because of the good way we treated them."

Her brothers and sister cast questioning glances at their sibling. "We didn't have any land," the oldest boy stated.

Mr. Charlton took a slow sip of tea, his eyes peering sternly at his daughter over the glass rim.

Rowe wiped his mouth on the edge of his napkin. "I meant no offense to you or your family. That once was a way of life for many people. Fortunately, it is no more."

Sophie straightened a little in her seat. The younger siblings were silent again as they sensed the tension from the adults. Their father cleared his throat.

Sophie composed herself. "Reverend, are you married?"

"I was. My wife died three years ago in childbirth."

"I'm so sorry!"

"You didn't know." He swallowed the last of his tea. The youngest daughter rose to refill his glass, but he declined. "Thank you, Rosemarie, but I believe I'm beginning to grow full. As I was saying, my wife and child died three years ago, when I was completing my studies in seminary. I worked as an assistant minister in a church until a friend informed me of positions out west for ministers, teachers, missionaries, and so forth."

"And God led you here."

"Yes, to Assurance."

Rowe chose not to mention how he tried to apply for positions in Charlottesville, Boston, and Smithfield before accepting the offer in Kansas. Positions in the big cities had already been filled by applicants with more experience, so his rejection letters stated. Once he accepted that hard fact and trusted God's leading, it made the journey out west easier to bear.

He just didn't count on the loneliness following him.

"We're grateful you're here, Reverend." Mr. Charlton took him from his musing. "Our town hasn't had a preacher in some months."

"As you can tell with certain folks," Sophie put in. "The moral indecency in this town has grown considerably. I'm sure you noticed when you spoke to that Miss Pierce after church on Sunday."

"Marissa?" Rowe blurted out her first name as though they were on familiar terms and had to promptly correct himself. "I ran into Miss Pierce on my first day here."

"Is that so?" Sophie looked up from the last bite of beans on her plate and set her fork down with an abrupt clink upon the fine porcelain. "Children, would you please clear the table?"

Rosemarie, David Jr., and Bernard stood. She waited until they gathered all the dishes and glasses and took them into the other room to wash. "Do go on, Reverend."

Rowe disliked her sudden change in tone, as though she demanded an explanation for his speaking to another citizen of the town. "When I arrived at the inn, Miss Pierce walked past my wagon. I tipped my hat to her, but she was in a hurry."

Sophie raised an arched brow. "She was likely feeling shameful."

"Of what?"

Father and daughter exchanged glances across the table. Mr. Charlton played with the edge of the lace tablecloth between his thick, plow-calloused hands.

"Well, Reverend, we're not in the habit of speaking ill of others, but Marissa Pierce is not what you would call a, ahem, respectable woman." Sophie explained. "She makes her living in the most disreputable way as one of the local song and dance girls of Jason's saloon."

Sophie's self-righteous tone provoked Rowe to speak on Marissa's behalf. "You saw that she didn't appear disreputable on Sunday. Her dress was modest."

"Well, I detected a hint of rouge on her cheeks."

Rowe recalled seeing the blush that crept on Marissa's cheeks as he accused the saloon employees of robbery. "That was natural. She wore no artifice, as far as I could tell, and she carried herself like a well-mannered woman."

"She was vastly deceivin' you, Reverend. And, if I may speak boldly, she probably does more than just a song and dance each night."

"Dear Sophie! We may know where Miss Pierce works, but we don't know the details of her occupation, do we?" Mr. Charlton likely asked the question in order to give his daughter a chance to redeem herself of the outburst, but she gave an airy shrug instead.

"One doesn't need to stretch the imagination too far, Daddy. You told me about the saloon girls when we first settled here and warned me to avoid their...less than pristine presence. But I will stand down, for the reverend's sake." Inclining her head to Rowe, she gave him a small, apologetic smile.

For all of her practiced gentility, Rowe detected a sharpness that could undercut all but the most insensitive hearts. How did Mr. Charlton handle his daughter's demeanor on a daily basis, he wondered. The poor man.

He pushed his chair back to stand. "The conversation has been enlightening. It's getting late, and I should at least think of what Sunday's sermon should be before I retire for the evening."

Mr. Charlton also eagerly rose, no doubt grateful that talk of the local saloon and its employees was over for the time being. "I'll get your coat, sir."

Meanwhile Sophie walked Rowe to the door, hands clasped neatly in front of her. "It has surely been a delightful evening with your presence gracing us, Reverend. We hope you can come again." The golden eyelashes batted.

Rowe reached for his felt derby hat on the wall rack and placed it on his head. "The dinner was delicious. Few women have your talent with the stove, Miss Charlton."

"I'd be pleased if you call me Sophie. Daddy and I will consider you one of our closest friends."

Or potential ally, he thought. During seminary he saw how men and women placed themselves in a minister's esteem to use that relationship as a way to achieve authority over others. Sophie Charlton had the potential to become such a person because she wanted not only his esteem but his intimate affection as well.

She lightly brushed her skirt to clear it of imaginary dust. Though lovely in appearance, her coy manner didn't sway him in the slightest.

Mr. Charlton returned with his overcoat. Rowe pushed his arms into the sleeves. "Thank you both for welcoming me into your home."

"We enjoyed having you, Reverend," Sophie's father said as he put an arm around his daughter's shoulder. "See you on Sunday morning."

"Yes, till then."

Outside Rowe untied his horse from the hitching post by the gate and climbed into the saddle. The evening air, still warm from the hot July day, whipped his face and lifted his horse's mane. Giving a final wave to the Charltons, he rode the winding path from their house to the dusty main road.

On the way home his mind reeled with thoughts of

Marissa. Her voice, her resolute dignity. Many women were pretty, but she possessed a certain quality of spirit. She had determination, a hidden strength to endure hardship, and that registered with him. The image of Marissa in a saloon girl's short dress and tight bodice, kicking up her petticoats to a tinkling piano, just didn't match the woman with the wide-brimmed hat strolling to the lake. They were two completely different personas.

Despite what he told Sophie and her father, he realized he didn't have a mind to work on the sermon tonight. What the Charltons had hinted of Marissa and the goings-on at Jason's Saloon was too distracting to push aside. Making the decision to go into town, he rode past mostly closed shops and stalls.

The blacksmith was still in operation, as was McIntyre's Restaurant. People out this late in the evening were either proprietors whose trade demanded long hours or those returning home from visiting a neighbor. A few others lolled about for different reasons, as indicated by the lights emanating from the saloon.

Rowe chided himself for stopping his horse in the middle of the road to look into the establishment. What was he thinking? Did he hope to catch sight of gamblers or immoral propositioning? That would be something for the town newspaper to print about its new preacher. Out to steal a glimpse at the whiskey swillers and dancing girls.

Rowe thought of the unpleasant way his last conversation with Marissa ended.

Leading the horse onward to his cabin at the lake, Rowe criticized himself again. He had a congregation to concern himself with. It was his responsibility to see to their needs. While Marissa might need special pastoral care, he should not let her take precedence.

He arrived at his cabin, unsaddled his horse, and let it

drink from its trough. Repairs were always good at bringing the mind to focus. Rowe wasn't much of a carpenter, but he noticed that one end of the perimeter fence was falling apart. That was something he could fix in the morning.

The hinges on the old wooden door creaked as he entered the house for the night, trying, in vain, to keep his mind off Marissa.

Chapter 6

THURSDAY MORNING MARISSA entered the store of Zachary Arthur, the town's shoemaker. Friends of her mother's family for years, Zachary and his wife, Rebecca, always welcomed her in spite of her place of employment. Marissa figured a visit would help keep her mind sane until she came up with a way to leave Jason's Saloon for good. The smell of leather permeated the store from the rows of newly cobbled shoes on the two large shelves. A cold potbelly stove rested in the back. Contentment gradually came over Marissa as she settled into her surroundings. Zachary, a cheerful old man with white hair and smiling brown eyes, greeted her from the store counter. "Hello, Marissa."

"How do you do, Mr. Arthur?"

"Very well. Haven't seen you in a while."

She came closer to the counter. "The saloon's been very busy lately."

Zachary ventured onto the sales floor. His form started to bend with age, but his friendly demeanor was just as fresh and exuberant as she had always known it to be. "Rebecca asks of you all the time."

He referred to his wife, a woman of equally sweet and welcoming disposition. Of all the townspeople, the Arthurs had known Marissa the longest. Her best memories were in this shop, before life took her parents and grandparents, making its strange, sad turn for the worse.

"Tell her I'm doing alright."

"Is that true, Marissa?" His eyes showed wisdom and concern. "We're not blind to your circumstances, you know."

Marissa looked down at her feet, unable to conceal the truth. "You were the first to know of my arrival back in town two years ago. Despite my current...arrangements, you never shunned me, so I'll tell you. My contract ends with Jason in eight days. I'll be free to pursue my own calling."

"That is splendid good news, Mari!" He called her by her childhood nickname. "What are your plans?"

"I was to own a small share of a store in Claywalk." She remained silent on the details of her bad investment because it still stirred her blood with aggravation. "Either I would become a merchant myself or receive a portion of the profits."

"Are you moving to Claywalk, then?"

"There are no prospects for the time being. I'm not certain it's wise for me to spend money on boardinghouses without being employed."

Zachary regarded her with touching compassion. "Stay with Rebecca and me. We have extra room. My wife would love to have another woman in the house to talk to."

Marissa experienced glowing warmth in her heart at having been so welcomed. "Thank you for the offer, Mr. Arthur, but I can't do that. It would be wrong to live under your roof without earning my keep."

"Then pay us a couple of dollars each month, if it would make you feel better. Or work in the store and earn a living that way. I can put you in charge of the stock and order placements."

She glanced over her shoulder to see if another customer had entered. No one was there, but she lowered her voice. "You know I'm a saloon girl."

Zachary lifted one stooped shoulder. "Soon to be former, but why should that matter?"

"No one in this town will buy shoes from you if I work here."

"Child, do you honestly believe the entire town would do

such a thing? There are plenty of God-fearing people here who are forgiving and will accept you."

"You forget about Jason Garth. He has a mind to keep me in that saloon. I don't want him hounding after you because you offered to help me."

Zachary dismissed the notion with a toss of his hand. "Rebecca and I are not afraid of that man. Any power or influence that he has can't stand against the protection we have over us."

Marissa took note of his confidence, the same she had witnessed in her missionary grandparents. It was too extraordinary to contemplate how they lived each day without fear of what people or events might bring.

"I'll think about it."

Zachary sighed. "I guess that's your way of telling me the discussion is over. You got that strong will and stubbornness, alright. You know where to find Rebecca and me should you change your mind."

"Thank you, Mr. Arthur. I do mean that." Turning to leave, she stopped short of a half step.

Rowe Winford stood at the door.

Rowe had no idea how he had set foot in the shoe shop when his original destination was the general store to purchase a new hammer. He broke the handle when mending the fence that morning and smashed his thumb in the process. Grumbling to himself for being out of practice, he made the short journey to town on foot. Then he saw Marissa through the large display window of the store.

"Good morning to you, Reverend."

He knew the man who welcomed him. Zachary Arthur and his wife were in the first row of pews at church last Sunday. Their encouraging smiles took much of his nervousness away at delivering the first sermon in front of a half-empty sanctuary.

Still gripping the broken handle of his hammer, Rowe hastily shoved the tool in the belt loop of his work pants. He needed to think up a good excuse for his presence. "Good morning, Mr. Arthur. I, ah, was wondering if you carry any work boots."

Zachary inclined his head. "That I do. What size do you wear?"

"Size?" Rowe glanced down at his feet. "Twelve, stout."

"Hmm." Zachary tapped his chin. "I may carry several of those in stock. Let me check for you." He headed for the back room. "Oh, and Mari can help you look out here while you're waiting. She knows the store like the back of her hand, don't you, Mari?"

Marissa folded her arms across her chest. Her caramel brown eyes shifted from Zachary to Rowe to the shoe seller again. Rowe offered a smile, but she turned her face before he could see it. "Show the reverend what the store has, child. I think there's some McKays on the shelves." Zachary disappeared into the back room.

Marissa's dusky pink lips thinned into a straight line as her chest rose and sank, suppressing a sigh. Rowe studied her carefully as she turned, rather stiff.

Her greeting was forced politeness. "Reverend, how do you do?"

The maroon dress she wore flattered her dusky complexion. Tiny silver buttons reached all the way to her collar, where a delicate ring of lace framed her neck. A stray wisp of hair escaped her coiled black braid, the color and texture of it hinting at a mysterious heritage somewhere in her bloodline. Her eyes, slightly slanted in the corners, narrowed as she awaited his reply.

He straightened his posture. "Fairly well, thank you. I'd like to see a pair of those boots Mr. Arthur mentioned."

The spicy scent of lavender trailed after her as she went to the shelf on his right and lifted one of a pair of brown boots for inspection. "This one?"

Rowe pretended to inspect the boot. He hoped that he didn't look like a complete fool to Marissa. "Yes, it seems sturdy enough. I think this is what I need."

"Do you want to try it on first?" She handed him the boot and indicated to a low stool set up in the corner facing a mirror. "You can see how it fits over there."

Rowe crossed the room and had a seat on the stool. Untying his bootlaces, he proceeded to tug on the heels to get them off.

"Use the boot jack." Marissa reached on the floor beside him for a simple contraption comprised of two wooden planks.

After he removed his right boot, he tried on the new McKays. The snug leather hugged his foot at the heel and instep. "Could I try the left one too, please?" he called to Marissa, who had disappeared behind another shelf.

He walked around the store when he had both McKays on. "What do you think?"

She offered no opinion. "How do they feel?"

"A bit tight at the instep."

"The leather needs a chance to break in. I can show you a pair in a larger size if you want."

"No, you're probably right. New shoes never feel good at first. I'll see what Mr. Arthur brings out." Rowe sat down again and tried to remove the boots. They wouldn't budge, even when he used the boot jack.

"Here." Marissa knelt on the floor and started adjusting the bootlaces. "You may just need to loosen them a bit. Try now."

While she held the boot, Rowe attempted to pull his foot out. She tugged one way, he another. "What if I can't get them off?"

"Then you get to wear them home. After you pay for them." The makings of a smile formed on Marissa's face. Glad that she was no longer being taciturn, Rowe hoped to keep that pleasant expression there.

"Tell me that was your attempt at humor, Miss Pierce."

"It was. What we'd really do is go back into the storage room for the saw."

Rowe yanked his foot back, toppling over the stool. His back came in contact with one of the display stands. Several pairs of dainty ladies slippers fell into his lap.

"Are you alright?" Marissa hurried to his side, holding the boot that he successfully kicked off. A mischievous light in her eyes revealed the laughter they contained.

Mortified, Rowe jumped to his feet and rushed to place the slippers back on the stand. Zachary called out from the back room. "Did I hear something fall?"

Moments later the old man emerged with two pairs of boots in his arms. "These are all I carry in twelve, stout. Not too many men in this town have feet that size."

"As I'm learning," Rowe mumbled.

Marissa let out a chuckle. "Don't feel bad. I have a similar problem finding women's shoes. When I was a child, my mother sewed leather to the bottom of old burlap sacks."

Zachary huffed. "Shame on you, Mari, fibbin' to the preacher. Now, Reverend, I'll have you know I've been supplying shoes to this young lady since she learned to wiggle her toes. None of my customers ever had to resort to using burlap sacks."

Rowe grinned at Marissa and shook his head. A soft blush bloomed on her cheeks. "Your saleswoman has a unique sense of humor, Mr. Arthur."

"You've heard nothing yet." Zachary carried the shoes up to him. "Do you want to have a look at these, or did you like the ones she showed you?"

"I don't think those suited me. What was their make, Miss Pierce? Miss Pierce?"

Rowe caught Marissa staring out the shop window. A melancholy expression replaced her former mirth as she made eye contact with a tall, ashen-brown-haired man standing outside in the street. The leanness of his build only served to enhance his height, giving him a sullen and sinister edge. His face was hard, with lines etched in a frown around his thin mouth.

Marissa moved to the door. "Good day, Mr. Arthur. Good day, Reverend."

Rowe watched as she hurried across the street to the man, barely dodging an oncoming stagecoach. The man's face folded into a deeper scowl as she communicated with him. His lips moved in a reply.

Rowe couldn't make out his words, but judging from Marissa's defiant stance, she was not pleased by what was being said. The man glared through the window again, his malevolent countenance fixed on Rowe this time. Rowe held his gaze, unflinching. The lean, wiry man clenched his fists at his sides once and put a hand on Marissa's back, leading her away from the town square.

A second oncoming stagecoach blocked the view of their departure.

Shaking his head, Zachary turned from the window. "That Jason Garth is somethin' else. I wish poor Mari were free of him."

Rowe quelled the urge to march outside and tear the man's hand away from Marissa's person. He handled her as though she were his property. "So that's the saloon's proprietor."

"Jason is the owner of the saloon, alright. Marissa's an

employee of his. What he has some of those women doing in that rotten establishment is downright despicable."

"Mr. Arthur, what if you and I could work together to help Miss Pierce and gather the town back to the church?"

The old man twisted his mouth in curiosity. "I would like to see that happen, but how does Mari have a part in it?"

Rowe set the toppled stool upright as an idea came to him. He remembered Dusty stating that aside from the regular attendees, most people were occasional visitors, drifting in and out when they needed to hear a word of encouragement. "A dramatic conversion might draw the rest of Assurance to renew their own faith. Marissa already has your support, I gather."

"Rebecca and I offered her a place to live and work, but she won't take it. She worries about doing us more harm than good."

"She has the desire to leave the saloon. She just needs a push from people who care. It's as though Marissa knows better, and wants to do better, but is being held back."

"You hit the nail on the head, Reverend," Zachary agreed. "She wasn't raised to be in the position you see her in. Her mother came from good stock."

"What happened?"

"Elizabeth got mixed up with an actor fellow who became Mari's father. Gregory Pierce strolled into town one day with a traveling show, and before we knew it, Elizabeth went and fell in love with the man. They lived here for nine years after Mari was born, but Greg wasn't too keen on life in our little town. He wanted to go back to the cities, be onstage in the concert halls and on the riverboats. So he took Elizabeth and Mari on down to St. Louis." Zachary paused to set the two pairs of boots on the floor. "Well, Greg found that folks just didn't care for his old act. He fell on hard times and took to gambling. When the debts got bigger, he eventually left his family to fend for themselves. Elizabeth went to work in a dancehall then, desperate to make ends meet."

Rowe couldn't imagine what it was like for Marissa as a small girl, with no stable home. "Why didn't Marissa's mother come back to Assurance? Surely she had family or friends she could turn to."

"By that time most of the folks Elizabeth knew moved out to seek land of their own or build the railroad. Her own parents died on a missions trip farther west. Before Elizabeth got sick with cholera, she made Jason Garth's acquaintance while he was staying in Missouri. He was a businessman, startin' up the plans for his own saloon here. He had already drawn up her contract to work for him."

"Marissa's mother wanted to work for Jason?"

"She had no other prospects. But Elizabeth died before she could fulfill the agreement. She still owed him money."

"How did Marissa start working for him?"

"Mari was seventeen when her mother passed, still in need of a guardian. Jason told her that he would give her room and board if she agreed to take her mother's place."

Zachary paused again. Strong emotions came upon him, and his kindly face grew weathered and shadowed.

"Sir, I didn't mean to stir these sad memories," Rowe said.

The old man drew a breath and collected himself. "I think about Mari and her family often. I'll gladly share what I know if it serves to help her. Where was I?"

"You said Jason promised Marissa room and board if she took Elizabeth's place."

"Yes. So when she turned eighteen, he had a contract officially drawn up for her to work in his establishment."

Rowe felt sick to his stomach. "That's why she's there."

Zachary shook his head slowly from side to side. "Rebecca and I were so happy to see Mari when she came back after so many years. But on the arm of Jason Garth..." His voice trailed off as his recollection became too much.

Rowe observed the genuine love and concern Zachary held for Marissa. If Mr. Arthur and his wife had been given the opportunity, there was no doubt they would have taken her in as their own. "Were you and Mrs. Arthur friends with Elizabeth?"

"We knew Elizabeth from her grandparents. Rebecca and I would go to their home in the early days for Bible study. Her grandmother, a Comanche woman, married Hank Procter, one of the missionaries."

That explained the striking beauty that lent itself to Marissa's features.

"Thank you for sharing this with me, Mr. Arthur. I know it must have been hard—"

The old man suddenly jabbed a finger at him. "See here, young man. I didn't share this with you to see if all my memories were still between my ears. Mari told my wife and me the truth about her life so we wouldn't judge her. I expect you to put this new knowledge to work and help her. Hear me, son?"

Not expecting such a powerful reaction to come from an elderly man, Rowe was stunned. He put on the boots he came in with. "I'll go to her. My guess is, she's at the saloon. I'll be back to purchase shoes another time."

"One other thing. Yes, her conversion would be good for the church. But whether she converts or not, she needs our help. Understand?"

"Yes, sir," Rowe agreed. But he was still excited at the idea of saloon girl, rescued from a shady establishment, finding new life in the church. It was just what he needed to start his ministry with a bang.

Heading for Jason's saloon, Rowe completely forgot about the broken hammer and trip to the general store.

Chapter 7

MARISSA BEGAN TO set up the ale glasses for the evening crowd. Thursday night usually drew in fair numbers for the saloon.

Jason devised a skit routine for the girls that involved customer participation. They would go about the room and get men to do impressions of animals, famous people, or other fluff. The men could earn a kiss, a tickle, or quick cuddle. Jason said that it made men want to spend more time with the girls—private time, even—and would allow them a small sampling of what their money could buy.

She was very thankful only to have to dance and serve beer.

"How long is it gonna take with those glasses?" Jason demanded from behind the counter. "You have whiskey to dilute too."

"I'm working as fast as I can." As she increased her pace, her elbow bumped into a stray glass that hung precariously close to the edge of a table. It fell to the floor, shattering across her boots.

"Clumsy woman." Jason uttered a curse as he grabbed a broom that rested against the staircase and flung it in her direction. She picked it up from the floor, careful not to slit her hand on the larger glass shards. "You wouldn't have to rush and make mistakes if you hadn't wasted all that time talking to the preacher man."

Marissa swept as he approached, his boots crushing the glass beneath his heels into a gritty powder. Cigar smoke clung to his clothing like cheap cologne. "Just what were you two laughing and smiling about in old Zachary's store?"

Her stomach turned at the overpowering scent of rye whiskey on his breath. "He needed work boots. I showed him some."

Jason snorted loudly. "Since when did you start advising men of the cloth about what boots to buy?"

"Zachary asked me to help."

"And while you're helping old Zachary sell shoes, you're telling the reverend how to shut my saloon down. I know about his Sunday sermon. He's got every church-goin' man and woman in town talking about being a good steward with money, about not being deceitful. I even had Sheriff McGee come in to ask me if my dealings were fair."

Marissa dealt with a mix of trepidation and secret gladness that Jason's practices were being called to attention. "We can make the dealings fair and still earn honest money. Lower the drink prices and charge an entrance fee at a certain hour of the night, for instance. Or let the men have a free dance if they've already spent a certain amount."

He stopped her hands on the broom handle. "I knew you had something to do with this. It's your way of getting revenge."

"No, Jason. I want to be good to the customers and treat them with respect. I hate lying. Can't you see if we dignify them, they'll patronize the saloon even more?"

"I know what he's doing," he barked. "That preacher's making an example of you. He is using you to build his church. Draw in the sinners! I'm not about to change my ways because some new preacher skips through town and charms the starch out of your petticoat!"

She snatched her hands away from his. "You think that's what this is about, that I only want to do what's right to impress a man? You don't know anything about me."

Daylight shot in, illuminating the drab browns of the room and the tiny dust particles that floated about. Marissa gasped when she identified the tall man who stood at the entrance.

"You lost, Reverend?" Jason snarled.

Rowe closed the doors behind him, sending the saloon back into its murkiness. He kept his eyes on the proprietor, his face unreadable. "May I speak to Miss Pierce?"

This sudden interruption was sure to make things worse. Marissa looked frantically at Jason. He started fist fights when provoked, and there wasn't a time she could remember when he didn't finish them.

"Say something to make him leave," Jason uttered to her under his breath. "Say it, or I'll hurt him. Do it quick."

With a smirk he then gestured for Rowe to come forward. "Go ahead. Talk to her." Taking his time to go to the other end of the bar, he sat down on a stool to watch the impending exchange.

"Thank you." Rowe approached.

Jason drew a cigar from his vest pocket and lit the tip. Inhaling, he let a puff of smoke drift out of his nostrils. Marissa pictured a bull preparing to gore his rival. "Sure you don't want somethin' to drink, Reverend? A glass of milk, perhaps? I'm afraid we're out of holy water."

Marissa glowered at Jason, but Rowe didn't react to the insult. "No, thank you, Mr. Garth. I only came to speak briefly to Miss Pierce, and then I'll be on my way."

Rowe blocked Jason's view of the two of them as he faced her. He always kept his posture straight and tall, but in the dim confines of the saloon, his broad-shouldered frame became the focal point.

"Hello again, Reverend Winford."

"Call me Rowe." He persisted with familiarity. "We've been introduced."

"Rowe." Her voice sounded small and nervous to her ears. She spared a glance at Jason to see if he noticed the change in pitch. He pretended to study the mysterious smudges on the ceiling. "What brings you to the saloon?"

"One other matter." Rowe carried on. "I wanted to invite you to church this Sunday." The seriousness in his eyes let her know he was not being facetious.

Jason let out a snicker.

Humiliation crept into Marissa's cheeks and flooded her whole body. Didn't Rowe know where he was? More importantly, what she was? She swept the line of gritty glass between them into a pile. "I'm afraid I'll have to decline."

"But you should hear the choir. They'll be singing several beautiful pieces."

Was he naïve enough to expect her to actually attend? The sanctuary would be so abuzz with hushed whispers that no one would hear the sermon for the constant drone of gossip.

"You shouldn't be here. Why do you keep after me? Did Mr. Arthur put you up to this?"

Rowe shifted. "He told me about you and your mother—"

"My mother? You spoke about her?"

Jason made no attempts to hide his eavesdropping after that. The proprietor turned the stool so that he could view them both full face.

How could Mr. Arthur have exposed her life to a practical stranger? Rowe Winford had been in town for less than two weeks, and already he knew more about her life than its four hundred residents. "Zachary shouldn't have talked about my mother."

"He was only looking to help you."

"How? By advising you to come in here and tell me how bad a sinner I am?"

"No." His face darkened at the accusation. "He said none of those things. I came only to invite you to church."

"Thank you for the invitation. I will consider it. Now I have work that I must be getting back to. Will that be all, Reverend?"

Her abruptness was not scaring him away. He planted his feet to the floor as defiantly as she did. "Will you be in attendance this Sunday?"

Surely something vile could be said to make him leave. Marissa put the broom aside and placed defiant hands on her hips, peppering her words with extra emphasis. "Yes. Yes, I will be there, if you want the church to see what a saloon girl looks like. You can warn all the decent, upright women of what will happen to them if they don't do what you tell them. Satisfied?"

Anger flashed in his eyes. The muscles clenched in her stomach. She knew she set something off inside him that wouldn't benefit her to see.

"It was *my* idea to invite you to church, if only for the sake of showing you a courtesy that I hope you are well-mannered enough to accept."

Marissa recoiled as if she had received a physical blow from him. Rowe continued. "Only God can judge. Any negative opinion that you have of 'decent, upright women' reflects your own feelings of inadequacy."

Marissa had been called names and received taunts all her adult life, but nothing struck so close to her core as the truth he unleashed upon her that moment. Inadequate was the way she perceived herself, to say the least. His words reaffirmed what she believed for so long.

And if a man of God could say it, who was to argue? The emotional blow that had been dealt her personified into a pain that made her hands throb.

Rowe spun on his heel and gave Jason a curt nod. "Good day to you, Mr. Garth."

The saloon doors were pushed open with a bit too much force and slammed shut to announce his departure.

After a few moments Jason put out his cigar. "Well done. He won't be back for a while."

Marissa returned the broom to its niche behind the counter and prepared to measure out the night's whiskey. "I did what you wanted. Please leave me to finish this work."

Jason snickered. "If the way the reverend spoke to you is how he delivers sermons, he'll be gone back to Virginia again by the end of the season."

What had gone through his mind to make him lash out at Marissa? Rowe fumbled through his sermon notes. Church was about to start in ten minutes, and here he was once more, disorganized and unable to focus on the day's topic.

Marissa had preoccupied him ever since he stormed out of the saloon on Thursday. His anger subsided only when he arrived home and started hammering on the fence, and by then it was much too late to go back and apologize. It was doubtful she would want to hear anything he had to say after he'd spoken those cruel words.

Why should she graciously accept his invitation to come to church? Of course she would be wary of accepting an invitation when he came upon her in a place where she never wanted him to find her again.

And that comment about inadequacy. How could he give her such an analysis? He was sure he had seen only an inkling of the talent, intelligence, and abilities that God placed within her to survive all this time on her own. Very few young women would have the fortitude to last very long, if left in the guardianship of one such as Jason Garth.

"Forgive me for judging her, Lord," he prayed more than

once. "I offered to help her, but I failed. I let my temper get the better of me."

It'll be a miracle if I ever speak to her again. There went the plans for helping her and the church.

Music began to filter through the door of the study. The organist played the entrance hymn, and that meant people were filing into the pews. Rowe threw on his coat and prayed that God would use the sermon to touch someone's heart.

What had gone through her mind to come here today? As Marissa told herself repeatedly, she had no business at the church.

Early that morning she awakened while Jason and the girls were still in their rooms, sleeping off the effects of the previous Saturday night's work. Dressed in a forest green taffeta gown with white lace gloves and a small, matching veiled bonnet, she crept down the stairs as quietly as possible. Then, with her grandmother's worn and faded white Bible in hand, she tiptoed outside to walk the short path to her destination.

The doors to the church were closed, yet the unified song of the congregation rang out. Marissa almost thought she heard Rowe's baritone among them but decided against it, not knowing what type of singing voice he possessed. If it was anything like the way he spoke, though, it would be deep and rich.

Her hand rested on the door handle. For years she hadn't been in a church. Were services held the same way she remembered when she attended with her mother and father? Would she be welcomed into the sanctuary or ushered out without delay?

Only one way of knowing.

The congregation progressed to their second hymn as she walked in. Their backs were to her as they sang facing the pulpit or followed along in their hymnals. Albert Pate played on the organ. In the soprano section of the choir his wife led the women in a measure of high notes. Mrs. Pate and Marissa's mother had been friends once, but the woman never did acknowledge Marissa, except on the first day that she returned to Assurance with Jason. She overheard Mrs. Pate talking with the liveryman's wife in the general store. "It appears Elizabeth raised up a soiled dove. I knew nothing good could come of her marriage to that Gregory Pierce."

Marissa scanned the pews. The more notable of citizens were closer to the front: Sophie Charlton and her family; the mayor Humphrey Hooper and his wife; Tom Euell, the newspaper editor. Zachary and Rebecca Arthur sat just behind them.

Finding an empty pew in the back of the sanctuary in the last row, she sat down at the far end closest to the door. The interior hadn't changed much since her last visit as a child. The old altar cloth of blue had been replaced with royal purple, but the pews, the location of the organist, iron lamp sconces, and brass candleholders, even the hymnals, remained the same.

Of course the preacher was a new addition.

Rowe led the congregation in "Amazing Grace," singing the lyrics by heart. It was a familiar song to Marissa as well. She pondered over the words and their meaning. *Amazing grace, how sweet the sound, that saved a wretch like me.* She didn't know whether she liked the song for its message or for the memories it brought to mind.

Surely the Lord's faithfulness didn't extend to a woman like herself, else she would not be in her current situation. Her mother wouldn't have suffered. Both her mother and grandparents had placed their trust in God, and look where it had gotten them. All gone from the earth, fallen to sicknesses, while she was left alive to carry on a lonely existence.

The song ended, and the congregation sat down. Marissa scooted further down in her seat so Rowe wouldn't find her amidst the people. No doubt seeing her would make him feel all the more smug in his ability to draw even the nonchurch-goer into the assembly.

Rowe turned the gilded pages of the large Bible on the podium. "Today I would like to talk about the sin of gossip and how we should have a heart for the Lord. Turn with me to Proverbs sixteen, verse twenty-eight."

What a concept. What need did God have of anyone's heart, as powerful as He was? Opening her Bible, she flipped the time-worn pages back and forth until she found the correct chapter in the Old Testament that Rowe directed everyone to turn to. Save for Genesis, Exodus, and Psalms, she had forgotten the order of all the books.

As the sermon began, she tried to read the verses for herself. *A froward man soweth strife: and a whisperer separateth chief friends.* Marissa understood what was being said in them, but not where the deeper meaning emerged. How did Rowe glean profound teaching from what looked like two simple sentences?

"The same message applies to us today," he explained, looking up from the Scriptures. "We sin when we gossip and spread rumors. It can damage lives irreparably. Instead, we need to maintain a quiet life. The way to do that is to not entertain those who slander and to gently remind them to refrain in their behavior..."

Marissa curled her toes. She knew where Rowe drew inspiration for the sermon, and she had no desire to be his muse. *God, lead me.* She found herself praying. The action made her afraid and embarrassed. The last time she prayed, she had been a child, kneeling beside her mother. When Elizabeth died, it felt like God left her too.

"We need to seek forgiveness, repent, and ask God to lead

in the right direction." Rowe closed the sermon with two more verses and a prayer. Marissa bowed her head respectfully, as she remembered seeing her grandmother do, as she herself had done when she used to say her evening prayers at the foot of her bed. Her mother had always been beside her, even when that bed turned to a straw pallet and then to a frayed, unwashed blanket on the cold, hard ground.

As she sensed the prayer drawing to a close, Marissa rose silently and slipped out the door. There. She had gone to church and honored his invitation. But that did not mean she had to stay to talk to him or subject herself to the glares and whisperings of the congregation.

Marissa hurried down the road, eager to put as much distance between her and Rowe as she possibly could.

Chapter 8

SINCE HEARING ROWE'S sermon on the dangers and sin of gossip, Marissa felt a glimmer of hope that the people of Assurance would take heed of the message. Already she could tell that a few had been listening on Sunday. When she went to deposit the saloon's earnings into the bank the following morning, there were decidedly fewer snickers and sneers as she stood in line for the teller. The little improvement she saw inspired her to open the Bible again to see what other principles it contained.

Taking a break from her duties Wednesday evening, Marissa read Christ's words to His disciples and contemplated the message. *Take my yoke upon you, and learn of me; for I am meek and lowly in heart: and ye shall find rest unto your souls.*

She looked up from the old Bible and stared at a faded advertisement of her parents' riverboat skit hanging in the corner of her small room. How the disciples must have felt when Jesus gave them this instruction. No longer having to shoulder the problems and distresses of their times, they could rely on their Master to come to their aid.

If someone offered to shoulder her burdens, she would fly. There would be no worries about money or where she would stay or where her next meal would come from. Someone else could handle those troubles.

But there was no one. Jason kept her because she needed to pay off her mother's debt and because she increased his profit. The town made her the object of their ridicule. Since her mother died, she relied on herself and would continue to do so if she wanted to survive.

But you don't have to rely on yourself.

Looking up from her Bible, Marissa blinked. Where had that thought come from?

The door to her room snapped open and Jason burst in, crossing the floor in three loud stomps. "That old sot Jedediah and his gang drank half a case of my bourbon tonight and wanted to put their bill on credit. They haven't paid me for the last one back in May."

"Did you allow them to do it again?" Marissa was used to Jason complaining about his customers' habits when he was the one who encouraged their bad business.

"No." He spoke slowly, irritated when she didn't share in his grumbling. "And I told him that he and his leech friends can't have another drink in my establishment until their bill is current."

"That's good, Jason. Maybe you'll see that money sooner rather than later."

"Or lose my best customer while I wait for him to try and come back."

"Jedediah can't be that great if he owes you so much money."

"He drops his coin on the girls too."

Marissa pictured the spindly-legged, pot-bellied man and shuddered. "I'm grateful I've never seen that man's money."

Jason cast a critical eye on her figure. "Don't think you're not too good for it. He just likes his girls small. If you weren't such a tall treetop woman, he might make you a bit richer."

Marissa quelled her instinct to trade insults. It didn't seem to be the right response anymore. He gave her the meanest look he could muster when his words garnered no reaction.

"Since when did you start readin' that?" His focus shifted to the Bible in her lap.

"Since my grandmother passed it down to my mother and she gave it to me."

Her hands instinctively went to cover the Bible, but she stopped. Why should she be ashamed of reading it?

"Ever since last Sunday you've been carrying that Bible and glancing at it every spare chance you get. I know where you went that morning too, because I heard your steps go out your room."

"I'm not supposed to rise before noon on Sundays now?"

"Simone watched you from the window and saw how you were dressed. She came and told me where you were likely headed."

The fact that he had the ladies scouting for him gave her chills. "I'm your best and longest-standing employee. You know I'll keep my loyalty to you until my contract is finished. Why should you care where I go on my days off?"

"Tsk, tsk, darlin'. Don't get defensive. Simone was only curious." Jason shrugged. "But we both think you're not church material."

Marissa rubbed her hands in a massaging motion. He only said it to hurt her feelings. It couldn't be true. After all, she just read how Jesus forgave the woman at the well. That woman also lived a sinful life, and the Lord accepted her. The biblical example strengthened Marissa to defend herself.

"You and Simone don't always have to be right."

"Hold on a minute." Jason pushed himself in front of her and cupped her chin in his hand. His fingers dug into her flesh as his lips curled into a nasty parody of a smile. "I know where this sudden interest in the Word comes from. You're sweet on the reverend."

He cut her off as she started to protest. "No man like Rowe Winford wants a slatternly woman like you. You may not entertain the men in this saloon like the other girls, but where you work still defines your reputation."

Bile threatened to rise in her throat as he continued his verbal assault.

"You are a whore in his eyes, like you are in the eyes of everyone else in this pathetic town. Better stick with me, if you want to see any gain from it."

The Bible lay at their feet where she had dropped it the moment he seized her. Jason launched a wad of spittle on the floor near the worn, white leather cover and exited.

The week after delivering what many in the congregation declared to be a rousing sermon, Rowe was forced to turn to the heavier aspects of being a minister. Midweek one of the town's founders passed away in his sleep. The family made haste with the arrangements, and on Thursday Rowe performed his first funeral service in Assurance.

He presided over the entire service. It included comforting and counseling the man's widow, surviving children, and close associates. After locating a gravedigger, he consulted with the undertaker so that the family would have some of their burdens lessened.

By the time it was over, he was exhausted and had to drag himself home, where he slept for the remainder of the day. In the evening Rowe awakened and read a recent letter from his younger brother Nathaniel back home in Virginia.

You must find it hard adjusting as a lone reverend, ministering to the needs of a small town. How is it, to be planted on the infinite plains of western America while your entire family is in Virginia?

Rowe finished the letter and picked up a blank sheet of stationery to reply. The pen hovered over the paper as he debated whether to write about the climate or the people he met.

You should be ashamed to think of that soiled saloon girl

when your sweet wife lies cold in the ground. He heard the evil voice again. Though inaudible to his ears, it jarred his mind with guilt and condemnation.

Rowe bowed his head, fighting against it. Clammy sweat formed on his brow.

Help me, Lord, to live the life You planned for me.

Expecting the sense of loss to seize him again and run off with him to a dark, lonely place, he struggled to find words to write to his brother. It was time to forget the past, to move forward. He had to find a way to get past the temptation to do otherwise.

Marissa's last few days of work flew by. On Friday, at the end of the evening, Marissa left two sets of red and black dance costumes draped over a chair, having no more need of them.

Sorting through her everyday blouses and skirts, she arranged them separately in leather valises. Tomorrow morning she would find a pair of strong hands to deliver her things to the local hotel where she would be staying until she found employment. The money would last for a good month or two, enough time for her to acquire something, surely.

God, help me. If I don't find work, I will not last long. Her gaze swept the small room that had belonged to her for the past two years. The bed nestled against the wall, the blanket turned down for her last night here. The chair and little table looked pitiful and bare since the removal of their frilly coverings. She removed the riverboat advertisement from the wall and tucked it safely in one of her books. Shelves lay empty as books, lamps, and toiletries all were packed and stored away.

Her Bible lay on the bed, one of the last things to be packed. The very act of holding it and turning the pages gave her a comfort that she missed in life.

The saloon din downstairs rose as the hour grew late.

The tinkling piano gave entrance to Simone's routine. At Marissa's urging, the older woman had taken her place for the hurdy-gurdy dance. From the sound of glasses clinking and men cheering, she was a good replacement.

Marissa changed into her nightgown and brushed out her hair. For an hour after the saloon closed, she read familiar passages from the book of Psalms. A thin blanket covered her legs on the bed.

Falling into an uneasy sleep, she started when someone turned a key in the latch of her bedroom door.

"You thought to lock your door and take the night off?"

Jason's voice chafed her ears. The recesses of his face swallowed the light of the candle he held. Marissa instinctively drew her legs closer to her body, tucking the Bible at her side. What time was it? The darkness outside and the quiet of the saloon told her it was late. Two or three o'clock in the morning.

He came to the side of the bed, reeking of strong spirits. Something was different about him. His usual spiteful humor was replaced by something darker, something cruel.

"What are you hiding?" He indicated to her right arm. She shifted in bed.

"Nothing."

"Show me."

"There is nothing to show. Leave me be, Jason."

"You lie!"

Her shoulder hit the wall at a painful angle as he shoved her roughly against the headboard. Seizing the Bible that was under her arm, he flung it across the floor.

Marissa's heart thundered against her chest. Pain coursed down her left arm in waves as she held her shoulder. "I will be gone tomorrow morning. Don't do this. My contract is out—"

Jason struck her across the face before she could finish her sentence. The hard blow sent her crashing against the wooden headboard. Her vision blinded to pinpoints of yellow light.

"Your contract isn't out until I say it is! You'll leave when I tell you to leave!"

The coppery taste of blood formed in her mouth. Jason clamped down on her leg and dragged her from the bed. The splintery wooden floor scraped her bare knees and hands. She pushed to get up, but he sent her on her back with a kick to the stomach.

"I should have done more of this to you earlier. Then you would know how to behave with a man." He started unbuckling his belt.

"No!" Her abdomen throbbed as she pleaded with him. Each breath felt like drawing in heavy gulps of fire.

He whisked the belt from his pant loops and lashed her across the torso. Her body instinctively curled up into a tight ball as he whipped her, her screams drowning out the sound of each lash.

"What's going on, Jason?" Simone appeared in the doorway, along with two other frightened saloon girls.

"Get to your rooms!" He paused in his whipping to address them.

That pause was what Marissa needed to escape. Groping for something to throw at him, her fingers found it in a heavy porcelain pitcher and washbowl stacked on the floor, too big and odd-shaped to be packed into a trunk. She hurled the pitcher at his head with all her might.

Once it left her hand, she didn't stay to find out if it hit her mark. Scrambling to her feet, she made for the door. Simone and the other girls jumped out of the way before she collided into them. Marissa raced down the hallway and flew down the stairs, leaping the last several when she lost her balance. More pain seared through her body.

Above, she heard Jason order the girls to pursue.

Her bare feet trampled on sharp rocks stuck in the unpaved road outside, but she didn't slow down. She ran as fast as she could through the town, searching for a place to hide.

Stark moonlight cut a path through the road. The shops and stalls had been closed and boarded up for hours. All the lamps in the houses had long since gone out. No one was outside. Not the sheriff, a passerby, or even a late-working blacksmith showed himself as she searched left and right for help.

Hooves pounded behind her. Jason's curses carried in the air as he pursued on horseback. "You can't leave me! You owe on your mother's debt!"

Marissa's lungs tore with each frantic breath. Her mind willed her to go faster. Wind stung her bruised face, forcing tears to flow toward her ears. Jason had passed the point of anger. He was out for a kill. She veered on the left path at the fork in the road, toward the lake.

Moonlight failed to illuminate the path as it did the town road. Stumbling in ditches and grooves left by wagon wheels, her foot twisted painfully on a large stone. She fell and clawed her way back to her feet, ignoring the agony that raced up her left leg.

"Marissa, I see you. I hear your breathing."

If she could get to the forest of trees surrounding the edge of the lake, she could hide there until Jason rode down the path. It would wind around and take him back to town. Then she could return to the fork and take the right path, where an old, abandoned cabin stood at the end of it. The cabin would provide shelter and a hiding place until morning.

Bramble and twigs stabbed her feet as she came upon the first line of trees and forced herself through. Low-lying branches caught in her hair and tore at her nightgown, ripping the lightweight fabric at the shoulder. Her skin was cut and scraped as she darted between the tree trunks.

Jason skidded his horse to a halt some distance behind her. Marissa dropped to her knees on the forest floor, hoping the brambles hid her white nightgown from the moonlight.

The trees hid what little moonlight there was to see him. Marissa barely made out the outline of his horse as it stood in the middle of the path, pawing the ground restlessly. Sweat burned her eyes as it ran down her face. She listened for Jason's clomping steps and wondered if he would dismount and search for her on foot.

Minutes stretched like hours before the horse and rider went onward down the left path. Marissa slowly allowed herself to take deep breaths as the sound of horse's hooves faded.

Blood flowed from her nose. She wiped it on the sleeve of her nightgown. With head pounding and a wave of nausea assaulting her, she picked herself up and pushed through the remaining trees.

The lake edge waited at the end of the small forest. Moonlight reflected off the shimmering surface, lighting the way to the path around the right side. She hurried along, dizzy, legs protesting every inch of the way.

The old cabin was just down the path. An oil lamp's glow shone from one of the downstairs windows. Someone had moved in recently.

Marissa spurred herself on, and the ground shook beneath her. She spun in time to see an unsaddled horse rushing toward her. She leapt aside. A hand caught in her hair.

Jason jerked her head back. Marissa cried out as he pulled her to him, his nails digging into her scalp. She raked her own nails into the flesh of his hand until he let go. Grabbing hold of her nightgown, he ripped the already torn and tattered garment at the sleeve.

Marissa broke free and stumbled backward, blurred vision

and dizziness overpowering her other senses. The ground tilted to the left and right. Jason was a large, menacing haze that fast closed in.

"Get away from me!" She threw her arms in front of herself in defense. The action further upset her delicate footing, sending her toppling upon the grass in front of the cabin.

Jason pounced. She braced for attack, her head and heart pounding as one. *God, help me! Where are You?*

A movement occurred in her right field of peripheral vision. Another person. A man's voice.

Through half-closed eyelids Marissa saw the figure run up upon Jason and block his attack. The figure drove him backward, away from her. Arms swung. Jason swore, reaching for the knife he always kept in his pocket.

The distinctive sound came of bone cracking.

The knife clattered harmlessly in the dirt. Jason fell to the ground on his hands and knees beside it, howling as blood streamed from his nose.

Marissa saw no more. Pain, fatigue, and the taste of blood from her injuries made the nausea finally overtake her. She turned and vomited in the grass.

Chapter 9

ROWE FLEXED HIS fingers as the feeling returned to them. He meant to push Jason away, not be forced to punch him in the nose. The saloon proprietor left him no choice but to intervene.

He heard a woman screaming for help and ran outside to find Jason attacking Marissa as though she were some forest animal. The initial sight of her, filthy, bleeding, her gown in tatters, caused a reaction within him that awaited no thought. He dashed from the front door to jump in front of Jason. Absorbing the blow meant for Marissa, he shoved Jason back before he could recover and strike her again. Jason threw wild punches, but Rowe effectively dodged them, long enough to deliver a swift blow that struck the saloon-keeper on the nose.

When it was over, Jason stumbled to his feet and loped down the road to his horse. The animal carried him away at a fast gallop to town.

Rowe crouched beside Marissa now as she wept softly, her head sloped on her chest in a miserable fashion. He smelled the sickness that she had expelled in the grass. His pulse raced when he saw the dark stains streaking her cheeks and chin—blood mixed with tears.

"Marissa, can you walk?"

She didn't raise her head. "My leg..."

He couldn't see much in the dark, but her left leg appeared to be swollen around the ankle. "I'm going to carry you into the house. Put your arms around my neck."

"N–no..."

But he had already hooked an arm beneath her knees and around her back. He stood up with her slowly, adjusting her weight in his arms so that she wouldn't slip.

"I'm too heavy," she murmured into his shoulder.

Rowe carried her into the cabin and kicked the door shut behind him. Going into the study proved to be a challenge, but he managed to place her upon the settee and moved the lamp closer to inspect her injuries.

The nightgown alone told the story of her night's struggles, bearing streaks of dirt, leaves, grass, and blood. Where it had been torn or ripped away from her skin, he saw the various scrapes and cuts along her shoulder and arms. The left ankle was swelling and inflamed.

"Please allow me to look." As he reached out slowly for the gown's hem, she jerked back like an animal cornered.

"Don't touch me." She eyed him suspiciously between strands of hair that fell in her face.

"Marissa, I carried you into the cabin. I want to help you." Rowe studied her pupils for signs of shock. Her heavy breathing punctured the room's silence.

"Where's Jason?" She hugged her knees at her own mention of the man's name.

Rowe clamped down his jaw in silent anger for the terrified state Jason's actions had brought her to. "He's gone. He took off on his horse. You're safe."

She remained with limbs drawn until her curled body took up very little space on the settee. "He could be waiting in the woods."

"I promise that Jason will not harm you here." Rowe spoke as though the words themselves were weapons of defense. "I won't let him."

Honey-brown eyes caught the light of the flame from the mounted opal font lamp above the desk. He knew then he would do anything in his power to protect her.

"Am I safe from you?"

First Marissa was pursued by a drunk, raging man. Now she sat alone in a cabin in the woods with another male. He understood her reasons for being fearful, but the distrust still stung like salt water on an open sore.

"I would never harm you. I want to help. First, your ankle. May I see it?"

She gradually relaxed until her legs extended across the settee. Rowe gingerly took the swollen ankle in his hand. The reddened skin was warm to the touch. "It might be broken. Can you move your leg?"

Marissa nodded, and he had to ask her to demonstrate. Maneuvering her ankle in a circle, she winced. "It hurts."

"It's not broken at least. It's just a bad sprain. And you've got some splinters." He examined the filthy, blackened soles of her feet.

She drew in a ragged breath as he pulled the sizeable splinters out with his thumb and the edge of a fingernail. He hated to cause her pain, but it was necessary in order to prevent infection.

Rowe left her seated to go upstairs for the washbasin and pitcher. On a shelf near the washstand he kept clean linens, a bottle of Dr. Tichenor's Antiseptic, and a jar of liniment. He took them and returned to the lower level of the cabin.

Marissa watched from the other room as he heated some water on the stove and poured it into the basin. He carried it into the study and set it on the floor beside her.

"I would have left the saloon a long time ago if I had the money. This is my fault."

Rowe lathered a clean cloth with soap and wrung out the excess water. "It is not. Jason is the one at fault for not having self-control." He pushed the wild, tangled sea of black hair away from her face, biting down his jaw when he uncovered the developing bruise across her cheek, and the dried blood under her nose. "Jason's a disturbed man to beat a woman."

To his relief Marissa allowed him to clean the dirt and debris from her face. She had a small gash on her forehead with swelling in the surrounding area, which he dabbed carefully with the antiseptic.

"Jason did it because he didn't want me to leave." She frowned when the antiseptic burned. "His anger's gotten worse since the customers discovered that he dilutes the whiskey and overcharges."

"You told them about the price inflation?"

"No, you preached about it in a sermon. Men have been repeating what they heard from you and the churchgoers."

Rowe stilled his hand. "I gave a sermon to make the town aware of deceitfulness. I intended to expose Jason without getting you in trouble, but it happened, anyhow." Guilt settled on him, black as the stains on Marissa's feet.

"Oh, I don't blame you. I'm glad you told the church. I was too worried about myself and scared to do anything."

"I caused this to happen to you." He stared at the red-tinged water in the basin as ice cold sensations ate at him from the inside. Yet another woman he hurt.

Concentrating on the scrapes along her calves, he washed and dressed them. They were as shapely and strong as the black-seamed stockings of her dance costume had once indicated.

"If anyone saw the two of us like this, it would be scandalous," she noted.

"I could almost agree, except they would change their opinion if they knew what happened to you tonight."

Marissa shook her head. "They would think me cursed. I've been trying to get away from Jason and that saloon for years. I thought I had saved up enough money to leave town, but I got swindled out of an investment by so-called businessmen. No one's hiring in Claywalk, either. I'm here in Assurance with no family, no friends, and little prospect."

"You have friends, Marissa," he reminded her. "The Arthurs adore you."

"I don't want them involved in this."

"But they are involved. They know the events of your life better than anyone else, and that causes them to reach out to you more."

"What events of your life brought you here?" She shifted her weight on the settee as she eyed him curiously.

It was best to go along with her hasty way of ending an uncomfortable subject if he wanted to make any progress. Rowe had to bring it up again shortly if they were going to find a place for her to rest safely tonight. "I wanted a place to start fresh because I lost much after the war. My wife died delivering our son."

Marissa's eyes widened. "Did the boy survive?"

"No. I buried them both in Virginia."

Her voice was as soft as a child's. "I'm deeply sorry for you."

He picked up another cloth and started tending to her feet. "I understand your reasons for wanting to leave a place because I've also gone through intolerable situations. Unlike you, the faults were my own."

"Your loss was tragic, but you can't blame yourself."

"But I could have prevented that danger had I watched the signs. She wasn't strong enough."

"No one can ensure that birthing a child won't put a woman in danger. I'm sorry if I sound cruel."

"No, you don't." She sounded like the voice of truth, even if Rowe could not accept her as such. She hadn't seen how Josephine suffered, how weak a shell his wife became in her final hours.

In the dim light Marissa's cheeks held the tiniest hint of a blush. Her voice softened again. "Did you have other family to turn to for comfort when they passed? A sister or brother?"

"Yes and no. My family wanted me to farm instead of going into the ministry." His gaze traveled to the desk, where Nathaniel's letter lay folded atop a set of study volumes. "But it's different with you. You have the help and concern from Zachary and Rebecca. I urge you to accept it."

The muscles in her foot tensed. "You saw what went on tonight. I can't let that happen to them."

"It won't. They're strong people, like you."

She propped her cheek against her hand, fixing skeptical eyes on him. "You think running and screaming for help is strong?"

"Not just physical. I see your strength in character because you persevere. A lesser woman wouldn't have survived this long."

A single tear drop fell onto her cheek. "I feel like my strength is just about to give out."

"Then ask God to supply you with His. He never tires. He's waiting to be with you."

"Are you saying that because you're a preacher?"

"I'm saying it because I'm a man. I've had my share of hard times." Rowe sensed the bond beginning to form between them. It was a kinship of sorts, spun from having to face some of the severest adversities the world had to offer. Marissa wasn't truly all that different from him. He presumed to be the helpful one, yet she was giving him encouragement simply with her presence and by listening.

"Do you think God meant for us to meet?" Her question was so innocent, it immediately brightened his mood.

"I believe it so. Do you consider me to be a friend, Marissa? Have you forgiven me for the way I spoke to you in the saloon?"

"There's nothing to forgive. I had to say those things to

make you mad enough to leave, or Jason would have become violent toward you." Her tears had dried, and now the familiar mischievous glint lit her eyes. "But since you're on the floor, scrubbing my feet, I can hardly think of a better show of remorse."

He considered the implications and burst out laughing. His humor infected her until she was forced to join in. Their combined hilarity filled the downstairs and carried throughout the sparse cabin. Rowe was grateful the nearest neighbor was a half mile down the road. Marissa composed herself first and reached down to take his hand. He nearly twitched from the touch of her soft palms. "You are a very good man. Thank you for coming to my aid tonight. It didn't concern you, but you took it upon yourself to prevent Jason from doing worse."

Rowe let the cloth drop from his other hand and rose to sit beside her, sobering at the intense gratitude on her face. Whispering, he tucked a strand of hair behind her ear. "It did concern me. Very much."

Marissa didn't flinch or shy away from his touch as his fingers grazed her cheek. The room suddenly grew too warm, and he had to draw back and stand. "I have to take you somewhere else. You may have other injuries that require a doctor, and a lady will need to assist you with your nightgown. We need to inform the sheriff of what happened as well."

"No sheriff." Realizing how badly the nightgown was torn at the shoulder, exposing part of her back and collarbone, she gathered the tatters in her fist. "And I don't need a doctor. Other than a few scrapes and bruises, I'm fine. My ankle will heal in a few days."

"You can't stay here for that long. I don't have the supplies to tend to you like you should be taken care of."

"I didn't plan on staying here. Are you concerned for my reputation, Reverend, or for your own?"

Rowe winced as she returned to the use of formal address. They warmed to each other beyond bare acquaintance, and once again his poor choice of words placed them at a distance. "My concern is for you. For your health and, yes, for your reputation. I respect you too much to let you be subjected to more ignorant gossip just as you're on the verge of starting a new life. I won't get the sheriff, if that's what you want, but please allow me to take you someplace where I know you'll be safe and well cared for." Pleading against her unwilling stare, he added, "Give me that much."

Marissa nodded, if still somewhat reluctantly. Rowe finished applying antiseptic to the visible wounds on her arms and feet and bandaged them. The ankle had ceased its swelling.

"I'll give you a shirt and some pants to wear over your gown. You probably have already guessed where I'm taking you."

She nodded reluctantly. "I'll scare Zachary and Rebecca if they see me like this."

Rowe left her momentarily to return to his bedroom. There he pulled a carefully folded tan shirt and pair of dark brown trousers from a trunk. The trousers were from his days at university, before the war put additional muscle weight on his frame. Since moving west, he meant to have the seams let out to fit his current proportions, but they would suit Marissa for the time being.

"I'll saddle the horse while you put these on." He laid the garments beside her, along with a belt.

"I'll only bring trouble to the Arthurs if I go there. Jason will come after me when he finds out I'm in their home."

"Jason will not trouble you again."

"How do you know?"

"Because I'm going to see him this morning, right after I take you to Zachary and Rebecca."

Rowe left Marissa in the study while he went to empty the washbasin outside. He scanned the darkened trees around him. The trip to town might be dangerous if Jason was foolish enough to wait in the woods.

Marissa was dressed by the time Rowe returned to the cabin.

"The horse is awake and saddled." He came into the study and rummaged through the desk until he withdrew a gun from the bottom drawer, an old Colt Navy revolver with some bullets. "After the war I hoped never to use a gun again. That was Virginia, where such a vow could be upheld for the most part in the more civilized areas of the state."

Marissa regarded him with widened eyes. "Don't break your vow for me."

The Colt disappeared into a holster inside his waistcoat. "If a gun is required to protect you, then I will carry it, but I hope to get you to safety before I have to even think of using this."

Holding the settee arm for support, Marissa struggled to stand to her feet.

"Sit back down. Your ankle hasn't healed already." Rowe crossed the room and proceeded to lift her again.

"I'm too heavy for this," she protested.

"I'm carrying you, aren't I?" He took her all the way outside and placed her atop the awaiting horse. Climbing astride the saddle behind her, Rowe patted his waistcoat for the Colt.

Leaning against him, Marissa moaned. "I've caused nothing but trouble this night."

Rowe kept her securely astride the horse with his arm across her torso. "Are you going to let hopelessness cloud your every thought?"

"I didn't intend to sound hopeless. Do I?"

"Yes, you do. Whatever you do, don't give up."

Chapter 10

THEY MADE IT to town without trouble. Marissa directed him to the Arthurs' house. The faintest trace of early morning light dawned on the horizon as Rowe knocked on the door.

It opened a crack, and a sleepy Mr. Arthur peeked out, yawning loudly. "Who's there? Do you have any idea what time it—oh, it's you, young man. What can we do for you at this absurdly early hour of the morning?"

Marissa heard their conversation from the street. The cuts and scratches she sustained chafed against her clothes, and sitting upon a horse did absolutely nothing to ease her discomfort. Still, fatigue set in hard enough to enable her to doze in the saddle. Absently stroking the animal's brown mane, she continued to listen to Rowe and Zachary.

"Marissa's been hurt. She needs someplace safe to stay until she can recover."

Zachary looked in her direction. "Hurt? What happened?"

Rowe gave a short explanation of the chase through the town and into the woods. "I heard her scream outside my cabin. Jason was assaulting her. I managed to stop him, but as you'll see, she's had a very hard night."

Marissa looked down at the pommel of the saddle. The Arthurs should not see her this way. It wasn't just her pride at stake. She hated for people to worry about her, and there was no question Zachary and Rebecca would fret themselves ill over this pit that she had fallen into.

Rowe returned after Zachary closed the door. "He's gone

to tell his wife to prepare the spare room for you. He said you can stay as long as you need."

She encircled her arms around his neck so he could take her inside the house. Rowe handled her as though she were fragile glass, about to shatter with a mere breath of air. No man considered her delicate before. Most of the time she was practically tossed, dragged, and yanked across the saloon's dancehall floor.

Zachary and Rebecca waited for her inside, worried and nervous. Rebecca also was in her nightclothes. Her curly red hair, peppered with gray, spilled out of its loose topknot as she hastened to lead the way down the short hall to the spare room.

"Oh, good," Rowe said under his breath. "No stairs."

"I heard that," Marissa chided.

"Set her on the bed, Reverend," Rebecca instructed. "I have drying cloths, water on the boil, smelling salts."

"She's injured, Rebecca," Zachary murmured, "not suffering a fainting spell."

"You only told me that Marissa was outside and she couldn't walk. I didn't know whether she was conscious or not."

The bed was soft and welcoming, especially after the fast trot upon the horse. Marissa stretched her hurt leg upon the coverlet. Her nausea returned. "Could I trouble you for a glass of water? My stomach is all nerves."

Rebecca poured her a glass of water from the bedside table and held it to her lips. "Drink, my dear."

"Thank you." The cold, clean-tasting water settled her stomach.

The older woman examined her face while she finished her glass. Like Rowe, Rebecca gently felt her bruised cheeks and temples for deeper wounds. "Who could do this to your pretty face?" She spotted the long hem of Marissa's nightgown where Marissa had tucked it in the waist of her borrowed pants. Rebecca pulled a few inches of the fabric out. "Good heavens."

"What is it?" Zachary rushed over, and seeing the blood-stained, dirty fabric, recoiled. Rebecca rolled up Marissa's shirtsleeve and found more blood on the arm of the nightgown.

Marissa turned her eyes away from their horrified glances. "It looks worse than it actually is. I had a nosebleed, and I had nothing to wipe with."

Zachary became enraged. "You shouldn't have had a nosebleed. That no-account scoundrel should never have laid his hands on you."

Rebecca replaced the shirt over Marissa's nightgown. "Please step out so that I can wash her and give her a clean nightgown."

"I'll *kill* Jason for this." Zachary stomped from the room. Rowe followed after him.

Marissa heard Rowe's calm voice attempting to assuage the older man's anger. Their footsteps receded down the hall. "I'm sorry I'm causing you and your husband all this distress, Mrs. Arthur."

"Hush." Zachary's wife made her lie down while she began washing the dirt away from her back and legs. "Family owes no apologies."

Rowe kept one eye on the closed door, the other on Zachary as the old man paced about the room. For the past fifteen or so minutes, he had done his best to calm him, but the shoe seller was all but ready to go up in arms to the saloon.

"He had no right to touch her that way. No right." Zachary knocked a kerosene lamp over by accident.

Rowe breathed a sigh of relief that it wasn't lit. He went in search of rags to mop up the spilled mess. Zachary declined his help.

"It'll give me something to do while I wait for Rebecca to come out here. Go sit down over yonder at that table." The old man found a cloth and started cleaning, picking up the broken lamp first. "I wish that Jason Garth never set foot in this town, he and his gamblin' cheats. It's one thing to let your workers go if you don't care for their ways, but it's quite another to beat up on them."

"Mr. Arthur, I feel the same way that you do. What Jason did to Marissa makes me furious, but we can't go fist to fist with him. We can't repay evil for evil."

"Well, we can't just let him get by, either." Zachary got on his hands and knees, joints popping.

Rowe got down beside him and started mopping with the rag, unable to sit idle while the elderly man exhausted himself. "Jason won't get by. He'll get what he deserves, but not by our hands."

"No one else in this town'll take action. Sheriff McGee's got to be the laziest law enforcer this side of St. Louis. He sits in that little office in town and puts his big, flat feet up on the desk. The only thing he'll shoot is tobacco juice in a spittoon."

Rowe's own anger threatened to rise higher as Zachary continued to talk of the lack of law enforcement in the town and the saloonkeeper's free rein. "Your fury is making you say those things, sir. You're an upright man, and I know you don't really want to commit any violent acts against another person, even Jason."

Zachary let out a loud and weary sigh. Stretching his legs out in front of his belly, he sat, helpless. "I'm an old man. I couldn't raise my hands against anyone if I wanted to. But I'd sure try for Rebecca and for Mari."

"Marissa is safe and being cared for by your wife. That's all that matters."

Zachary wrinkled his nose at the strong scent of kerosene beginning to fill the room. "I don't want her to go back there. Dear God, help that child." He bowed his head.

Rowe's nostrils burned as he worked faster to combat the stench. "He is, Mr. Arthur. He placed you and Rebecca in her life."

"And you, Reverend. She wouldn't be under our roof if you didn't bring her here."

Rowe smiled. "She did resist. I kept telling myself along the way here that her stubbornness will one day reveal itself as character strength."

"That I am waiting to see." Zachary's gruff countenance melted into a more presentable expression.

Rebecca came out of the bedroom. Rowe stood as she entered, his stomach twisting in anticipation of her news. "How is she?"

Rebecca sighed. "She seems to be alright, other than the cuts and bruises on her body. I didn't see anything that looked dangerous, but I do want Dr. Gillings to examine her this morning."

Zachary nodded. "I'll call for him as soon as possible."

"I've already washed her and given her one of my nightgowns. She's sleeping now. I'll give her something to eat when she wakes up."

The first rays of morning sunlight shone through the patterned curtains. Rowe heard the neighbor's rooster crow. "I should be going."

"Thank you, Reverend," Zachary said. "We hate what Jason did to Mari, but we're sure glad she's with us now."

Hopefully, she'll stay with you. "I'll return to visit when she's well enough. Good day to you." Rowe removed his hat from a peg and took his leave.

It may have been a mistake to leave the Navy revolver in the saddlebag before going inside the saloon. He battled within himself about carrying it for safety, but seeing Zachary temporarily overcome by malice made him change his mind. Who knew what Jason was capable of, now that his attack on Marissa was thwarted?

Jason's clerks and serving ladies congregated in the dance-hall. From their frantic expressions and quick phrases about a doctor visit, Rowe surmised the boss wasn't on the property. "Excuse me," he called.

All of the employees turned their heads toward him as one collective unit. Some of the women gasped. One winked. The men stared him down with reproach.

"If you come here lookin' for the boss, you've got some nerve, Preacher," one of the clerks spat. "I'd get out of here if I was you."

Rowe faced him, not intimidated. "Tell me where he is, and I'll leave. I don't want any trouble."

"Then you shouldn't have come. Gettin' into Jason's business was your mistake." The clerk put his hands on his hips. "None of us are gonna give you any information."

He took in the various scowls, coy smiles, and blank stares and knew he would not make any progress with them. The workers were loyal to Jason.

"Maybe you should preach your sermons here." The lady who winked at him spoke. "We seem to be your favorite topic, and you come here enough."

"Shut your mouth, Nellie," the clerk warned. "You can go on now, Reverend. Your business is finished here."

Rowe exchanged glances with each and every one of the saloon's employees, memorizing their faces in case one of them would approach him in the future. He walked out of the saloon while entertaining the idea that he could get shot in the back. Blessedly he emerged outside, unscathed.

The sun made its steady ascent into midmorning as he rode around the corner and up the street to the physician's office, where Dr. Gillings' name was painted on the door.

"Is the doctor in yet?" he asked the female attendant at the front desk.

"He's tending to a patient at the moment. It could be for some time. The man has a broken nose."

That wasn't good to hear. There was no way Jason or anyone else would believe he had tried to shield Marissa peaceably.

"Is anything the matter, Reverend Winford? I could ask for the nurse."

"No, I'll wait. It's the patient with whom I need to speak." His neck grew warm as the attendant nodded her head in a slow, perplexed manner.

"Then please take a seat."

After about ten more minutes passed, the door to the doctor's examining room opened and Jason stepped out, holding up one arm in a self-conscious attempt to cover the wide bandage across his nose. He gave a start at the sight of Rowe.

Rowe stood up. "Jason, hear me. Breaking your nose wasn't intentional. I just wanted to get you away from Marissa."

Jason glared at him and headed for the door. Rowe followed him out, and Jason halted at the bottom of the steps.

"Where did you put my girl, Reverend?" Jason's voice sounded different, muffled by the bandages on his nose. "I know you're hiding her. She didn't come back to the saloon last night after you got into our business."

"I wasn't about to let you continue to brutalize her. No woman in her right mind would return to you after what you did. And she is not your girl." The man's sense of ownership disgusted him.

"She ain't gonna be yours, that's for sure. Customers have tried to put up a price for her, and she refused." Jason managed a twisted sneer, although his swollen face prevented the expression from having full effect.

Rowe willed himself to remain grounded. It was just an attempt to make him lose his peace. There was no need for him to engage in another round of violence after last night's demonstration. "You've spoiled many things for Marissa, but her life is not one of them. She can have the life of a respectable woman."

"You think you can give that to her, Reverend? You think your Bible readin' and sermons and church dinners will satisfy a woman used to dancing and serving up drinks all night? Think she'll want to turn in her fancy garters for prim lace?"

Rowe thought of the difficulties that lay ahead for Marissa. Could he, a simple minister, be there to help her? She acted as though she didn't desire anyone's aid, with her maddening independence demanding its freedom.

"Marissa has already shown you what she thinks of the things you've given her. That was clear before she met me."

A spark ignited in Jason's eyes as they glittered with a fierce jealousy, brimming on hatred. "You best stay in your church and out of the lives of men like me. I don't take kindly to meddlers, Bible-thumping or not, understand?"

"You understand that if you lay a hand on Marissa again, it will be more than meddling that you will be taking kindly to. Good morning, Mr. Garth." He sent one last meaningful glare before deliberately turning his back and walking away.

Turning from wrath was much easier to do in Virginia.

Chapter 11

MARISSA SLEPT UNTIL ten in the morning, when Rebecca awakened her to see Dr. Gillings. The brown-suited, respectable-looking physician nodded to her as he came into the room and set his medical bag on a chair that had been pushed beside the bed.

"Miss Pierce, Mrs. Arthur tells me that you've had a frightful night. I would like to see the extent of your injuries, if you have no objections."

Marissa sat up in bed, grimacing when she used her legs to push up. "I'd forgotten that I twisted my ankle, but it didn't fail to remind me."

Dr. Gillings pulled the sheet down and began inspecting her left limb, poking and prodding like everyone else had done.

"Is it broken, Doctor?" Rebecca asked.

"No. It's mainly swollen from bearing weight. Tell me, Miss Pierce, how long were you on this leg after you injured it?"

"I don't remember. I just had to keep running because I was being pursued."

"Hmm." He compared her swollen left ankle to her right. "I will give you a nettle poultice to ease the inflammation. Keep the leg elevated and stay off of it for a few days." He avoided her as she attempted to make eye contact.

"You know what happened, don't you? You know about Jason Garth." She raised her head in question to Rebecca.

"Mrs. Arthur didn't tell me." The doctor scribbled some notes on a small pad. "I treated my first patient today for a broken nose. That's all I'll say about it."

Rebecca gaped at Dr. Gillings. Marissa cleared her throat. Apparently Rowe didn't share with the Arthurs all the details of how he came to her rescue. If he was reluctant to carry the Colt for protection, how guilty he must have felt for inflicting an injury upon Jason for her sake.

Dr. Gillings examined the rest of her, checking her bandaged cuts and scrapes to see if they were properly dressed. She told him about her stomach where she had been kicked. He felt along her sore abdomen and declared that none of her internal organs were damaged.

"The bruising will heal on its own. You'll have to sleep on your side or back for the time being." Dr. Gillings completed the rest of his examination in several minutes. "Whoever bandaged your feet did a very commendable job. The person very likely prevented you from getting an infection from those splinters."

Her heart swirled when she thought of Rowe tenderly washing her feet after he removed the splinters. "He cleaned the cuts on my arms and face too."

"This man has some experience with medicine. You were fortunate to cross his path, Miss."

Yes, I was, she echoed in her mind. Marissa caught herself. What exactly did she mean by that?

Dr. Gillings left her some bottles of rubbing alcohol and salve for her bruises. He gave further instructions to Rebecca on how to care for her, including brewing a tea of ginger root for inflammation and pain relief. Before leaving the room, he promised to visit again within three days to check her progress.

"Well, young lady, how about some breakfast?" Rebecca suggested, after seeing the doctor out. "Zachary brought some fresh-cured bacon and a basket of eggs in this morning. The bread's still warm in the oven."

"That sounds good, Mrs. Arthur. I would much enjoy it. Oh!"

Rebecca dashed forward. "Are you alright?"

"Yes." Marissa propped herself higher in bed. It dawned on her that all her clothes, linens, and other belongings were still at the saloon. She was supposed to have them out this morning. Now what could she do? "It just occurred to me that everything I own is still with Jason."

"Well, you most certainly are not going back there. I'll speak to Zachary about it."

"No, Jason will hurl him out. Tell him to find Timothy, the livery stable hand. He'll send his cousin to get my valises for me." *If Jason hasn't already tossed them from the top floor window.*

The older woman nodded. "I'll tell Zachary to do that. For now, rest while I get your food ready."

Zachary must have caught Timothy before any customers arrived at the stables, for Marissa's trunk and valises were delivered to the Arthur residence that afternoon. She observed from the bedside as he lifted the lid of the trunk. His countenance soured.

"What is it?"

He lifted one of her dresses, the green-laced one that she had last worn to church. The delicate lace was ripped from the collar. The embroidered bodice was slashed in the middle. Another gown, a maroon-colored frock that brought out her coloring to great effect, was slit all the way down from the work of a knife. Dress after dress followed the same pattern. Petticoats and stockings were destroyed in similar, horrifying fashion. Soon the trunk lay bare of its tattered contents.

Zachary shook his head in utter distaste. "I've never seen a man so vindictive."

Marissa swallowed her hurt and anger. She spent years acquiring the few gowns to her name. Being a tall woman, most things had to be sewn to her proportions. That was a timely and costly endeavor, even when she made her own clothing. Now she possessed only a dirty nightgown to her name and oversized men's breeches on loan.

Zachary reached deep into the bottom of the trunk and pulled out a stack of torn pages. Once gilded, the edges were now brown and burnt. They crumbled like ash from his hand to fall back into the trunk. "A devil, that man is." He picked up the mutilated cover of Marissa's heirloom Bible.

Marissa held the tears threatening to fall from the loss of her only remembrance of the family she once had. She didn't know much about her grandmother's God anymore, or if she should even pray to Him. How could He allow trouble after trouble to fall on her?

"We'll get you some clothes, Mari. Don't worry." Zachary's reassuring voice broke into her dark thoughts.

Marissa simply nodded.

Rowe discovered that word got around quickly in Assurance. That Sunday after his scuffle with Jason he noticed an upsurge in church attendance. Men and women he had never seen before took up space in the pews, studying him as he delivered the morning sermon. As they didn't open their Bibles or take notes, he surmised that their presence had more to do with his latest involvement in the affairs of Jason's Saloon rather than an interest in Paul's letter to the Ephesians.

His ears burned as he heard murmurings in the congregation when he came to the verse about not grieving the Holy Spirit. They thought him a hypocrite for reading it. Rowe wondered what his colleagues back home would have thought. Here he was, a university-educated man, brought up to be a gentleman, resorting to fisticuffs with a coarse barman. How his peers would grimace if they knew he did it all for a saloon girl. The implications alone were enough to revoke his ministerial license.

As Rowe closed with the benediction, his eyes met those of a portly man seated in the first pew. The man wore a silver star pinned on the front of his shirt and an amused smile plastered on his face. Rowe guessed who he might be.

The service ended. Before Rowe could get down from the pulpit, the portly man was out of his seat and lumbering towards the steps. His voice matched the size of his barrel chest. "Reverend Winford, I don't believe we've had ourselves a proper introduction. My name's Julian McGee. I'm the sheriff." Between sentences he grabbed Rowe's hand and pumped it up and down. "I hear you're taking the law enforcement burden off my shoulders."

People chuckled in passing. Rowe wanted to sink into the background of a Last Supper painting that hung outside the hall of the sanctuary. "Sheriff McGee, I hope you don't think—"

"Easy, Preacher. I ain't here to arrest you. I just wanted to come and see how you do in church. I already know how you do outside of it."

"Sheriff, you need to know that my actions were in defense of an employee of Mr. Garth's." Rowe remembered Marissa's wishes about not informing the sheriff, so he kept her name to himself, although he was certain everyone in Assurance knew who it was that Jason pursued.

"From what I hear tell, Mr. Garth and the employee were on your land. A man's got to defend his property. No charge for that."

"That's not what I meant."

Sheriff McGee laughed. A thin sheen of sweat shone on his wide forehead. "I know what you meant. You were protecting one of those gals, but I can't do anything about Garth's carrying on unless I catch him in the act."

"What if the girl comes forth?"

"She'd need a witness, one that saw her get beat. Who's to say someone else didn't do it and she blamed it on her employer? Can't say I trust any word coming out of Jason or his employees."

"I see." Rowe's strategy was shot before it got off the ground. Sheriff McGee thumped him on the back before leaving. "You took care of him, though. Don't think about it anymore."

Rowe did think about it. That week he inquired about Marissa's health twice, once after church on Sunday when the Arthurs shook his hand and then during the noon hour Tuesday, just before he made rounds to visit one of the town's shut-in elderly. He went to Zachary's store for a report on her progress.

"Dr. Gillings says she should be up and walking in a few days. Rebecca's having a time keeping her in bed." Zachary chuckled.

"Will you let her know that I stopped by the store?" He wondered if the question sounded too eager, but Zachary gave him no indication that it did.

"I'll be sure to tell her. You still looking to purchase a pair of work boots? I can order those McKays in a twelve and a half, stout."

"Do I need to pay for them now?" Rowe took his mind off Marissa to factor in the cost of shoes, since he had already spent a good part of his earnings that month on the materials for a new fence.

"You can pay me when they come in. If I can't trust a preacher man, who can I trust?" The shoemaker went back to stitching the toe of a child's soft leather ankle boot.

In the days that followed, Marissa's injuries began to mend. Her ankle returned to normal size, and she could put weight on it. The superficial cuts and scrapes had scabbed over. Marissa felt better on the inside too, now that she was away from Jason and the saloon.

Rebecca hovered over her constantly, dressing her bandages every morning and giving her cups of ginger tea on a regular schedule. She wanted desperately to move around but dutifully held still while Rebecca applied pungent-smelling salve to her fading bruises.

"You are so kind to me, Mrs. Arthur, but truly, I can walk."

"You'll do no such thing," the older woman scolded, pulling the covers up to Marissa's chin after applying the salve. Marissa gave up on reminding her that it was August and that she didn't have the chills. "When Dr. Gillings finds your ankle to be satisfactory, then you can walk. Until that moment you will remain in bed."

Marissa sat up and fluffed her pillows. "The good doctor could have left me with a pair of crutches. Lazing about after a few days becomes…tedious."

Rebecca put the salve and medicines away. "You won't find many people to side with you on that."

"No, but those shortbread cookies you make really do help."

Rebecca laughed. "I remember they were your favorite when you were little. I can see that hasn't changed."

"Except that I can eat more of them now."

They were silent for a time. Rebecca straightened the room while Marissa idly studied her empty trunk resting in a corner. The tattered clothes had been removed, and the brittle pages of her grandmother's Bible were collected and thrown away. The reality of where she was and why she was there consumed her thoughts.

She wondered if Jason was looking for her, or if someone had told him of her whereabouts. He might be searching the town. The safety of the Arthurs was her primary concern. They were honest, good-hearted people who didn't need to bear the brunt of Jason's spitefulness.

Perhaps he went to Rowe and demanded the preacher to tell him where she was. Rowe wouldn't do any such thing, of course. The man had shown her such strength and caring. And when he touched her cheek, a wealth of emotions that she thought she didn't possess came charging to the surface.

"Marissa, did you hear me?"

She looked toward the sound of Rebecca's voice. The woman stood impatiently at the window, hand on her hip.

"I'm sorry. My mind drifted away."

"I agree. I've asked you twice whether you wanted more light in the room so you can read."

"Um, yes. Thank you, Mrs. Arthur."

Sunlight drifted in as Rebecca drew the curtains. Marissa perused the stack of classics that Zachary gave her to read. "Mrs. Arthur, have you received word from Rowe?"

"Who?"

"I mean the reverend." Marissa swiftly opened the cover of the first novel so Rebecca couldn't see her embarrassment for the slip in formality. "I had fallen asleep before I could express my gratitude for him escorting me here."

"He is aware of your gratitude, I'm sure. If not, you'll have a chance to thank him when you heal."

So she would see him again in a very short time. The thought made her heart pound inexplicably.

Rebecca came and sat beside her. "Marissa, I've been meaning to ask you something very important."

She braced herself, expecting that Rebecca had noticed her preoccupation with the reverend.

Rebecca folded her hands neatly in her lap. "You carried

your grandmother's Bible with you for all these years. Did you read it often?"

Marissa gave an inner sigh of relief. At least this question was an easier one to address. "From time to time, but not very much."

The woman didn't give her the scorn she expected. "Do you know about Jesus Christ?"

"I know He's the Son of God and that He died on the cross."

"But do you know why He died, and for whom He died?"

Marissa drew her brows in confusion. What kind of question was she being asked, if the answer seemed so clear? "He died for everyone."

Rebecca nodded. "Yes, but He died to pay for our sins, so that we could have eternal life with Him in heaven. With Him we can have a life of peace and abundance here on earth as well."

Marissa turned her head as the familiar hurt and bitterness crept back into her heart and made her hands ache. "That kind of life wasn't meant for me."

"Why would you say that, when you were brought up in the faith? I remember your grandmother teaching you scriptures."

"I've forgotten many of them. It's done me little good."

"How so?"

"Where was God when my grandparents died? Where was Jesus when my father dragged my mother and me all around Missouri, gambling away our food and supplies? He left us like flea-bitten mutts when the money ran out. Where was *anyone* when I was left alone?" She tossed back the bedcovers angrily. "Even Jason does well for himself, but look at me."

"The wicked will never prosper," Rebecca said firmly. "Don't compare yourself to that man."

"I have nothing to compare with. I've lost my money in an unfair contract. I am unemployed. No one will hire a saloon girl. I've been beaten, and all of my possessions have been destroyed." Marissa swallowed the catch in her throat. "Even God has ridden Himself of me."

"That is not true, Marissa. God says, 'I will not leave you as orphans. I will come to you.'" Rebecca took her by the hands, squeezing urgently. "You must believe that."

A part of her wanted to believe that there was still hope. The pain welling inside of her painted everything sad and bleak. She had begun praying again recently, so why did it have no effect? Things had actually gotten worse. "But I was an orphan. After all I've been through, no one in this town wants anything to do with me."

"I do. Zachary does. We've always loved you like the daughter we never had. More than that, God loves you. I beg you, Marissa, seek Him out."

Marissa thought of the times she spent praying with her mother, asking for God to bring them out of poverty, to provide them with decent work. All that praying did was callous her knees. God didn't love her. If He did, He would not have allowed her to pass for little more than a common strumpet. "If you don't mind, Mrs. Arthur, I'm tired of seeking charity where it can't be found. It's time that I took a stand for myself and make my own way."

Marissa half-expected Rebecca to put forth another argument or plea, but she merely closed her eyes for a moment and opened them again to peer out the bedroom window. Without another word, she departed from the room.

Marissa raised her head to see what was outside but found nothing except a rooster, scouring the dirt for dropped food.

Chapter 12

ON WEDNESDAY ROWE was busy at his church study writing a sermon when a burly-chested man burst into his study shortly after one o'clock.

"Reverend Winford, I've got to see you."

Rowe arose to greet him. "Is it an emergency, Mister—?"

"Keith McCauley, and no sir, it ain't an emergency. But I got a really big matter I need you for." The man panted from running. Sweat marks stained the front of his shirt. "I need you to unite me in matrimony today."

There was no fooling in the man's wide, earnest eyes. Rowe pushed the sermon aside. "Mr. McCauley, I'll be more than willing to conduct your marriage ceremony, but I need time to prepare."

"I have my papers." Keith pulled folded documents from his pocket, smoothing the crumpled edges as best he could. "The marriage license. Just got it today in Claywalk, my girl and I did. She don't want the justice of the peace marryin' us there. She says she wants the rev'ren in Assurance to do it, 'cos that's where she's from."

Rowe read the name of the bride elect on the document. "What does your fiancée, Miss Alice Carson, have to say about the expedient wedding date?"

Keith hung his head. "Well, you see, I said I would marry her when I was able to leave the railroad and earn my money an' all, but things happened."

"What things?"

Keith scratched his neck, looking everywhere about the study except directly at Rowe. "I ain't been the best steward with my money. I hurt Alice with my venturin' to the dance-hall most nights. It's time I do what's right by her."

"That's honorable of you, but why do you want to be married today? Is Miss Carson with you?"

"She's on her way here. She wanted to stop at her ma's house and change into her best Sunday dress. I went on ahead because I wanted to spare her of hearin' me tell you this."

"Tell me what?"

Keith hesitated. "We should be 'shamed, sir. And we are 'shamed. Mighty so."

Rowe had an inkling of what the man was trying to say. He patted his shoulder. "I'm not here to pass judgment on you or your fiancée. If you don't want to tell me, I won't press."

"So you know?" Keith glanced at him sideways.

"I think I have an idea."

That seemed to put him at ease. "I wasn't even thinkin' about marryin' her right away, but when she told me that she was expectin', I know I needed to be a proper man to her."

"You're doing the right thing."

"A child needs a father. Mine wasn't around too much for me. I don't want my little boy or girl to grow up without knowin' their pa."

"That won't happen now."

"That's why I need you to marry Alice and me today. We can't live in sin any longer. Please, Rev'ren."

Rowe went to the bookshelf for the book containing his outlines for ceremonies. He skimmed through the pages. "Do you and Miss Carson have any vows you'd like to present to each other?"

Keith scratched his neck again. "No. She just realized her condition today when she was feelin' poorly. We went to get the license and ran straight here. I think I hear her comin' now."

A woman's soft footsteps padded down the hall by the entrance to the sanctuary. Marissa stuck her head in the open doorway seconds later. Her skin was luminous, and her hair gleamed in a glowing, vibrant picture of health. As her sweet smile formed, all the battered images of her from days ago fled Rowe's mind. "I'm returning the clothes you were so kind to lend." She held up a wrapped bundle. Her lips parted slightly when she saw Keith.

"Missy," Keith greeted her, equally caught off guard. His eyes darted about the room again, this time avoiding hers.

Rowe suddenly understood. Marissa was Keith's reminder of all his time spent in the saloon when he wasn't courting his fiancée.

"I didn't expect to find you here this afternoon, Keith," Marissa spoke first, awkwardly. "I thought you'd be on the Claywalk line."

"I'm gettin' married today."

She gasped. To Rowe's surprise she dropped the bundled clothes on the desk like delivered laundry and let out a gleeful cry. "Congratulations, Keith. I'm so very happy for you."

Keith's nervous mood washed away, and he ceased scratching his neck. "Thanks, Missy. You're the first to wish me well."

"I know how much you wanted to settle down. You told me how lonely it is, laying track work across the prairie for monthly stretches at a time."

"Yeah, I'm just sorry for all that bad dancin' I put you through."

She shook Keith's hand and patted the top of it with her left. Were they good friends, or did she simply recognize

Keith as a frequent saloon patron? Rowe never witnessed her come so alive around another person.

"Keith, what in the name of decency are you doin', touchin' that painted cat?"

Rowe viewed the shrill lady that marched into the study. Her flat-soled boots slapped the floor. From her slightly green pallor and the way her arm covered her abdomen in a protective gesture, he knew her to be only one person. Miss Alice Carson.

Alice bristled up at Marissa. "Remove yourself from my future husband, you no-good, common slattern."

"Alice." Keith's eyes bulged. "Don't speak that way in front of the rev'ren. You're in a church. Missy was only congratulatin' me on the marriage."

"I'm sure she was. Jason's women see more of you than I do. Don't matter if you're in the saloon or you ain't."

A vein in his neck pulsed. "All that's gonna change, Alice. I'm gonna be a father."

"Must you say that aloud before we're married, Keith?" Alice covered her face in a show of humiliation.

Rowe had to do something before more havoc ensued between the three people in his study. It was easy to see why Alice would be angry at finding Marissa near her fiancé, but her words were a whip that lashed out uncontrollably. "I can begin the ceremony whenever you're ready, Miss Carson. Would you care for some tea first?"

As Alice measured Marissa up and down with contempt, her expression showed just what she imagined doing with that tea. "No, Reverend Winford. I'd rather you marry Keith and me right away."

Marissa's joviality from earlier had packed itself away tightly in a little box. Standing straight as a rod, her only movement was in the constant furling and unfurling of her hands. "You're getting a good, kind man, Miss Carson."

"As I am marryin' him, that knowledge hasn't escaped me."
Rowe pickled at Alice's caustic tone. "I have to ask you to
refrain from your conversation, Miss Carson. As your fiancé
stated, you are in a house of God."

Alice shut her mouth, shame written across her lips.

"I should be going," Marissa excused herself.

"Wait." Rowe stopped her just as she was halfway out the
door. "Let me have a word with you when the ceremony
concludes."

Sighing, she seated herself in the chair facing his desk and
reached downward to tug the bottom of her slate-colored
skirt over the tops of her boots.

Keith ushered his fiancée out. Rowe followed behind them.

The newlyweds waved good-bye to Rowe as they left the
church. Marissa's wagon was fixed alongside the steps, where
the horse chewed lazily on the grass. Rowe blew a puff of
air, grateful that she hadn't stolen away while he was uniting
Keith and Alice in matrimony.

She was still in the chair when he returned to the study,
pulling at her skirt as he saw her do before. The hem was
curiously short, revealing the brown tops of boots that
looked like a smaller version of the McKays he once tried to
squeeze his feet into.

"Thank you for waiting and for returning my clothes." He
placed the book of ceremony outlines back on the shelf.

"If Keith hadn't been getting married today, I'm certain
he would have stopped to ponder why I'd be returning such
items to you." She gave a slight laugh, although nothing
about her indicated she was feeling the least bit humorous.

He placed the bundle of clothes in a drawer. "Have you
fully recuperated from your injuries?"

"Yes, I'll have to visit Dr. Gillings tomorrow for Mrs. Arthur's peace of mind."

"How did you get her to let you leave her sights today?"

"I promised that I'd take the wagon instead of riding a horse."

"I asked Mr. Arthur about you." Rowe moved in his seat for a comfortable position. Since when had the chair become so high-backed and rigid? "I hope you'll forgive the new Mrs. McCauley for her comments. Brides sometimes do forget themselves on their wedding day."

Marissa made a small sound as she massaged her fingers. "Hmm. One can hardly blame her. Keith visited the saloon often. Seeing him with a former employee would stir her defenses."

"She still shouldn't have spoken to you that way. You handled yourself well against her rudeness."

"It becomes second nature when you hear it enough."

"You don't have to hide it from me, Marissa. I know those words hurt you."

"It doesn't matter. Once a saloon girl, you never quite lose the title. Even a woman pregnant out of wedlock can scorn." She rose so hastily that he mirrored her movement without thinking. "That was wrong of me to say about Alice. Now I'm being rude. I should return to Mrs. Arthur before she worries."

"I'll walk you outside." Rowe vaulted around the desk to reach the door first. While holding it open for Marissa, he had the opportunity to observe her feet again. They were definitely men's boots He was curious as to why Zachary hadn't given her a pair of ladies' shoes instead but politely remained silent. Her light steps made the thick-soled boots glide along the floor like dance slippers.

Rowe offered his arm to her before they descended the

steps outside. The hearty breeze pushed them from behind, making her cling to him.

"I'm pleased to see you in good health," he said as they came to the wagon. She started on her hands again, massaging and rotating each finger clockwise. "Do your hands trouble you?"

"They do when I'm upset. You were correct about Mrs. McCauley's words hurting."

Rowe studied the skin of her palms for redness or irritation. "I don't mean to be rude or forward, but I don't understand why you do that."

She shrugged. "My hands ache when I'm upset. Some people blink their eyes rapidly when they lie, or their neck muscles twitch when they're anxious."

"You're a good observer of people's features."

"I learned that in my former profession. It saved me from many an unwelcome encounter."

Rowe assisted her when she put her good foot on the wagon platform to step up. His hands went to support her waist. "What do my features tell you?"

Pausing with one foot on the platform and the other suspended in midair, she swiveled her neck to gaze at him. "You haven't lied to me, and I've yet to see you twitch."

Good. She was unaware of how clumsy and doltish he became when she was around. He determined never to let her see it.

"However," she added, settling into her seat, "you do move about restlessly."

"What do you think it means?" he asked, putting a hand on the seat back.

Her diaphragm expanded and contracted beneath her dress. "A constant purpose or passion, maybe. Only you know which."

Marissa's nearness was heady. Rowe peered at her as he

sensed tender, invisible threads weaving them together. Warm. Delicate. He grew afraid that if he broke her gaze, they would break.

"Will you come to church on Sunday, Marissa?" He switched to a pastoral tone, trying to keep the hidden emotions from his voice.

Her eyes flicked away. "I don't know. I don't want to be a distraction."

"You won't be." He didn't know if he was lying to her—or himself.

"You know I would be, after all that...happened." Marissa shifted away from him, fumbling for the reins. Her face awakened with some untold sentiment. Sensing her discomfort, Rowe moved to untie the horse's tether then got out of the wagon's path.

"Maybe when things calm down," she said. "Then I will think about coming. Thank you for the invitation."

The horse's head rose up in attention with a snap of the reins, and the animal pulled the wagon away.

Chapter 13

MARISSA'S ENCOUNTER WITH Rowe and the strange, indescribable sensation that passed between them came back to haunt her as she shivered in Dr. Gillings's modest office. Despite the warm temperature in the room, her skin prickled beneath her white, tucked bodice.

Rowe made contact with her before with handshakes, accidental brushes of the arm, and when he applied bandages to her wounds. What happened outside the church yesterday was altogether peculiar. Her whole being responded to it.

It was terrifying.

What force made her so abruptly aware of him? And how cruel it was, for how could there be anything between a man of God and a woman from a den of iniquity? She banished the notion from her mind again, as she did numerous times that day. These feelings surfaced because he had shown her kindness. It was foolish to imagine anything else.

Besides, she had her livelihood to think about. She couldn't continue to hide from Jason in such a small town. Marissa didn't mention it to the Arthurs, but she knew that she had to come up with a more permanent arrangement, for their safety as well as her own. Eventually she would have to leave Assurance.

"Looks like you'll be receiving a clean bill of health, Miss Pierce." Dr. Gillings put all his medical instruments away as Marissa set her feet on the floor.

Rebecca thanked the doctor for his time. "I appreciate you caring for her. Her recovery was more swift than I could have imagined."

Dr. Gillings escorted them out. Back on the street Rebecca turned to Marissa. "You're so quiet. Does your leg hurt?"

"No." Marissa cast a tentative glance in the direction of the woman who cared for her like a mother. Despite her terse refusal to accept Rebecca's invitation to follow Christ, Rebecca maintained a loving and sweet disposition, bringing her tea, food, and making sure she got enough rest. The attentiveness left her awash with guilt. She had nothing with which to repay the woman for her kindness.

Marissa came out of her brooding when Rebecca touched her shoulder. "I was thinking that we should pay a visit to the seamstress. Perhaps Mrs. Walsh or Linda will be on hand to make you dresses to wear for work at the store."

Marissa cheered up momentarily at the mention of clothes that fit. Now if something could be done about her feet. Zachary had been gracious enough to give her a pair of men's boots until he could fashion a pair of ladies' shoes in her size. The boots were comfortable, but every time she looked down and saw the tops of them, she felt more than a little self-conscious.

At the door of the seamstress she had a change of heart. After all that had transpired lately, she didn't want to give Linda Walsh more grist for the gossip mill.

"On second thought, Mrs. Arthur, let's find a few bolts of calico fabric from the general store. I can sew my own dresses, and it will be less expensive."

"Nonsense. This is my gift to you. Let's go inside."

They found the store empty of all the Walshes except for one family member. Linda sat by the Wheeler and Wilson sewing machine as she embroidered a lovely white fabric with deep blue threads. "Hello, Mrs. Arthur." Greeting the older woman cheerily, her expression immediately blackened at the sight of Marissa.

If Rebecca noticed the abrupt change of face, she gave no

acknowledgment. "Miss Walsh, we have need of your talents. Marissa needs several tucked bodices and a skirt or two, a Sunday dress, and some ready-made undergarments."

Linda assessed Marissa's form. "She's very big. I'll need to measure her for sleeves and hem."

"We'll have to have these clothes as soon as possible."

"You can have the bodices by tomorrow if I only have to fashion the sleeve length. A skirt too. The dress will take longer."

"How long?"

"About a week, if I pause from my other customers. My parents will ask that I obtain a percentage of the payment today."

"Done."

Marissa started to dissuade Rebecca from extra spending, but the woman quieted her. "I said, consider it a gift. You can help me with the housework and in the store. Now I'm off to get some sorghum and molasses from the general store. I may even sit with Mr. Decker and his wife for coffee. See you in about an hour."

Rebecca made the impending ordeal sound as pleasant as gathering prairie violets and larkspurs. Marissa stifled the urge to pull her back, not wanting to be left alone with Linda's sarcasm.

The bell on the door chimed when it closed. No sooner did Rebecca leave than Linda's true nature surfaced. "What do you need new clothes for all of a sudden?"

"Mrs. Arthur thought I should have them."

"Why should she care about you?" Marissa, by instinct, formed a retort in her mind, but she held it at bay. "Mrs. Arthur has known my family for years."

Putting the sewing machine aside, Linda instructed her to stand in the dressing room. Marissa removed her skirt and bodice before a tall mirror in order for the measurements to be taken.

"How did you get so tall anyway?" Linda spoke to Marissa's reflection in the mirror.

"Most of the women in my family were tall. My father was almost six and a half feet."

"Well, it makes you hard to sew for, and costly." Linda put the tape around her waist. "You could make do with a tighter corset."

Marissa sighed. "Not every woman is meant to be whittle-waisted." The temptation to trade insult for insult was great. She bit her tongue and listened as Linda described the white fabric she had been working on before Marissa and Rebecca came inside the shop.

"That's going to be a dress for Sophie. The material is imported from France, the very same cloth that the ladies of Paris use for their dresses. Very expensive."

"How nice."

"Don't you wish you could afford one?"

She refused to let Linda's childish pettiness make her angry or envious. "Linda, I know we've bickered in the past, but it's time to stop. There's no need for it."

The girl scoffed. "You're only saying that because you want Reverend Winford on your side. I'm no fool. Sophie told me how you tried to talk to him after church that Sunday. You can't compete with her."

"I am not about to compete with any woman for the attention of a man." A thread of unwelcome tension laced her tone. What exactly did Rowe think of a young lady like Sophie?

Linda scoffed at her again after a short interval of silence. "Why aren't you saying anything?" Kneeling at Marissa's feet, she measured the length of her legs for a skirt hem.

"Maybe after the fitting. I'm afraid you'll stick me with a pin."

Linda placed her remaining pins in a cushion and stood. The measuring tape dangled from her neck. "Lift up your hair so I can measure your bust."

She did as instructed. The seamstress gasped at the ruddy, healing scabs on the back of her shoulders and arms. "What happened to you?"

The reaction made Marissa tense. "I don't want gossip, Linda. Don't ask if you can't resist telling everyone."

Linda's voice grew low as she took in the cuts and fading bruises. "Mr. Garth is responsible for this, isn't he?"

"Yes." Marissa let her hair fall down again to cover herself. "Promise you won't say anything."

Linda continued to stare, awkward.

"Promise."

"I won't tell a soul."

"Not even Sophie."

"I promise."

Marissa still had her doubts from prior experiences with Sophie and her friends. "I'll take you upon your word, then."

An hour went by, and Marissa found herself becoming more at ease with Linda since they had reached an understanding, or at the very least, an agreement to remain silent.

The bells on the door chimed as someone entered. Rebecca's voice called up front. "Are you ladies still measuring?"

"We're finished, ma'am," Linda called back. She handed Marissa her clothes from a rule-lined table. "I'll work as fast as I can today so you can have a bodice and skirt this evening."

Unsure of how to dispel the girl's discomfort, Marissa uttered a simple thank-you.

Saturday evening Rowe drummed his fingers on the desk where the new Bible lay. Light from the lamp reflected its gilt-edge pages, casting tiny gold beams across the walls of his home study. He should be putting the finishing touches on his sermon for tomorrow, but he found himself distracted once again.

He picked up the Bible. It was an expensive gift, but when Zachary told him about Marissa's Bible being destroyed by Jason, he wanted to do something to ease her distress of losing a keepsake. So he had gone to Claywalk today to buy her a new Bible. If word got out in Assurance about his gift, the church elders would beat a path to his door, demanding an explanation. He didn't have one for them or himself.

He recalled what he sensed when he helped Marissa onto the wagon outside church. Several theories could explain what happened. Rowe listed them as he listened to the wind whistle through the trees outside.

The most obvious was that he was glad Marissa recovered from her injuries. Another acceptable explanation was that he was new to Assurance. After a day of preparing sermons, of course the distraction of a friendly visit caused a positive reaction.

Rowe heard the horse snorting outside. He got up and looked out the back window to find the animal trotting the yard in circles. The setting sun highlighted the sheen in its chestnut coat. The horse tossed his mane before heading to the yard's perimeter.

Rowe returned to his desk and raked his fingers through his hair. The third explanation was a bit more daring, but still reasonable. He found Marissa to be pretty. It was natural for a man to admire a woman's beauty, the same way it was natural to admire a landscape or a flower. The horse's neighing outside sounded like chortling laughter. Rowe gave up. Who was he trying to convince? The attraction he felt was similar to what he experienced when first introduced to

Josephine. God rest the woman's gentle soul, how could he do this to her memory?

Rowe's mind brought back the day of her funeral. So peaceful she looked, with her light auburn hair dressed in soft waves about her shoulders.

"She appears to only be asleep," one of his nieces had remarked.

But Rowe knew the hours of agony Josephine endured in her labor and of the fever that swiftly overtook her after it was discovered that their son was stillborn. It was his fault both of them were taken away so soon.

After the mourning period was over, part of him wanted to keep Josephine's memory alive. He still felt that way today, though the faces of the past were becoming increasingly blurred in light of his new surroundings.

And the faces of the present. One, in particular. Why did this lost woman have to matter so much?

The wind rapped on the window glass like a knock. *How could you?*

"I'm not." He found himself talking out loud to no one. The grief was finally going to have its way, make him descend into madness.

You don't love Josephine anymore. You let her die. Now you let her memory depart for a woman no real man of God would spare a second glance.

Was this why people perished out west, because the land conspired with the hidden recesses of their minds? Dusty was right about the devil being in the town. *Something* here was intent on making him regret ever stepping foot on that train to Kansas.

The wind picked up speed, and Rowe saw his horse go into the small sheltered area where the hay and water trough were kept. The door of the cabin beat against its hinges. He went to bar the latch before the door threatened to slam inward.

A rainstorm was coming. Clouds darkened the sky and blotted out the last of the orange sunset. Rowe went to the cabinet near the stove for matches to light the rest of the lamps. When he came back to the darkened study, the gilded pages of the Bible cast bigger points of reflected lamplight on the wall.

Maybe he shouldn't give the Bible to Marissa. It was a bit extravagant. Still, she deserved it after all she had been through. He would give it to her, then leave her be.

He started to wrap it in red paper that was also purchased in Claywalk, and as he worked, he also began to steel his heart. He'd done his part in helping the Arthurs get Marissa out of the saloon. What she did with the rest of her life was up to her and God. If he wanted to be a successful preacher in the town, he had to distance himself from the situation, physically at least. Hopefully in time, the rest of him would follow.

Chapter 14

ARISSA RETRIEVED A pair of newly soled kidskin walking boots from behind the counter and proceeded to wrap them. "Yes, Mrs. Barnes, your shoes are repaired. They were finished yesterday."

The gray-haired matron regarded her with sharp, narrow eyes as Zachary totaled the cash amount. "Aren't you Arrow Missy?"

It took her aback to hear her stage name on the lips of a genteel woman. Her fingers halted in the process of folding the corners of the wrapping paper. "I used to go by that name, but I don't work at the saloon anymore."

"She's my employee now." Zachary gave Marissa's shoulder a pat. "She'll be able to help you with anything you need in the future."

Mrs. Barnes pressed her thin lips together and narrowed her eyes. "As you say, Mr. Arthur."

Marissa watched her collect her boots and leave the store. "She doesn't like me very much, does she?"

"She has to get used to you. You've only been working a week. Once you're established here, no one will concern themselves with your former life."

He kept speaking as though she was going to work in the store permanently. His constant attention and training signified he wanted her to stay.

More shoppers came into the store. Some reacted to her presence like Mrs. Barnes, wary and skeptical, while others paid for their shoes and left without so much as a glance in her direction. Zachary reassured her as much as possible when he saw her mood sinking. "It gets easier. This is new to them, and it'll soon wear off."

"Do you mind if I sit with Rebecca in the back room to catalog the stock for a while?"

He weighed her request with a critical eye. "Mari, I don't want you hiding back there. It won't do you or the customers any good if you're not on the sales floor."

"I won't hide. Let Rebecca teach me how to catalog or remove shoes just for an hour. I promise I'll come right back out."

Zachary gave his reluctant permission, and Marissa stepped around the front counter. The bell chimed on the door as another customer came in.

"Has my order arrived yet, Mr. Arthur?"

Marissa jolted at the sound of Rowe's voice. She hadn't seen or heard from him since their last encounter at the church when she returned the borrowed clothing. When the Arthurs went to church on Sunday, she opted to remain at home and prepare dinner.

"Reverend Rowe! Good to see you." Zachary pushed a stack of receipts into her hand. "Give these to Rebecca, Mari. She'll need them for the record books." He turned his back to her and resumed talking to Rowe.

Marissa clutched the receipts. Zachary had all but kicked her into the back room. Rowe didn't even greet her as she walked off the sales floor. Bits of their conversation reached her ears as she paused just inside the stockroom.

"...I would have given it to her sooner, but my obligations kept me from leaving the church..."

She? What other woman could Rowe be referring to, and what was he presenting to her? A pang of jealousy hit Marissa like an unexpected slap to both cheeks. How had he managed to find a lady so soon?

Slumping onto a nearby stool, she figured exactly how he

managed. Rowe was charming, friendly, handsome, and a gentleman. Linda Walsh practically swooned when she first saw him, and the majority of the town's women did the same. The fact that these desirable qualities were in a godly man—a *preacher*, no less—made for a most eligible bachelor indeed.

Marissa dug her nails into her palms, where they began to hurt. What reason did she have for being offended that he chose to give another woman a present? Hadn't she raced away from him last week at church after he helped her into the wagon? Perhaps he had seen too much of her curtness for his tastes.

Or perhaps it was simply that he preferred a lady like Reverend Thomas's wife. That woman would cook kitchen-hall-size dinners for the church, entertain houseguests all day, serve the poor, and sing like the star of an opera company. Never a day went by when she hadn't had a cheery smile upon her face.

Marissa wasn't ignorant of her own personal characteristics: independent, tall, watchful. Those weren't the traits that men normally admired in women, especially preachers' wives. Vivaciousness, finishing school manners, a knack for making everyone feel graced to be in her presence. That's what men wanted to see in a female.

There were positive qualities to her person, of course. She was helpful, intelligent, and usually polite. She could cook, sew, mend. Her stature allowed her to lift and carry more than the average woman. Those were skills needed for a life on the prairie. She knew seven or eight forms of ballroom dance. That was a rare talent to be admired.

But could a preacher appreciate a waltzing wife?

Stop thinking about it. It was absurd to even consider the idea that her former background would not show negatively on Rowe's duty as town preacher. It was better to not dwell on courtship and marriage for the time being, especially when she left her old saloon life less than two weeks ago.

She stood up from the stool and approached Rebecca, who sat at a table with her back turned, poring over the account ledger. "Mrs. Arthur, your husband told me to give these to you."

"Thank you, dear." Rebecca took the receipts from her. "You look upset. What's wrong?"

Marissa hated that her face was always so transparent. Amid the neatly stacked crates of nails and cobbler's tools, she took a seat across the little wooden table from Rebecca. "The customers are wondering why I'm here instead of at the saloon."

"And?" Rebecca prompted, as though she knew there was more to be revealed.

"Reverend Winford is here speaking to Mr. Arthur about a gift he's going to present to a woman. Mr. Arthur sent me away, and the reverend was so excited about the gift that he didn't bother to greet me."

Marissa cast her eyes down in embarrassment as Rebecca nodded in understanding. She moderated her previous statements. "It's none of my business, of course, but a courteous 'hello' would have sufficed."

"The reverend most likely wasn't aware of his manners, given his excitement."

Marissa busied herself with stacking leather into a neat pile on the table, anything to occupy her sensitive, aching hands. *I truly should not feel this way. I'm so jumbled up inside.*

"Marissa, would you mind helping me with the supper tonight? I'm afraid my fingers are going to be so cramped from all this ledger writing."

"I wouldn't mind at all." There would be more work for her hands and something else to dwell on.

For the remainder of the afternoon she helped Rebecca, arranging crates and learning the store ledgers. Zachary didn't come into the back room and order her to go out on the sales floor, as she expected him to. When the workday was done and she was at home, she prepared a dinner of chicken and vegetables on the stove. All the while her mind wrestled with the idea of Rowe and the unnamed woman. Who was she?

Marissa pictured the unmarried young ladies of Assurance and thought of those who could catch his eye. Linda Walsh was fresh and pretty, but she wasn't ready to leave the shelter of her parents' wings just yet. The sisters Amelia and Leslie Mason already had beaux. Several other women were ruled out until the remaining choices were Margaret Rheins and Sophie Charlton.

Both women were flirtatious and coquettish. Marissa could see how a man would be attracted to Sophie's petite, outward appearance. Linda already told her that Sophie had her eye on the reverend. Did Rowe finally succumb to her persistent charms and helpless gestures?

"Let him have Sophie, if she's what he wants." Marissa forced the overly analytical thoughts aside while she checked on the chicken.

Rowe would probably marry a rich farmer's daughter or townswoman when the time came. It was expected of men from his background and education, and there wasn't much she could argue against it.

"Mari, is the chicken cooked?" Zachary called from the main room of the house. "Our guest is here."

The Arthurs never said anything about having a guest over for supper tonight. She hoisted the pan from the stove with two mitts and carried it to the dining table.

"Good evening, Marissa." Rowe stood in the room's center, waiting.

The roasting hot contents of the pan came close to dripping all over the floor and the front of her dress. "It's you." Marissa set the pan in the center of the dining table as he approached.

He produced a beautifully wrapped present in dark red paper, her favorite color. "This is for you."

Confounded, Marissa looked to Rebecca and Zachary for an explanation. They merely smiled and nodded encouragingly. "Thank you, but what is the occasion?"

"You are. Open it." Rowe held the present out.

Marissa took the gift. It was square-shaped and heavy. She tore the red paper away to find a Bible, bound in soft ivory leather. She gasped. "Rowe, this is extravagant." Too fancy, is what she wanted to say. How much did he spend?

Zachary went to admire the book. "It's lovely, isn't it? He wanted to show me the Bible before he presented it to you."

"You both knew about this?" Marissa grew sheepish as Zachary's smile broadened. "That's why you shooed me away to the back of the store and why Mrs. Arthur wanted me to help with supper."

"We had to keep you distracted," said Rebecca.

Marissa opened the Bible toward the middle, where a silk bookmark rested atop the book of Psalms. Jason's voice suddenly echoed in her head, *That preacher's making an example of you. He is using you to build his church.* Was this gift an attempt to get her to join the congregation?

Reading the first psalm to herself, she stopped when she discovered him staring intently at her, the same way he did when he helped her into the wagon. What was behind those dark blue eyes? She had to find out if he honestly sought her friendship or if he merely needed to make an example of her for the rest of the town.

For a moment that seemed like an eternity, she returned his gaze. "Thank you again."

They stood, awkward, with the Arthurs as their onlookers. "Mr. Arthur told me about what happened to your grandmother's Bible. I tried to find you another one like it."

"It's lovely." Marissa really did think so, but the very nature of the gift, its similarity to her old Bible, even the wrapping paper in her favorite color, everything was too well thought out.

"I think we'd better eat before that chicken gets cold," Zachary suggested when the silence stretched too long.

Marissa put the Bible on top of the dish cabinet, where it couldn't be in danger of gravy stains and grease smudges. "That was highly sweet and thoughtful, Reverend."

Rowe seated himself across from her. His endearing face tempted her to reconsider her suspicions, but for the time being, she deemed it best to remain vigilant.

The supper ended just after eight, with everyone finishing off the light yellow biscuit cookies that Rebecca Arthur was famous for. Zachary regaled Rowe and Marissa with stories about the early days when Assurance was first settled as a missions town.

"Zachary, let him get up and stretch his legs. He's sat listening to you long enough." Rebecca rose and began to clear the dishes from the table. "Mari, would you mind entertaining our guest on the porch while we clean up?"

Marissa set her napkin on the table and proceeded to rise. Rowe hurried around the table and pulled out her chair for her. So this was how proper women were treated when they dined with men.

Zachary winked at Marissa when Rowe wasn't looking, and she blushed. Was everyone conspiring to make her a lady?

Marissa and Rowe left the table to go out into the quiet

evening. The last trace of sunset skimmed over the horizon like a smear of orange paint blending into an ever darkening blue canvas. From a distance the vaulted store fronts of the town square formed angular silhouettes that dared to compete with the majestic backdrop of the wide, rolling land.

"If Virginians could see this, they would envy the homesteaders," Rowe said with awe in his voice. Leaning over the front porch rail, a smile crossed his face. "Did the Arthurs seem different to you this evening?"

Marissa cautiously rested her hands on the rail, more aware of his confident, inherent strength when they were alone. "They could have seen your gift-giving as something more than what it was."

"Such as?" The sun set against the planes of his face.

Since they were alone, Marissa saw no need to mince words. "It hasn't slipped by me that the three of you have been working together. The Arthurs want to make a respectable woman out of me. I assume you do too, but for a different reason."

"I'm afraid I don't follow."

He was more astute than that. It was just a Southern gentleman's polite way of obtaining information without being forceful. "They want me to believe in Jesus, and you want me to join your church. That's why they gave me a job at the store, and that's why you gave me the Bible."

With a thoughtful frown he tilted his head. "I still don't see how those are devious aims. You sound as though we were all plotting something malicious against you."

"So you do have an aim. You admit to wanting to see me become a member of the church."

"What's wrong with that? We all need to accept Christ for our eternal salvation."

She held onto the porch rail as though she'd fly away like the dry brush in the prairie winds. Preachers and their preaching. Did they never stop? "And wouldn't it help church membership if you had a saloon girl give her testimony?"

"I'd never manipulate a person into doing something they were averse to. Why are you speaking this way?"

His voice contained a sorrowful note. Marissa was ashamed of herself for ruining the evening. Things could have been said with more tact. "Because I feel manipulated. Jason said that you might use me as an example for the town, that I could help you draw in the sinners."

"Jason seems to be very good at twisting the truth."

"Is he right?"

"No. After what he did to you, how can you give anything he says a serious thought?"

Marissa stared off in the distance. Rowe only knew a portion of the despicable, lecherous things Jason had done. If he were to find out about everything, including the rape... she bit her lip. He could never know. It was too disgusting. "Jason may be a horrible man, but he's no fool when it comes to recognizing people's motivation."

Rowe spoke with great deliberation. "Marissa, you've been around so much of his cynicism that you think I'm using you when I'm trying to encourage you. If you join the church, I want it to be because you choose to."

"And the gift of the Bible? Was it also to encourage me?"

Solid and austere, he straightened his posture. "Yes. I told you that I gave it to you because Jason destroyed the one you inherited."

"That's an acceptable reason."

"Good. Now are you done doubting my intentions?"

The door swung open. Zachary padded onto the porch in his gray knitted socks. "Oh, you're still here, Reverend? I thought Marissa was watching the sunset so long she forgot it went down for the night."

Neither of them laughed at his jest. A cricket hiding

somewhere in the grass chirped twice and immediately ceased its noisemaking, as if it too realized that a cheerful evening serenade was not welcome.

Zachary frowned from one person to the other. "Say, you heard about the fair in Claywalk next week, haven't you?"

"I haven't," said Rowe.

"Well, there's dancin', food, games. You'll like it. You've been there a few times, haven't you, Mari?"

"When I was a child," she replied, hoping that her flat monotone wouldn't arouse more suspicion as to the heated nature of the previous exchange. Zachary knew something was amiss, she could tell. Naturally curious and sociable, he was going to inquire about it from her later on.

"If you're not too busy, Reverend, why don't you go to the fair with Mari? You need to take a breather from all that church work, and she needs to have some good clean fun for once."

"That depends on her answer, sir." Rowe turned to her. "Would you like to accompany me to the fair next week, Marissa? I would be honored if you would attend."

There was no saying nay in front of Zachary. Her only excuse would be she had nothing to wear, and Zachary would tell her that what she had on could be washed and pressed in time for next Saturday.

"Yes, I will accompany you. Do you dance?"

"Not in years, but perhaps you could refresh my memory."

Their stiffly polite dialogue seemed to satisfy Zachary, who held the door open for Marissa. "We better go back on inside, Mari. Rebecca will come behind me if she thinks we all went out here for some fresh air and didn't include her."

Marissa accepted the opportunity to return inside the house. "Have a good evening," she murmured quickly, slipping past Rowe.

"Good evening, Marissa. Till next Saturday, then."

Through the screen door she viewed his retreating steps from the house. One week until she had to speak to him once more. After the way she accused him and nearly rejected his gift, it would be a wonder if he showed at her doorstep again.

Chapter 15

On the Monday before the fair Marissa returned to the Walsh seamstress shop for her newly fashioned clothing. Everything that she ordered from Linda was designed for function, not fancy enough for wearing to festivals or parties. With neutral brown and navy skirts and basic white blouses as her choices, she had no idea what could be put together for Saturday.

Chiding herself, Marissa didn't think she should give the fair too much attention. After all, Zachary wanted her to go just so she would have a chance to get out of the house. No one expected her to be the belle of the ball, so to speak. Rowe would dance with her out of courtesy, *if* he hadn't changed his mind about being her escort.

Marissa felt odd at the thought of dancing with Rowe, as if tiny butterflies in the pit of her stomach stopped fluttering and suddenly took to swan diving. She had danced with dozens upon dozens of men, so why did the thought of dancing with this one man upset her so?

As Marissa entered the seamstress shop, Linda leaned on the front counter, her face contorted in a mix of worried brows and downturned lips.

"Are you alright?"

The young seamstress twiddled the pearl buttons on a pair of ladies' gloves. "No, I'm completely wretched. Sophie is angry with me, and I've caused the store to lose business."

"How?"

"The new cloth that Sophie ordered just came in, and she wanted me to make it up in time for the fair. When I said that I didn't have enough time to sew the fancy design she wanted, she refused to buy the cloth and left here in a big huff."

"That sounds like Sophie. I'm sorry you got caught in the middle."

Linda eyed her speculatively. "Do you want the white fabric made into a dress for you, Marissa?"

She jerked her head up. "Are you sure Sophie won't mind?"

"She doesn't want it anymore. Sophie told me to sell it and give her the profit."

Linda placed the fabric on the counter. It was fetching, with blue thread delicately woven throughout its borders. Marissa touched the loose edge of the fabric bolt. The material gave off a soft sheen as it glided through her fingers. "This is pretty, but I don't want to ruin friendships over a dress."

"My family's store will be ruined if I don't sell it." Linda pushed unruly tendrils off her damp forehead. "The cost to import it was more than what we earned in the first half of winter."

Marissa eyed the fabric. "The material itself costs as much as a fully sewn dress, correct?"

"Yes. I'll subtract the import price if you buy it. I'll lose money from shipping, but it's not everything, at least."

It was a fair offer. Marissa wouldn't be able to afford it if it was made into a gown. However, she could fashion something simple on her own. Rebecca might be of help. "Instead of making my dress, sell me this fabric, and I'll do it myself. Sophie can't say anything about that. You'll make money for the shop too."

"That can work," Linda agreed. "I do thank you for this." The seamstress was hesitant at expressing gratitude, perhaps embarrassed for the time spent taunting Marissa, right alongside Sophie.

"Thank you, Linda, for sewing my clothes so quickly."

Marissa paid what was owed and left the store with a small start to a new wardrobe and an extra fabric bolt under her arm. Already her mind fashioned the design of the dress she would create for the fair. The next several days would mean long nights in the company of thread and needle, but at least she wouldn't look like she went from stocking shoes to running to the ticket booth.

"Thank you for coming. Stop in again." Marissa handed the newly purchased gaiters to Hunter Myerson, one of the ranchers who lived about five miles from the town.

"My wife will enjoy these." Myerson stuffed the neatly wrapped package in his rucksack. "It'll help take her mind off the ones she muddied on the way to church last Sunday."

"We'll be getting more shoes in next month. Invite her to take a look the next time you come into town."

"I'll do that. Have a good day, Miss." The rancher collected the rest of his purchases from the trip and left.

Marissa glanced at the clock in the corner. Four customers visited since the store opened, and now it was set to close in two hours. Aside from utilitarian work boots, shoes were still low on people's priorities in a small town. The general store got the most business, as more residents came in for hardware and tools.

The Arthurs had already gone home, due to Zachary having some trouble with his back that morning. Marissa basked in their confidence of her abilities, leaving her in charge as a learning experience.

She busied herself with straightening behind the counter.

"So this is what you'd rather do than pour drinks."

Marissa froze at the sound of the all too identifiable, chilling voice as Jason entered the store. Her body drained of its life-giving warmth as he presented her an awful smile.

Tobacco-stained teeth displayed themselves behind long drab-brown hair that hung in greasy strands about his shoulders. The door shut behind him, and he slid the bolt into place. Her stomach dropped.

"Can't say that this place doesn't hold its charm." He casually tossed a glance about the room. "But a shoe shop don't suit you, darlin'."

Around the nose his face was oddly misshapen and slightly bulbous, giving the eyes a squinty appearance. For over two weeks she had managed to avoid him—probably because he was cooped up waiting for his nose to heal. She should have known the respite wouldn't last.

Marissa drew a long, deep breath until her lungs couldn't hold any more air, exhaled, and willed her voice to stay low and calm.

"A shoe shop suits me just fine, Jason. Unlike my prior place of employment, I'm in a respectable position."

"As a cobbler's assistant? Where's the money in that?"

"It's not about money. It's about being fair and honest to customers as well as earning a decent living. I don't go to bed feeling guilty."

Beneath the counter there was a magnifying glass and a dull pair of scissors. Nothing that she could use to defend herself if the situation called for it.

Jason edged two paces closer to the counter. "Since when did fairness and decency become important to you?"

"Since the day I saw how you truly dealt with your customers and employees."

Loud, raucous laughter sounded throughout the interior of the shop. "And here I thought you were going to say since you gave your life to Christ. I thought for certain that preacher man would've convinced you to already."

In a fleeting moment Marissa cast her vision away from Jason. "He tried."

"And what happened, sweetheart?" Jason feigned concern. "Didn't you want to save your immortal soul, or was it the good reverend you were thinking about giving yourself to?"

She held her ground. "He has little bearing upon the decisions I make."

"Of course he doesn't, darlin'. As sure as you're born." Jason picked up a wooden shoe last and examined the bottom side with detached interest.

"It's true. As a matter of fact, what you did to me the night I left the saloon and the years leading up to it made me see how much I needed to leave that place. No man had to tell me."

"You haven't been the same since Winford came here."

"I wouldn't expect you to see things for what they really are. Now, please leave. You have no business in this store."

"Is that any way to treat a payin' customer?" He put the shoe last back and started pacing around the room. "Old Zachary wouldn't be too happy to hear about this."

"He would if he knew to whom I was speaking." Marissa watched his every movement, every footstep for where he might veer, and every hand motion for the slightest twitch.

"That senile old coot wouldn't be able to do a thing about it. Neither would your preacher beau. Is Winford gonna thump me on the head with his Bible?"

"His fist to your nose seemed to do the trick."

Snarling at her defiance, he shouted, "You are my woman that I've looked after for three years. You belong to me. I took you from your ma when she was on her deathbed."

Marissa lifted her chin and met his wild, possessive gaze straight on. "My mother was feverish when you lied to her about erasing her debt. She thought you would look after me until I turned eighteen, not have me assume her job. She didn't tell you to use me or my body. Or beat me."

Jason snatched an item from his waistcoat so fast that

Marissa jumped backward, expecting a firearm. Snickering at her reaction, he slapped the item on the countertop. A piece of paper. She looked closer. It was the old contract that bound her to him.

"Read the fine print." With a stained thumbnail, he indicated to a paragraph near the very bottom of the last page. "There's a clause that states you have to work for me if the business starts goin' sour. You have to continue until the business restores itself before you can leave."

Marissa dared to take her eyes off him long enough to read the tiny letters of the paragraph. He was right.

> In the event of debt, slowing sales, or infrequent customers, this employee hereby agrees to maintain employment with employer until the state of the business has been restored satisfactorily.

Her own signature mocked her from the bottom of the page.

"Guess you should have read more carefully before you signed, eh?"

"I trusted you." Her eyes flew back up to meet his. "I was eighteen when you gave me this contract, and I didn't have anywhere else to go." She picked up the three-page agreement, scanning the paragraphs to see if there was anything else she had missed. "How am I to know when your saloon has been restored satisfactorily? You could have me working for years."

"Ain't the law grand?" Jason took the contract from her. "I'd better see you back at the saloon by the end of next week, or I'll get a circuit judge to enforce this. You'll go to jail."

"I'm not going back to your saloon. When I tell the judge what you've done to me, he won't enforce that contract."

"You'll have to prove it first." He slid the papers back into the pocket of his waistcoat. "You'd have to hire a lawyer, which I don't believe you can afford. And even if there is a witness from town, he won't get himself involved to help a woman with your bad standing."

Marissa grew sick at the truth of his words. Just when she thought she had broken free of him, he snatched her back like an animal chained to a sturdy post, slackening long enough to let her think she had escaped his hold.

"Don't forget that I can sue the Arthurs for stealing my employee while she's still under contract. You don't want to hurt their business because of your mistakes, do you?"

"Get out of here, Jason." Her voice trembled slightly as she held back utter distress. Rebecca and Zachary gave her a home and entrusted her with so much of what belonged to them. Everything they worked so hard for could be destroyed because of her.

Jason beamed, proud of the control he regained. "I wonder what Rowe Winford would think of you now. The woman he thought to redeem is going back to the den of iniquity."

"Rowe sees beyond who I once was."

"You try to hide it, but I know you're sweet on him. He won't have you as his wife. You're far from the gentle, sheltered woman he'll pick to marry. Do yourself a favor and stick to the only thing you're recognized for."

Marissa didn't take her eyes off Jason until he exited the store. When he swaggered out of view, she bolted from the counter, locked the doors, and ran into the storeroom. There, in the midst of crates, shoes awaiting repair, and spare display shelves, she gave herself over to a flood of tears.

Chapter 16

ARISSA KNEW SHE couldn't stay locked in the storeroom with the crates and ledgers forever. Eventually someone would notice that the store had been closed for over an hour and would alert the sheriff. Given that Jason already promised to get the law involved in their dispute, Marissa had no desire to see McGee's face sooner than she had to.

She lifted her head from her hands and wiped the tears from her face. Crying was not helping matters. Other women could resort to such means in assurance of rescue, but she did not have the privilege of being a damsel in distress. She used to be, *still was*, a saloon girl. No one save a judge could get her out of that predicament.

But what judge would hear her case? Jason had the binding agreement and records to prove the slowing sales in his business. She was the one who looked guilty by running away.

Marissa stood to her feet and shoved a hand in her dress pocket for her change purse. Barely enough money to hire a wagon to Claywalk, much less a lawyer. She shot down the idea of asking to borrow money from the Arthurs. They did enough for her. She needed to solve this problem without them.

In the salesroom the clock on the wall struck half past four. Marissa saw no reason to reopen the shop. Head beginning to ache, she removed the money from the register and locked it in the storeroom before closing the front door of the shop behind her.

The main square of Assurance bore the usual afternoon activity, people making their last errands before going home for supper. The blacksmith across the way ceased his hammering to get up for a sip of water. He stared at Marissa as she crossed the street.

"Do you work for the Arthurs, Garth, or both of 'em now?" he called.

Marissa felt exposed to the hot sun bearing down on her back, as though it were calling the citizens' attention to her every movement. "I don't know."

"Well, that don't make no sense. You gotta know who's payin' you." The blacksmith took a large swig from his tin cup before tossing the last of the water in the street. Folding his large forearms, he acted like he was mad at her for not giving an answer. "Garth's been tellin' folks you still work for him."

"I'm sure he has."

"Well, is he makin' himself out to be a liar? I haven't seen you in the saloon for a spell."

Was this the sort of conversation she would be having with people for the rest of her natural born days? "Mr. Hastings, I don't intend to go back to that saloon. Ever. Now, I can't tell you any more than that. Good day."

Jason worked fast. She couldn't go back to the Arthurs' home yet. Best to get a handle on the situation first.

The sheriff's office loomed on the outside of the square. The black iron bars from the window of the attached cell gave a grim, gap-toothed smile at her. The last criminal to occupy that cell waited one hundred and eighty days before the circuit judge rode up to give him a trial. Then he was transferred to Arkansas to be hanged on charges of horse theft.

Leaving a job while under contract was very much like stealing. Marissa breathed street dust into her dry throat and choked. She hurried to turn her back on the building.

Step by step she trod the path to the church. One option existed short of skipping town. Rowe was no lawyer, but he had the clout to retain the services of one. If she were fortunate, the lawyer may even agree not to accept payment until after the trial proceedings.

Has there ever been a time in your life when you were fortunate? A snide voice infiltrated her mind.

"Can't believe I'm going here again," she muttered as she followed along the path. The church steeple was visible ahead.

That place isn't for you. Why would Rowe help you again after you accused him of using you to build his church?

Marissa considered the irony of her predicament. When would the day come that she could rely on her own resources?

Never. Jason's set you up to stay put with him. Once you're a painted cat, the color doesn't wash off.

A wagon and three saddled horses waited outside the front of the church. She pulled the heavy door handle. Her heels clacked on the floorboards outside the sanctuary as she hurried to the pastor's study.

Mrs. Pate blocked the hallway passage. "Can I help you, Miss Pierce?" Her tone was polite but not friendly. The steel-haired lady eyed Marissa as though she would burst into a saloon song and dance at any moment.

"I must see the reverend. It's urgent."

Mrs. Pate put a finger to her lips. "If you would, the choir will be rehearsing in the sanctuary in a few minutes. The reverend has been detained in his study all afternoon. What if you come back tomorrow, hmm?"

Marissa gritted her teeth at the woman's curt dismissal. "I wouldn't be here if it were not urgent." She skirted past the woman to knock on the door.

It opened before she could put her hand to it. Rowe stuck his head out. "Is something wrong, Mrs. Pate? I heard voices."

Mrs. Pate jabbed a finger at Marissa. "I tried to get her to leave and come back tomorrow, Reverend, but she was too stubborn to listen. I told her that you were busy."

Marissa looked at Rowe imploringly. "I'm in bad need of your help. Otherwise, I wouldn't have come."

The tense conversation he had with her last week appeared to have been forgotten or forgiven. His countenance bore no grudge. "Miss Pierce is as welcome into the church as anyone, Mrs. Pate. I'm never so busy that people can't at least inquire of me whether I can see them."

"I'm sorry, Reverend." Mrs. Pate tugged at her sleeves. "I didn't think you'd take kindly to having your studies interrupted." Excusing herself, she returned to the sanctuary.

"Forgive Mrs. Pate. I never asked her to attend the door. She can be cordial but also very set in her ways." Rowe returned to his desk, where he pushed aside his books. "Now, tell me what's wrong."

Marissa took a quick breath. "Jason's going to send me to jail."

"What? You're shaking. Breathe slowly."

His solid presence and deep, soothing voice provided enough calm for her to continue. "Jason came to the store. He says I have to go back to the saloon, or he will tell a judge that I broke my contract. There's a clause that says if the saloon is in trouble, I have to work for him until business picks up again."

His eyebrows rose. "You won't do it, of course."

"I'm still under contract. He can sue the Arthurs for taking an employee of his." She flattened her palms against her dress. "Rowe, I can't let Jason harm them because of me. I hate to ask, but would you help me retain a lawyer? I'd pay the fee, of course, but I need you to convince a lawyer that my case is worth taking up. It's hard enough for any woman to get legal counsel, but no one will even think to help a saloon girl."

Rowe took a decisive step toward the wall rack and pulled his coat on over his shirt. "This time we're going to see the sheriff."

She panicked, thinking of the iron bars. "No."

"Yes. Marissa, the reason Jason has gotten this far in his dealings is because no one will speak out against him. If we had gone to Sheriff McGee the night Jason hurt you, he could have been arrested already."

"You don't know that."

"It was a good chance. I saw him come after you, and I'm sure at least one employee in that saloon saw or heard what was going on."

Marissa lowered her head. "Simone and the other girls saw him strike me, but they'll never talk. Going to Sheriff McGee now won't help, either."

He placed a hand on her shoulder. His touch was warm, where her hands felt like they had been soaking in ice. "You came here because you wanted my help. Can we try it this way? If it doesn't work, we can seek legal counsel."

His use of the word we proved that he viewed her problem as his own. Marissa's courage strengthened with the knowledge that she had an ally who wasn't given to losing his nerve. If she held onto hers long enough, they might have a chance of convincing the sheriff to take care of Jason. Maybe.

"Jason's giving me a chance to return to the saloon. If I appear before the sheriff, what's to stop him from putting me in a cell?"

"What do you hope to accomplish by avoiding the sheriff? This isn't a big town. He can find you." Rowe opened the door to the study and ushered Marissa out, keeping behind her as if she would try to dart under his arm and hide under the desk. "I'm only saying that we can't duck our heads in the sand and hope this all goes away. It'll just get worse."

Marissa heard Mrs. Pate hit a high C from inside the sanctuary. It was off-pitch. "There goes the last note I'll ever hear as a free woman."

Rowe shook his head and put on a half-smile. "If

Assurance ever gets a theater, I think you'd make a great comedic actress."

She was temporarily stunned by his shift in humor. "People consider that to be even worse than a saloon girl."

"What do you want to be?"

She sensed he was trying to distract her from panicking again. It was sweet, but the fear of being tossed in jail with only Sheriff McGee for company still crawled up the base of her spine. "I'll worry about that later. Let's just get this awful business over with."

Sheriff McGee pursed his thick lips in a gesture of concentration. "Let me get this straight, Miss Pierce. You signed an agreement without readin' the provisions, and you want me to get you out of it."

Marissa knew Rowe's idea of going to McGee would be a lost cause. She and the reverend stood before the sheriff, urgently pleading for help while he listened to them from his seat in the town jail, stretching a plump leg on the table. A jar of chewing tobacco and a rifle shared the table with his limb. Moving a wad of the tobacco around in his cheek, the sheriff gathered enough saliva to launch a brown stream into the spittoon on the floor.

Some of the liquid splattered onto the toe of Rowe's boot. He clenched his jaw. At least now he had an idea of the man's unprofessionalism, Marissa thought.

Rowe spoke. "That contract is unconscionable, Sheriff. Marissa can't work for a man who's violent to his employees."

McGee's small eyes shifted to her. "Why did she do it in the first place?"

"I was eighteen years of age when I signed Jason's contract. I was too worried about keeping a roof over my head and food in my mouth to comb through the fine print."

Sheriff McGee shrugged as though he wasn't about to comb through the matter, either. "An agreement is an agreement. You signed it, Missy. Is that what they still call you?"

"No, because I don't work there anymore, and I'm not going to ever again."

He chortled at her resolve. "You realize you could be jailed for violatin' a contract?"

The small cell behind him beckoned for an occupant, with its rusted iron bars and stain-covered straw pallet. Marissa set her chin in a stubborn line to keep it from trembling.

"Show him your scars," Rowe suggested.

Marissa was hesitant, but she rolled up the sleeve of her blouse. The bruises had completely faded, but the scars were pink and newly formed. Rowe pointed his finger at them. "Those are the work of Jason Garth. He chased her through the streets of Assurance and beat her in the woods when she refused to stay in the saloon. If I hadn't intervened, he probably would have killed her. Should she be jailed because she couldn't work under those conditions?"

McGee leaned forward in his chair to study her scars. "Maybe Missy was handled roughly by some men during her work hours. It does happen in that trade, Reverend."

Marissa snatched her arm away and glared at the sheriff. "How is it that I'm the one you're suspicious of? Are you saying that my past precludes me from the protection of the law?"

"I keep telling you, you're under contract. There's nothing you or anyone else can do to get you out of it."

"Would you say that to another woman who needed your help? Reverend Winford, perhaps we've wasted our time."

"No, we haven't." Rowe leaned forward. "Sheriff, that man Jason Garth is dangerous." His voice rang with authority in the small room. "You can't tell me he has a right to Marissa as an employee."

McGee sat upright. "Like I told you before, I need proof. A few scars don't tell me anything."

Before? Since when did Rowe converse with the sheriff prior to today? Marissa regarded him with suspicion. He promised not to say anything.

Rowe went on. "What more do you need to be sure he abuses women?"

"Do you have the contract?"

"No." He checked his coat pockets before glancing at Marissa. She shook her head.

"There's nothin' I can do then. She could get a man to speak on her behalf to the circuit judge, but he'll need incontestable proof too. That's the only way she's gettin' out o' that agreement."

Rowe clenched his fists. Marissa thought he was going to bang them on the table. "She's not going back to Jason. Something will be done to keep that from happening, I can assure you."

"Reverend, this town's been official for twenty years. It won't do you no good to be upsettin' things."

"Maybe that's what's needed for people to wake up to the atrocities happening around them."

He beat Marissa to the door. He held it open for her to pass through before letting it slam shut on McGee.

Marissa paced the front of the jail building, arms folded and distraught. "I knew McGee would do nothing." Her raised, upset voice drew the interest of passersby on the street, but they were the least of her worries. "Now he'll watch me to make sure the contract is enforced. I have to leave on the next train that stops in Claywalk."

"No, you don't. You're anxious and upset."

"Of course I am. When did you speak to McGee about this? I just heard him say you talked before."

"It was in church. We talked about Jason and the saloon. As you preferred, I didn't go into detail about what happened." Marissa faced Rowe again, pivoting sharply enough to kick up dust with the quick spin of her boot heel. "The longer I stay in this town, the worse it gets. For me, for you, for the Arthurs."

Several men and women stopped what they were doing to listen to the conversation. Rowe guided her away from them, taking her up the street. "You are not going to let Jason run you away from your birthplace."

Marissa quickened her steps to match his. "Perhaps it's best that I leave. Just start again somewhere new. I'll go across the state, back to St. Louis."

"Your distress is making you talk this way, but it's a very bad idea."

"It couldn't do worse than this one. People get pardons from other states. It isn't unheard of." Deep down Marissa knew she sounded irrational, but reason had its chance to shine in McGee's office, and it failed miserably.

"You don't know how you'll fare in St. Louis. In large cities there are more violent acts and thousands of Jason Garths. A change in location won't solve the problem."

Marissa was beginning to intensely dislike Rowe's ability to point out the flaws in her logic. "Then what will? No one here will help."

"I don't know. We have to pray hard about it."

"And find a lawyer." She wanted to make sure Rowe didn't dispense with practicality.

"Yes. But on the upside, even if Jason charges you, he'll have to wait until the judge makes his rounds. It could take months before the judge rides to Assurance."

"I don't want to think about sitting in a cell that long."

"How much time did Jason give you to return to the saloon?"

"By the end of next week." Marissa remembered the sneer on Jason's face when he said it.

"That gives us about ten days. We can see about visiting a lawyer in Claywalk when I take you to the fair this Saturday." She had forgotten all about the fair. "Or we could go to Claywalk now and find one."

"I'll go tomorrow, first thing in the morning. In the meantime, you should go home. Mr. and Mrs. Arthur are probably worried about you."

"There's no way I can rest or face them until this is resolved."

"Procuring legal counsel will have to wait. It's after five, and most businesses are closed." Rowe reached out and tucked a loose strand of hair behind her ear. "Things will turn out right, Marissa."

The gesture caught her off guard. It wasn't forward, but it certainly wasn't something a casual male acquaintance would do in the middle of town square. She turned about to see who had been privy to it. The people who stopped outside the sheriff's office were making their way up the road. Two of the women, the middle-aged Mrs. Rheins and her daughter, Margaret, returned Marissa's gaze with knowing. They started talking to each other, keeping her in their sights.

"Marissa?"

Rowe's handsome face emanated concern and thoughtfulness. Did he realize that he just caused a scandal?

"You're right. I should go home." She retreated two steps from him. "You'll tell me as soon as you find a lawyer?"

He nodded, with a conflicted, haunted air, giving the impression that he was far away in thought. A frown line appeared between the bridge of his nose and forehead.

If Marissa stayed long enough to question what he was thinking about, she'd give the approaching women more gossip fodder. She headed in the direction of the Arthurs' home.

Chapter 17

W HY COULDN'T HE have just told Marissa that she had a hair out of place?

These desires were getting worse. He wanted to feel her dark hair glide between his fingers, to touch her cheek.

Two women saw him do it. Rowe heard the concealed tones in their voices as they greeted him on the street. He recognized them from church.

"Good afternoon, Reverend." The older one, Mrs. Rheins, had a clipped British accent. She gave him the same scolding eye his mother used when he got caught stealing bites of apple pie filling.

"How do you do?" Her daughter Margaret's high-pitched greeting reminded him of Sophie Charlton. The two girls often sat together in church, distracting him with their giggles and whispering.

"Good afternoon, ladies." He smiled. They did not reciprocate.

"Was that Marissa Pierce you were speaking to?" Mrs. Rheins asked with artificial lightness in her voice. Rowe dreaded where this was leading.

"Yes. We had some business to attend to." That didn't sound right.

Mrs. Rheins lifted her head and tilted it like a sparrow hearing an odd noise. "Oh? Well, it is known of her recent plight and all. I hope she's not in any more trouble."

He couldn't lie, but he wasn't obligated to disclose every detail either. "She sought my opinion on a matter."

"Undoubtedly, I'm sure. As I'm sure you provided the necessary comforts to ease her mind. That is what we need our ministers for. Comfort." The woman's words dripped in double entendre.

"Are you going to attend the fair this Saturday, Reverend Winford?" Margaret's question allowed him to change the subject.

"Yes. I wouldn't miss it."

Mrs. Rheins glanced at her daughter in calculation. "Margaret has yet to find an escort. If you're not otherwise obligated, I wonder if you could take her. I'd feel better if she went with you, Reverend, as opposed to a chaperone that I would hold in question."

Both mother and daughter fastened their hopeful brown eyes on him. The sound of a horse's hooves clopping on the other side of the road was strangely reminiscent of the ticking of a clock.

"I'm sorry, but I promised to escort someone else."

Mrs. Rheins retained her poise, but Margaret looked as though she had taken a tumble from the bird's nest. Rowe hoped they wouldn't ask who he was bringing to the fair.

"We did inquire of you rather late," Mrs. Rheins recovered. "Perhaps Margaret will see you there. She's looking forward to the dances, aren't you, dear?"

Margaret nodded, and her chestnut curls bounced in an imitation of Sophie's coiffure.

"If you don't mind my asking, is it Miss Charlton that you will be escorting? I'm told that you and her family have become well acquainted."

Rowe thought back to the conversation he overheard between Sophie and Linda, where Sophie discussed her plans to invite him to supper. It was possible she considered his visit the beginning of courtship. That was how Josephine reacted when he attended a party at her family's estate. He had to tread carefully with Sophie and her friends.

"No, Mama." Margaret put the emphasis on the second syllable of the word, sounding decidedly upper crust. "Sophie is being escorted to the fair by Chad Hooper."

"The mayor's son? A fine choice. You have yet to find a young man of equal repute."

Margaret folded her hands behind her back and studied her two-tone boots. Unfortunate girl, Rowe thought. She couldn't look forward to the fair because of her mother.

"We should be going now. Good evening, then, Reverend." Mrs. Rheins led her daughter away from the square.

Relieved that his interrogation was over, Rowe journeyed back to the church to gather his study materials before going home. He had a challenging task in the morning, finding Marissa a lawyer. Then there was the fair to think about. An hour's drive away. An hour alone on the wide open prairie with Marissa. How could he keep his thoughts civil if he was already abandoning his will to think of no woman but Josephine?

The Saturday of the fair turned out to be promising, despite the few raindrops that fell the previous evening. Golden sun lit the wide, tranquil blue sky. By the time Marissa and Rowe set out in the morning, the ground was dry.

"It's good to get out of town." Marissa settled on the wagon bench as Assurance sank beneath the horizon behind her, eaten up by the plains. It was equally refreshing to be away from the watchful eyes and gossip, but more than that, she was anxious to meet the lawyer that Rowe found for her. Two days before, he said he talked with a counsel in Claywalk and that the gentleman was willing to speak to her concerning the contract. Mr. Jonathan Boyd, esquire, was supposed to be in attendance at the fair.

Rowe drove the team of horses. "Other than the train to Kansas and the trip to Claywalk, I haven't seen much of the countryside."

"Our windy, flat plains probably don't compare with Virginia's forests, do they?"

"Virginia is lovely, but that doesn't make this state any less beautiful."

Through her thin shawl she felt his body heat. She awaited their time together in Claywalk half in anticipation, half in dread. The wagon wheels rolled along the long narrow dirt road. Tall grasses waved the horses forward. Marissa imagined Virginia as a lush green landscape brimming with tall, leafy trees whose branches blocked the sun. She wondered if Rowe's statement about the land applied to his opinion of people as well.

Marissa smoothed the folds of the blue and white dress she and Rebecca lost hours of sleep over, no longer fooling herself into believing she didn't care about what he thought of her appearance.

They talked of their individual birthplaces on the way to the fair, describing the locals and the typical climates. Hearing Rowe speak of crowded cities and large buildings made her curious.

"Did the war also prompt you to leave Richmond?"

He explained God's calling for him to be a minister after the war. "After I gave my life to Christ, living in Richmond no longer appealed to me. I'd seen death and families divided on a dehumanizing system that should never have been in place in this country."

"I would expect to hear that from a northerner but not a Virginian."

With a shrug he said, "I was drafted under a conscription

law. I didn't get to choose whether I'd fight. You'll find that those of us in the South had differing opinions of the war, as did those in the North."

"There was violence here in Kansas too. I'm grateful that it ended when it did. Now the country can start moving forward."

They left the somber subject behind as their wagon began to run adjacent to the train tracks leading into Claywalk.

"I haven't attended the fair since I was eight or nine." Marissa shielded her eyes and scanned the distance. The white tops of schooners dotted the town outskirts. Booths and colorful tables decorated the first three streets. Fiddle music drifted between the shouts of excited children and the buzzing chatter of adults. "Where did you agree to meet Mr. Boyd?"

Rowe took one hand off the reins to grab his hat, nearly losing it in a sudden gust of wind. "He told me he would be waiting near the hitching posts. Shorter man, goatee. There he is. See him under the fair banner?"

Marissa spotted the man Rowe described. He was below average height, wearing a light suit of summer wool. A gleaming gold watch chain dangled from his waistcoat. He opened the lid of his watch, then studied the attendees as they filtered between the poles holding the banner.

"I guess we need to hurry." Rowe swung down from the wagon bench and secured the horses. Marissa took his hand as he assisted her in climbing down.

"Mr. Boyd." He got the man's attention as they approached.

"Reverend Winford, good to see you again." The lawyer shook Rowe's hand before acknowledging Marissa. "And this must be the client in question."

"Yes, this is Miss Pierce. She's being kind enough to accompany me to the fair today."

"Gotta keep a watchful eye on these city folks so they don't hurt themselves out here, right, ma'am?" Mr. Boyd pumped her hand up and down.

She liked his friendly manner, quite different from the unflappable lawyers her father used to consult for his debts. "How do you do, Mr. Boyd?"

"Good. Let's talk over yonder, where I can hear you over the racket." He led them to a patch of grass away from the ticket line.

What the lawyer had to say could determine whether Marissa breathed a sigh of relief or turned herself in to the sheriff. She felt as anxious as she did the first day Jason put her to work.

Rowe's steady and reassuring hand on her back was a welcome signal to bring her mind away from speculation.

Mr. Boyd began. "I read up on contractual laws since I last saw the reverend. I'm basing the facts on what he said since I don't have the contract in front of me. From what it seems, this is a civil matter. Your employer can file a lawsuit against you and the people you work for now if he chooses. That's the bad news."

"What can possibly be good news?" Marissa imagined the Arthurs losing their home and business because of her.

"The good news is no criminal action can be taken against you. Your employer can't have you put in jail for simply quitting your job. He has to wait until a circuit judge comes into town to try the case."

"So Jason was bluffing." Marissa looked up at Rowe. "What about after the trial?"

Mr. Boyd continued. "If the judge finds you violated the contract—and I'm sorry, Miss Pierce, there's a good chance he will, since you did leave the saloon before your termination date—he will order you to pay the damages. If you can't pay, your employer is free to pursue a case against the owners of the store you work at currently."

Her heart sank to the murky place it was before. "What about the contract itself? Those clauses that stated I had to work until the saloon increased its sales. They were vague."

"You can argue unconscionability. It's up to the judge to decide if he agrees with you or with the saloon proprietor."

"What does that mean?"

"It means the terms of the contract are so unreasonable that no person should have to be subject to them."

Rowe chimed in. "I think we're getting ahead of ourselves. Mr. Boyd did say that everything has to wait until the judge arrives, whenever that may be."

"Right." The lawyer took a handkerchief from his coat pocket and wiped fingerprints from the cover of his watch. "So long as you don't try to skip town or hide from the law."

Marissa wasn't sure if Sheriff McGee would be satisfied with that. "What if my former employer insists that I'll try to run away?"

"You'd best convince your town's sheriff that you won't."

"I'll speak for you," said Rowe, "even if it means pestering McGee all day long."

Mr. Boyd cleared his throat louder than necessary. "If you don't have any further questions, I hear the fruit turnovers calling my name."

"No, that's all we have for today. About your fee." Rowe proceeded to reach behind the lapels of his coat for his billfold.

"No fee. The initial consultation's always free of charge. You know where to find me if you need my help again."

"Thank you, Mr. Boyd." Rowe turned to Marissa after he left. "Are you ready to get your ticket?"

"I suppose, even if it means having to keep a watchful eye on you."

He played along. "Yes, we city folks just don't know what to do with ourselves this far from home."

Marissa allowed herself to laugh now that the lawyer disappeared among the food vendors. "But this is your home now. You're officially a resident of Kansas and a citizen of Assurance."

He turned serious. "I hope you'll still consider this your home too and not move away when this legal battle with Jason is over."

She moved her shawl higher on her shoulders, in spite of the sun reaching its zenith. "I don't think anyone would miss me too much, other than the Arthurs, and they'll understand. Eventually."

"I'd miss you."

"Don't say that." It scared Marissa to hear the honesty in his words. For a man with strength, in physique as well as character, Rowe wore his feelings too far out on his sleeve. "You have a church to build."

"What does that have to do with me missing you if you go?"

"The town would think it unseemly if you pined after my friendship."

The breeze upset Rowe's hat again. He took it off and adjusted the inside band. The wind tousled his hair at the crown. "Maybe it's more than friendship I seek."

Marissa got chills from the base of her spine to the top of her neck. She hoped he hadn't intended for her to hear what he said. Even if she was attracted to him, she hid it. Why couldn't he do the same? "I didn't hear what you said over the music."

She thought preachers were good at concealing their annoyance, but Rowe was as bad at that as he was at keeping quiet. His eyes darkened a shade bluer than the evening sky. "You don't have to be tactful. We're not near the town gossips."

"I don't want to talk about this. Zachary wanted us to go the fair because it would be fun. We should buy our tickets."

He didn't move as she walked by him to the ticket counter

and stood in line. If this was any indication of the rest of their day, Marissa hoped that it would go by fast.

Twice in one week Rowe had three women chastise him as though he were a sulky child. First Mrs. Rheins and Margaret, and now Marissa.

She was being stubborn, but this time her willful nature had nothing to do with the Assurance townspeople and everything to do with him.

He scared her off.

Rowe noticed how careful she was not to make eye contact with him as they stood side by side in the ticket line. The last thing he wanted to do was upset her. Why was he having so many slips of the tongue?

The dress she wore was fetching. Its heart-shaped neckline made a pretty portrait of her honey-bronzed skin. Today she let her hair hang free down her back, and every so often, the breeze would lift the silky strands to tickle him on the wrist. The rinse she used smelled faintly of rosewater. It combined with her lavender fragrance, making him think of stepping into an English garden.

It was torture.

Rowe tried to get his nose to take in the smell of grease from the dough frying at a pastry table. It didn't help. He smelled grease and flowers.

"How many, sir?" The attendant had a thick roll of tickets sitting on the counter.

"Two, please." Rowe took four coins out of his billfold and placed them in front of the attendant.

He didn't want to admit it, but if Marissa were to leave Kansas, he would run right after her to get her to come back. She was right to tell him that he shouldn't pine away, though. He'd done too much of that already for his wife.

Rowe took the tickets from the attendant and handed one to Marissa.

"Where to first?" she asked as they walked through the vendor tables.

"You can point me to the ring toss." Rowe stopped to reply before venturing back into his musings.

Here he was, trying to shed his past and his melancholy. Was Marissa just another distraction? A pretty face, a damsel in distress…a new way to get his mind off of Josephine?

And what of Marissa? What is she scared of? That I'll judge her? That the town will shun her? Many people were doing that to her long before he arrived. It couldn't be the full reason for her aversion to him.

The wind kicked at his back. *You'd be sinning if you were to become involved with her.*

But he was already involved, far in over his head. And he couldn't think straight enough to know his own motivations about it, much less hers.

The fair was in full swing. People from both towns gathered at the field's center to hear the band play their fiddles. To one side young men and children filled the gaming stalls, throwing darts, hitting and missing their targets. A man sat in the dunking booth, jeering at whoever tried to aim a ball at the mechanism that would send him under the water. Rowe decided to join in the festivities.

Marissa read the show lineup on a sheet of paper tacked to a post. "I want to see the lassoist and horse trainer. It also says here the dancing starts at five."

The scent of smoked sausage and corn fritters wafted from a nearby vendor. Rowe looked to the gaming stalls. "Mind if I try to dunk the man over here first?"

They approached the booth. The man sitting above the water continued to heckle the participants.

"Is that the best ya got?" he cried as a burly man threw a

ball and missed. The man threw again, and the ball harmlessly bounced off the side of the target and onto the ground. "Better luck next year, when you strengthen that arm. Who's next?"

Rowe paid the attendant for two turns and stepped up to the white line where he was to throw the balls.

"Oh, a fancy city man." The long-john-wearing heckler remarked upon the cut of Rowe's coat. "Let's see if yer as big and strong as you look."

Rowe threw the ball at the booth, missing twice. On the third try the ball hit just above its target.

"Guess they only use their arms in the city to hail a carriage driver."

"May I try?" Marissa asked when Rowe went for a second turn.

"What's this?" the heckler called out. "Sendin' a little woman out to do a big man's work?"

"She's bigger 'n' you, Grover," an onlooker shot back.

Rowe looked on in fascination as Marissa blocked out the taunts and concentrated on the mark, pulling her arm back to let the ball fly.

It found its target. Grover hit the water with a big splash, succeeding in drenching himself and anyone else standing close by.

Marissa turned to Rowe and the attendant. "I grew tired of his taunting," she put it plainly.

"I see why your aim is famous." Rowe shook his head, amused and impressed.

For her effort the attendant presented her with a prize of a stuffed doll.

"Well, that suits you more than me." Rowe rubbed the back of his neck. He said that for his own benefit, and she rewarded him with a teasing smile. The day at the fair could have a chance of going well after all.

Chapter 18

THEY SPENT THE next hours playing more games, including darts, which Rowe fared much better in, and foot racing. Marissa cheered him on as he beat the other eight men and took home a prize of a bread and cheese basket.

His relaxed humor throughout the day made her chuckle. Unlike the other men she knew in her former life, who only approached her because they wanted a drink or something that she was unwilling to offer, Rowe genuinely enjoyed her company.

Maybe she had been too hasty in discouraging his friendship.

Affection was a better word. She heard him say he wanted more than friendship. The notion left her as frightened and vulnerable as the first time a man put hands on her. Rowe could lose his job if he wasn't careful.

She forced herself to put aside her heavy thoughts. For now she and Rowe had time to themselves without one person from Assurance giving them so much as a curious glance or frowning lip. Marissa visited her favorite seasonal purveyors at a slower pace while Rowe ventured from stall to stall, eyeing the wares and talking amiably to the vendors.

She left a table filled with lotions and toiletries to catch up with him when she collided with another woman.

Marissa skirted back, while Sophie nearly toppled over. Whirling back to Marissa, her pretty heart-shaped face turned up and puckered like a bulb onion.

"You did that on purpose!"

"I'm sorry, Sophie. I didn't even see you."

"I saw you, though." Her eyes swept over Marissa's dress. "You're the one Linda sold my fabric to."

"You told her you didn't want it."

"Look at the mess you made of it. A potato sack has more elaborated stitching than that rag."

Sophie's escort, Chad Hooper, approached.

Sophie continued, unaware that Mr. Hooper was in earshot. "Tell me how Rowe would choose to take a woman like you to the fair instead of me."

"You really would have to ask him yourself."

"He had to take you out of town in order to be seen with you."

"Perhaps he did." Marissa excused herself, nodding courteously to Sophie's escort. "Good day to you, Mr. Hooper. Sophie."

Sophie's eyes bulged when she realized her escort had heard everything. Marissa left them to sort it out. Her own escort was a short distance away.

Rowe handed her a raspberry tartlet while nibbling on his own. "Where did you run off to?"

"Not off. Into." She indicated with a nod of her head in the opposite direction.

Rowe saw Sophie and her escort behind them. "Oh."

"Sophie's starting to bicker already. Is there any way we can avoid having an unpleasant afternoon?"

He swallowed the rest of his tartlet. "Let's not allow that to spoil things for us. I've been hearing lively music all day. Come. Let's see who's onstage."

Marissa groaned. So much for their getting away from the people of Assurance.

Rowe didn't see how Marissa could be surprised or upset by Sophie's presence. A fair would attract both citizens of Claywalk and Assurance. If Miss Charlton wanted to bicker and quarrel, the best thing to do was not give her an audience. Five o'clock arrived to the strains of the fiddles. He gazed surreptitiously at Marissa as she tapped her foot and clapped in time to the music.

That dress was a work of art on her figure. The blue embroidery curled about the bodice to wrap itself around the narrowest part of her waist. She shimmered like an angel when the sun cast light upon the sheer fabric.

The tallest woman he had ever danced with stood about five feet four. How would it be to glide along to music with the tall, regal grace that was Marissa?

The grand stage began to clear for the dance. Couples walked upon the wood floor, hand in hand. Men who came by themselves searched for a lady with whom to partner. Younger ladies in their teens rushed to their escorts and beaux, giggling, while the older, more mature women waited alongside the stage, anticipating being asked to dance.

Rowe noticed the attention being paid Marissa. More than a few passing glances came from the men as they started to approach her. He offered his arm before they had a chance. "May I have this dance before I have to get in line?"

A tiny smile played across her lips. "I would be delighted to dance with you."

The band played a waltz. Her eyes sparkled, displaying nervousness and gaiety all at once as she followed him out on the floor. "Let's see if I remember this." While taking her hand, he stepped forward on his left foot and counted the beats. "One…two, three, one…two, three."

Rowe had been told he was a natural dancer, with good

timing and a firm lead, but he felt like an amateur compared to Marissa. He missed steps, stumbling once when his nerves got to him. Thankfully she didn't seem to notice.

He spun her around the floor, past other dancers and onlookers whose faces he recognized. For a moment they were not themselves but other people free from their problems and recent disputes. Here he was, a man unencumbered with pain over his deceased family, free from the weight of Assurance's expectations of him to be the figure of moral authority. Marissa was a woman without her sordid past and current troubles, a grand lady who had but one aim, to dance with the man whose eyes saw only her.

"Pardon me. Might we trade partners?" Chad Hooper tapped Rowe on the back. Sophie appeared demurely beside him.

Rowe met Sophie's blue, saucer-plate eyes with their gold fringe. He was reluctant to let go of Marissa's womanly softness for Sophie's petite fragility. Something about another man holding Marissa, in time with music or not, struck chords of possessiveness in him. Mr. Hooper, on the other hand, appeared too eager to please his escort to cause any rivalry.

Rowe gave Marissa's hand over to the other man. The look she fired off at him said that he should have refused Chad's request. It was obvious that Sophie had put poor Mr. Hooper up to it.

Chad danced off with Marissa while Sophie rose on her tiptoes to rest her hand on Rowe's upper arm, as she couldn't reach his shoulder. Rowe didn't like her perfume. It was too powdery.

"My, you do look handsome today, Reverend."

"Thank you, Miss Charlton. Your face shows your delight at being here." He placed his hand up against her shoulder blade for the dance position. His hand could have easily covered over half the span of her waist, she was so tiny.

Sophie waited patiently for him to begin. He led her into the dancer's circle, where Marissa and Chad moved just along the edge. Though he was forced to bend over to keep from jerking her off her feet, she seemed to take pleasure in every moment of what felt like complete awkwardness to him.

"How are you enjoying the fair?" she asked.

"I'm enjoying it very much, Miss Charlton. I haven't had such entertainment in years."

"How grand to hear that." Even her teeth were dainty when she smiled.

Everything about her was practiced and artificial. Yet if he had never met Marissa, would he have clamored for Sophie's attention like so many men? *Charm is deceptive, and beauty is fleeting.* The proverb floated in his head.

"You know, these country festivals aren't as good as the ones I remember in New Orleans, but the people here do their best."

Rowe considered a response to her half-compliment, half-criticism. "I doubt much of the country can compare to the culture of your beloved city."

Her curls bobbed as she inclined her head in resignation. "I learn to make do. Now I must applaud you for escorting Miss Pierce to the fair."

"Why, may I ask?" Narrowly avoiding a misstep that would have crushed her toes, he smoothly regained himself.

"For reasons previously mentioned, no other man could chance his reputation being seen with her. But you, as a preacher, well, no one would think anything scandalous of you."

"I'm afraid I still don't understand your meaning." His

manner grew short and curt as his movements fell out of rhythm to the music.

Like using a pair of fans, she batted her thick fringe of lashes. "I don't think I could be clearer, Mr. Winford. It's obvious that you're taking pity on her."

Rowe stopped dancing. His feet planted themselves into the stage. Dancers twirled at the last moment to avoid crashing into the two of them. The male leads gave him vicious looks.

"No, no, Miss Charlton, that is assuredly not why I am escorting Miss Pierce. She is a remarkable woman that I find very engaging. You are terribly mistaken."

Sophie's face colored at having been declared erroneous. "She's fooled you. You are placing yourself in the clutches of a harpy."

Rowe dropped his arm from her back. "I'm getting a bit heated in this climate. If you don't object, I will escort you to Mr. Hooper now."

Her face colored as though she wanted to throw a fit, but she wouldn't dare cause a scene. Having no choice, she accepted his arm and allowed him to lead her over to where Marissa and Chad still danced.

"Calling it quits already?" Chad released Marissa as Rowe neared.

"I'm afraid so. Miss Charlton's presence is consuming enough that I wasn't able to speak and dance at the same time." Without pause he took Marissa's hand and spirited her away.

Marissa glanced over her shoulder repeatedly as the distance widened between them and the other pair. "I believe our preacher didn't provide the exact truth for why he stopped dancing."

Rowe increased his pace. Must she always remind him of his occupation, first and foremost? Was that all she saw him as? "Would you have me tell Mr. Hooper that his companion's presumptuous manners are insufferable?"

"You could be doing him a tremendous favor."

"He more than likely knows but is still smitten by the appearance she puts on for the world to see." Turning to face Marissa, he took her into the waltz position again as the music changed. "I came to the fair with you, and I want to enjoy our time together. You are by far the loveliest woman here."

She stared at him with her almond-shaped eyes. He felt like he was gazing upon Solomon's lover from Song of Songs, because to him she was every bit as lush, vibrant, and full of passionate life as the descriptive words of that book.

As they waltzed, Rowe battled against Sophie's claims. If Sophie thought he was doing all of this out of pity for Marissa, the other congregation members assumed it too. Or thought worse, as Mrs. Rheins so thinly concealed. Was he prepared to deal with the whispers of his congregation?

The music sped to a polka, and Rowe led her again around the stage. Marissa abandoned herself in complete joy as he wheeled her about in a series of unexpected turns. She threw her head back, laughing delightedly as they skipped by everyone.

By all appearances he was courting her, plain and simple. If a list were made, all of his actions would further prove such intent. He gave her presents. A gift of a replacement Bible was still a gift. He visited her for supper and escorted her to a social function. If she had a male relative, that gentleman would demand to know what Rowe's aims were. And to be honest, Rowe had no precise way of answering. Was it infatuation or the Lord leading him out west for a real chance to begin again?

The polka ended. Marissa's dress still twirled when he released her. Her cheeks were flushed a dark, dusky pink.

"I've danced with plenty of men before, but I can't remember it ever being this exhilarating."

So does she find me exhilarating, or my dancing? Rowe's blood pumped harder in his veins as she dabbed moisture from her brow with a handkerchief. Her skin glistened in the setting sun, reflecting its gold, red, and tawny rays.

"I don't think I'll have enough stamina for another number," Rowe commented between breaths. "You dance wonderfully, Marissa."

"Thank you, but I had a good lead."

He gazed heavenward. "The sun's beginning to set. We should head back to town before it gets dark."

They made the walk to the wagon. Marissa climbed in as Rowe loaded their prizes and souvenirs into the back. After making sure the souvenirs were stationary, he climbed up beside her. They sat silently during the ride out of town, enjoying the music that slowly faded into the distance behind them.

At length Marissa sighed.

"What's the matter?" Rowe asked. "Did you want to stay and dance longer? We can still turn back if you like."

"No. I was just thinking…tongues will surely wag tomorrow morning in church. Sophie will assist in that part, I'm sure."

"It's easier said than done, but you have to get past what they think." Rowe wanted the message to apply to himself too.

"Yes, but you could lose your position because of me. I don't want you to be without work."

"And you think that not being seen together will solve that problem?"

Staring at her hands in her lap, she voiced her reasoning slowly. "I don't want your reputation sullied because of your association with me. A minister can't do what other men can. That's why the locksmith can spend the night gambling while the church organist had better be at home with his wife. The integrity of what the locksmith produces is not compromised by his card dealing."

"You're comparing what we have to something immoral and illegal in most states. Seeing you is not a crime, Marissa. I can't control how people choose to think about us."

"Us?"

"Us." He reached across and tilted her chin. Marissa gazed at him with wide, uncertain eyes, the brown irises growing larger as the sun kissed her face. *God, what am I doing?* Words spilled out of him. "I feel something very strongly and deeply for you. I've been wrestling with it ever since we met. Can you tell me that you haven't experienced similar feelings?"

Her countenance registered hurt, concern, the possibility of rejection. As if he could be the one to reject her.

"I would be lying to you if I said no," she said quietly.

He leaned his face in, close to hers. Marissa shut her eyes. Closing the distance between them, he felt her whisper-soft lips as he kissed her. Lingering, tender warmth remained with him when he withdrew.

"I'm scared for you," she whispered.

"Don't be." He kissed her mouth again, harder, then pressed his lips against her temple. The result was a mix of pleasure and a sweet yearning to savor the moment. "I can withstand a few rumors and useless chatter."

"You know it will be more than that. Will the town take your sermons to heart from now on? I want to believe you, but I think you're wrong." She tried to hide her desire for more kisses, more embraces, but the effort with which she held herself back was visible. Rowe felt the longing too and controlled himself by moving away to the end of the wagon bench.

They continued the journey home, each absorbed in their

own thoughts. The horses pulled the wagon along until they reached fellow travelers going in the same direction. As Rowe observed their happy, contented faces, he wondered just how many would be frowning at him in church tomorrow morning.

Chapter 19

RAIN AND STORMS assaulted the town for the next three days. The hot late August air brought with it frequent lightning that lit up the night and hail that rattled off the roofs of homes and storefronts. The storms were so bad that church was canceled Sunday morning. Marissa breathed a sigh of relief. Without church as a site for the gossip mill, perhaps chatter about her and Rowe being seen at the fair would die down more quickly.

Rain muddied the streets of Assurance until midweek, when the sun came out and dried the mud to grayish clay. The wind followed right after, blowing unlatched doors wide open and sending mud clusters, dried grass, and sagebrush tumbling down the streets. The townsfolk who were able to come out of their homes to resume chores and business were not pleased with having the extra cleaning to do.

Marissa was sweeping the entranceway of the store when Rowe came loping up the steps. He was hatless, wearing a work shirt stained with mud and sweat marks. The sleeves were rolled up above his large forearms. Her heart sped to an impromptu drum tap.

"I've come to see if my work boots came in," he announced, but he shot her such a look of boyish abashment that she knew it was an excuse. "I just helped a man in town with a roof leak. Now I have to raise my fence that sank in the mud, so some new work boots would sure help out." To further his explanation he held up the metal toolbox he carried in one hand.

"You really are the strangest preacher I've ever seen.

Reverend Thomas never carried building tools around town."

Marissa stepped inside the store to return the broom to its corner near the back wall.

"That may have had something to do with his age, from what I hear." Dropping the toolbox, Rowe followed her inside. "You shouldn't be in here when you're so downright muddy and filthy." Marissa stuck her nose out and sniffed. "You don't smell too good either."

His face fell, like that of a crestfallen child. "I'm sorry. I just couldn't resist the chance to see you after being cooped up in all this rain. I promise to be spanking clean tomorrow if you go boat riding with me on the lake."

Marissa found herself carried along by his boyish enthusiasm. "Where did you get a boat?"

"Mike O'Hare lent me his fishing boat as thanks for the roof. So, you'll come to the lake tomorrow afternoon?"

"Yes." Her hands tingled with excitement. She couldn't let this go too far, as tempting an idea as it was. He may pretend that their dalliances would have no effect on his ministry, but she knew better. The lake would provide a quiet place to tell him. What was one boat ride?

His jubilant smile told her he expected it would be more than a boat ride.

She retreated, dropping her voice in an implied warning. "I will meet you there at two." A final meeting to end what barely had started. Then they would go their separate ways. It was the right thing to do. Necessary. Painful.

"I'll hold you to your promise." Innocently ignoring the warning in her tone, he went outside to pick up the toolbox. "You left your dustpan out here," he called through the screen door.

"I'll get it when you leave."

He climbed down the steps, giving her a smile so generous that Marissa felt its effects in her heart long after he was gone.

Mike O'Hare's fishing boat proved to be the right size for the two of them. Made of lightweight but solid birchbark and white cedar, it had two planks for seating and a set of oars attached in the center. It glided smoothly out on the water like a fish venturing toward open sea.

Marissa trailed her fingers across the lake's cool, rippling surface. "I'm glad we were able to do this."

Rowe manned the oars. "I am too. This morning I thought it was going to rain again." Varying shades of gray clouds smeared the sky.

"The weather here can be fickle. What looks like a bad storm one minute will be blue skies the next. See how the wind's moving those clouds."

"It's moving the boat too." Rowe increased his control of the oars.

They talked as the boat drifted farther toward the middle of the lake. Rowe told her of life growing up in Virginia, fishing in the James River with his wild brothers. Marissa listened intently as he described his scholarly father, his farm-laboring grandfather, and the humorous arguments they had over the dinner table. When he described his late wife, Josephine, she heard the bittersweet fondness of remembrance in his voice.

"We never get over the death of someone, do we?" she asked.

He stretched his long legs as best he could in the boat. "You always remember the person. The pain of the loss subsides in time."

"Do you think of her often?"

His eyes darkened, reflecting the lake's grayish surface. "Josephine was my first love, and for that she will always have a place in my heart." He changed the subject. "Tell me about your family."

"My mother was a short-hire cook before she met my father. Oh, how I miss her food. She could bake the sweetest strawberry pies and season meats as though they had been smoked and cured for hours." Her mouth watered as she pictured her mother chopping garlic, onions, and rubbing meat with ground peppercorn and rosemary.

"Judging by the dinner you prepared the other night, I'd say you inherited her skills."

"Thank you, but her food would put the great chefs to shame."

"Did her looks resemble yours?"

Marissa closed her eyes, envisioning her mother's appearance. "She was tall for a woman, a few inches shorter than me, with beautiful, thick black hair and green eyes. She carried herself with dignity and elegance, even during the last days when she fell ill."

"You miss her, don't you?" His mellow baritone was gentle and compassionate.

"Yes, I do. Some days it seems like so many years have passed. Other times I think I'll see her walk down the street, talking and laughing with my grandmother."

"What of your father?"

Marissa disconnected from her warm feelings of remembrance as she described Greg Pierce. "I didn't see much of him, except when he came home after a gambling stint. He was a firm, stoic man. Very tall, built solid like an ox."

"Was he affectionate when he saw you and your mother?"

"He didn't know how to be anything but a gambler. I can't fault him without criticizing my mother. She could have returned to Assurance without him, but she chose to remain in Missouri."

"Was your father near when your mother passed?"

"To this day I doubt if he knows what happened to her. He left my mother and me in the room of a dirty inn and disappeared with the last of our earnings. They weren't much, but he said he would make good on them and come back for us. I haven't seen him since."

Rowe lifted the boat paddle for a piece of driftwood to float by. "Men have failed you all your life." He didn't look at her, giving her the space to absorb his words.

"Not all men. Mr. Arthur is like the father I've never had. You're the first man to see past my dancehall costume."

His reflection in the water mirrored his show of remorse. "I've failed you too, Marissa. I didn't get there in time to save you from Jason. If I had given a little more thought to that sermon, he would not have reason to lash out at you."

"Yes, he would. Jason always finds an outlet to relieve his frustrations."

"Still, this particular instance is my fault."

"You love to blame yourself, don't you? Listen to me when I say this, then. I forgive you, Rowe."

He reached across the boat and took her hands in his, giving them a squeeze. Their eyes did all of the communication that rendered words unnecessary. Marissa's window of opportunity to end their courtship steadily closed as she allowed him to come dangerously near.

"Reverend, is that you?"

Marissa flung herself back so fast that the little boat pitched dangerously to its side. It recovered balance just before water could spill into the bottom. On the lakeshore the traveling orator Abel Yancey waded out with his fishing line cast. Behind him four men dragged two boats into the water.

"What are you doing out here?" Abel waded until the water reached his waist. He didn't seem to be worried that the volume of his voice scared the fish. "Who's that with you?"

Marissa sank to the floor of the boat. She thought for certain that the bellowing man had traveled to the next town. She hadn't seen him on the platform in town square for weeks.

Rowe studied her reaction before lifting his hand to wave. "Afternoon, Mr. Yancey. Fine day for fishing, isn't it?"

The speaker cackled. "Oh, you're not out here fishing, Reverend. At least not for catfish."

Marissa wanted to drown, but with no plans for a watery grave that day, she was forced to remain in the boat.

"We thought no one else was at the lake," Rowe admitted.

Abel's laugh issued forth for the second time. "I can see that. Who is the lady? Is it that Rheins girl?"

The men in the pair of boats paddled out. One boat got close to where a blond-bearded man took a good look at her face. "It's one of Jason's girls!"

Murmuring broke out among the men. Marissa heard an aspersion cast on her birth. With no further point in hiding her identity, she turned to face Abel. His jovial face deteriorated to a contemptuous frown that reached to the wrinkles below his hairline.

"How could you be seen with this woman, Reverend Winford? You know where she's from."

Rowe rested his hands on the oars. If he was just as embarrassed as she was, he concealed it far better. "I do, but that's all past. Miss Pierce has made herself into a respectable woman. We need to treat her as such."

Marissa liked hearing him say that, though he was only half right. Jason still had a rope around her ankle to drag her back into the saloon.

Abel lowered his fishing line. "How do you know she's respectable? None of us have seen her in church."

The blond-bearded man chimed in. "You're not courtin' her, are you, Reverend?"

Marissa gazed at Rowe. He didn't look at her before answering. "I'm not a man to dally with a woman's affections."

"So you admit it? You are courting this ungodly woman?"

"'Be ye not unequally yoked with unbelievers,'" Abel quoted.

Marissa withered under their attacks. How could she have thought she could see him again, even one last time? "I should be going home. Would you please paddle the boat to shore?"

Rowe gave no indication that he heard her request. "Mr. Yancey, I'm well aware of what the Bible instructs. Miss Pierce is not a heathen. The town will eventually see that."

"But why must you be involved? There are properly raised ladies that you can court instead of one trained up in a brothel. Don't let that harlot make a fool out of you."

"She's not a harlot. This is hardly the conversation to have out on the middle of the lake with a lady present."

The men scoffed at the mention of Marissa being a lady. He went on, undaunted. "Excuse me while I escort Miss Pierce home. To answer your question, yes, I am courting her."

He paddled the boat away. His jaw clenched tightly, and Marissa saw the veins in his neck. "Coming to the lake was a bad idea. I should have declined yesterday."

He said nothing.

She persisted. "They're right. We shouldn't be seen together."

"They're not right. Those men think that a person can't change. It's not Christian to hold someone's mistakes over their head forever."

"You told them you were courting me."

"I know what I said."

"Do you? You're digging yourself a grave. Abel is a well-known orator in these parts. He'll go from town to town, spreading the word about you and what he saw today."

"I can't control what he does, Marissa. I can't lie and say I'm not courting you."

Marissa held her head. "I was enjoying the attention too much. I would have been wise to make you go away."

"How do you intend to do that this time? I don't scare easily."

She thought of the rape, how Jason's crime made her unclean more than any dance in a saloon or spilled drink could accomplish. "You can't court me. If you knew everything about my past, you wouldn't be so quick to speak up for me in front of everyone."

The boat reached the shallows. Rowe climbed out and pulled it farther up shore, tugging with more force than necessary. "Then tell me what I should know."

Marissa opened her mouth, but the words wouldn't come. Just thinking about the act Jason committed, the pain that signified the loss of innocence, the bleeding that followed, made the fainting sensations return. She gulped for air.

"Marissa?" Rowe dropped the boat. His stone face became gentle. "Are you ill?"

She gathered her wits before he attempted to carry her ashore like a delicate wounded deer. "Enough. I'm not sweet, nor am I innocent." She scrambled out in the shallow water, wetting her boots and dress hem. "If you want to keep the remaining good standing that you have, you'll forget about me. I'm sorry I did this to you. Now let me return home—alone."

He started forward, hand outstretched, but her defiant stare held him back. And with one waterlogged boot in front of the other, she made sopping tracks for Assurance.

Chapter 20

Ow was your boat ride?" asked Rebecca.

Marissa had hoped to creep into the Arthurs' home unnoticed, but it was a difficult thing to do in damp clothes and squeaking shoe soles. The gray skies decided to open up on the way home, releasing a shower that put the appropriate ending on a sour afternoon.

"We went back to shore early." Marissa hoped Rebecca would think it was from the rain and not press her for further explanation. She removed her boots near the door.

"Why didn't the reverend escort you home?" Zachary asked from his seat at the dining table, where he was awaiting supper. The scent of stew floated in from the kitchen.

"I wouldn't let him."

"Why?"

There was no way to sugarcoat the truth. Best the Arthurs hear it from her before it was the tittle-tattle of the town. Marissa lifted the wet collar that clung to the back of her neck. "Because he told some men of the town that he was courting me."

Zachary eyed the pot of stew like a famished wolf when Rebecca went to take it off the stove. "What's wrong with that?"

"Yes," Rebecca came from the kitchen. "He's an upright man, close to your age, and really cares about you. I'd say that's wonderful news."

Marissa sank in one of the chairs, never mind her wet clothes. A damp circle formed in the table wood under her elbow. "You should have seen the disgust in the faces of those men. I imagine they're racing to town now to spread the word. Rowe will lose his position in the church for sure."

Rebecca set the stewpot on the table, then pulled up a chair. "If he chose to court you, the town would have to find out sooner or later. You can't hide those things."

Marissa fiddled with her shirt sleeve. "I *won't* let him lose the respect he needs to do his job."

Zachary frowned. "You think he's just gonna do what you say, Mari? From what I know of our new preacher, he's a pretty determined young man. Supposin' he comes to the store to see you tomorrow?"

Marissa's thoughts rolled over to the deadline Jason gave her to return to the saloon. "I won't be there."

"You can't hide out from people."

"No, it's not that." She looked down at her hands. It was time to tell them. "Tomorrow I will be returning to work at Jason's saloon."

"What!" Zachary and Rachel gasped simultaneously.

Marissa quickly explained the contract clause to them and how it had been presented to her. "Even if I don't go to him," she concluded, "I can't continue working at your store. Jason will sue."

Zachary's face reddened with anger. "You will not return to work for that man. Not if I have any say about it."

To protect them, Marissa tried to sound matter-of-fact. "He has a legally enforceable agreement until a judge says otherwise. I didn't want to tell you about it, but if Jason wins in court, my only choices are to work for him, be sued, or go to jail. You can be sued too for hiring me while I was under contract for him."

"How can you be jailed for refusing to work at that bawdy house?" Zachary's voice boomed with indignation. "Any officer of the peace would see that Jason's business practices are illegal."

"They have to be proven first, and none of the regular patrons will speak up because they like the drinks and the women. I spoke to a lawyer in Claywalk about it."

"But you said the saloon is having money problems." Rebecca twisted a napkin in her hands, her face lined with distress.

Marissa ached at how the woman was suffering on her account. She wished she had packed up months ago and run out of town. "It is having money problems, but again, the contract states that until the saloon recovers or shuts down, I have to honor my agreement. I'm such an idiot for not reading the fine print."

"That's nothing to be callin' yourself." Zachary was closest to the stewpot and pushed it away. Marissa didn't want anything to eat either.

"You're going to the store tomorrow. I won't leave you at the house by yourself. Have you told Rowe this?"

She nodded. "We already went to the sheriff. McGee said as long as there's a contract, he can't do anything if he doesn't have incontestable proof that Jason beat me." Zachary drummed the table in thought. "What if the reverend spoke to the judge?"

"I know you think highly of Rowe, Mr. Arthur. He's a good man, but his opinion is not enough to dispute a written and signed agreement."

Marissa exhausted her mind for solutions to her dilemma, things she could explain to the circuit judge. What could she say or do, short of showing them her old wounds and hoping they would believe her?

She pushed her chair away from the table. "I didn't want to bring trouble to you, yet it's already started. I will put a stop to it. That's a promise. Now please let me go rest and think. It's been a long day."

The Arthurs glanced at each other, then nodded reluctant assent. With a heavy heart she left the room.

Rowe wondered if he should have dispensed with being a gentleman and followed Marissa back home against her wishes. No woman should walk alone in the rain, even one who rejected his offer of courtship.

Muttering to himself, he loaded Mike O'Hara's boat onto his wagon and drove it into town to return it to its rightful owner. At first he was too distracted by his own emotions to notice anything around him. But after he dropped off the boat, he began to notice the stares of the townspeople he passed. Apparently the news had spread already of his tête-à-tête with Marissa. He guessed Abel and his friends had abandoned their fishing trip in favor of a more entertaining pastime. Gossip.

On his way out of town Mr. Charlton flagged him down so he was forced to stop. "Reverend, I'd like a word, if you please." The tone of Mr. Charlton's voice told him he'd better climb from the wagon or risk having his business trumpeted all over town. Rowe complied.

"I heard you were out on the lake with that dancehall girl, Reverend. I didn't think Abel Yancey was a fibber, but I had to ask you for myself."

Rowe kept his tone even. "He wasn't lying. Miss Pierce and I were at the lake together."

Mr. Charlton regarded him carefully. "Courting?"

Rowe heard that word so many times in one day he thought he would never be able to drive it out of his head. "Yes, but as she's no longer here, I don't think we need to discuss this."

"Where'd she go?" Mr. Charlton gazed at the wagon as if Marissa could be hiding within its bed.

"Suffice it to say she is not present." Rowe wasn't going to tell him why Marissa left. Especially since her warning about the gossip they would provoke had proved prophetic.

"For a man of God you've shown sloppy behavior." Sophie's father declared. "I don't know how preachers back East carry on, but in Kansas we expect more out of our church leaders."

If the weight of their condemnation were an actual stone, Rowe would sink to the bottom of the lake. "What would it take for you to see that Miss Pierce has changed? She's a part of this town just as we are. I can't—won't—shun her because you want me to."

Mr. Charlton held up a hand in an apparent attempt to appear reasonable. "We didn't say you should shun Miss Pierce, but do you have to go boating together? Surely there are other, more eligible young women you might consider."

Rowe stiffened at the thinly veiled reference to his daughter. "Thank you for your insight, Mr. Charlton, but I'll do fine to think for myself."

Sophie's father huffed. "No, Reverend. You're not doing much thinking at all. We hired you because we thought you had the credentials to lead our church. "

The Charltons were a very influential family in Assurance and the church. To fall out of their good graces was to lose favor with everyone. Rowe was treading on hot coals, but he had to stand up to the wealthy patriarch. "With all due respect, Mr. Charlton, you scolded Sophie for judging Marissa when she knew little about her. Now you do the same."

The man exploded. "Don't call me a hypocrite."

"You were in church when I preached about gossip destroying people. The town won't let Marissa make a new life. In a sense you're all condemning her to die."

"Jason and those strumpets are to blame for our problems. He sells immorality, and you made a purchase!"

The accusation incensed Rowe. Blood hammered in his veins and rushed to his head. "The people here allowed Jason to have the saloon. It's him we need to deal with. I came here to preach, not help start a witch hunt."

Mr. Charlton growled. "Then do your job before we find someone who will."

The next morning Rowe felt the sting of rejection all over again as he went into town. People stared at him but said nothing in passing. Was this what Marissa went through every day that she worked in the saloon? He began to understand why she thought there was no escape. The residents of Assurance were set in their ways. He wished he had more experience as a minister. His old seminary instructors would know what to do.

They wouldn't be caught in your predicament. The fiendish voice taunted him as a dry wind blew through the unpaved streets.

Rowe knew that today was Marissa's deadline for returning to the saloon. He wasn't certain if Jason would personally come for her, but he wasn't going to take any chances.

On his way to Zachary's shop he passed the newspaper office. For the first time in his life he feared the gossip column.

"Nothing I can do if it's already printed." He muttered the reminder to himself and walked on.

Residents gathered below Zachary's storefront. A commotion was going on inside. A woman yelled to get the sheriff. Rebecca.

Icy fingers spread across Rowe's back. He pushed through the crowd and clambered through the open door.

Jason was there with one of his clerks. Behind them the Arthurs and Marissa stood with their backs to the wall.

Zachary held his cane in front of him like a bayonet, ready to thrust it at the two barmen.

"You heard my wife. Get outta here before the sheriff comes to place you under arrest."

"The only person the sheriff is gonna arrest is you, old timer. I haven't done any thievin', but you sure have by taking my employee."

Marissa saw Rowe. Jason turned. "Look who's here, Pete. The meddlin' reverend don't know how to keep himself out of trouble."

Rowe had no weapon and couldn't tell whether the two men concealed firearms beneath their jackets. "You heard Mr. Arthur. They don't want you here."

"Doesn't matter what they want. I'm here to collect my property. Marissa is coming to the saloon with me now."

"No, I'm not." Marissa's refusal came out strong, although she had to be shaking inside. "I'll sooner march myself up to the jailhouse this instant before I go back to that filthy hovel."

"Unless you got a lawyer hiding in the back room, you best start marching, darlin'."

Jason and Pete made a space for her to pass. In all likelihood they would grab her as soon as she came within reach. Rowe went between them and moved to stand in front of Marissa.

"She's not going anywhere."

Jason laughed, but his eyes were hard and without humor. "Are you her lawyer now too?"

"No, but I can speak on her behalf."

"How so?" asked Pete. "You got no claim over her. Saving souls don't count for much when a name's signed to a piece of paper."

"Maybe not, but I have admitted to courting her. If she agrees, we'll be engaged shortly."

A collective gasp went up from the first row of onlookers

outside. The reaction continued down the line as those in front spread the word to those in the back.

Marissa surprised Rowe with a strong grip on his arm. Her widened eyes met his as though she were searching for symptoms of lunacy. "Are you insane?"

It was a desperate maneuver, but Rowe could think of no other solution that would work as fast. He took her shoulders in a firm, excited grip. "I remember there being laws in Virginia that a man can claim ownership of his wife's property and enter into contracts for her. If we marry, I have a sure say that you won't work for Jason."

The saloon proprietor made no further show of mirth. "Kansas doesn't have laws like Virginia."

"That's true, but Kansas has laws that forbid married women from engaging in any contract against their husband's wishes. That's factual for almost all the states."

Marissa put her cold, nervous hand on his. "What if the contract was signed before a marriage took place?"

Rowe dared to believe she was considering what he said. As he also weighed the implications of them being married, his speech became rapid. "No judge will force you to serve drinks or dance with other men all night if your husband doesn't want you to."

"A judge only has to look at a man like Jason and tell there's nothing respectable about working for him," Zachary put in.

Marissa clasped her hands in reservation. She spoke low so only Rowe could hear. "We can't marry. I told you that this has to end. You're not involved any longer."

"Yes, I am. I meant every word when I promised that Jason would never harm you again."

"At the cost of your own livelihood?"

"How could I minister knowing that I allowed you to go to jail?" He thought of the sacrifices he made in the past for his fellow citizens during the war. None of those acts compared to the cost he was going to pay for Marissa to be free. If marrying her meant his ruin as Assurance's pastor, then at least he could live out his days knowing that he kept her from being lustfully procured by Jason or any man.

"I can get Mr. Boyd to help." She put up a fight still.

"And if he loses the argument before the judge? No, this way you won't ever go to jail."

"Get out of my way." Jason dashed forward to seize her. Rowe blocked him. Pete moved to assist, but a man in the doorway grabbed him before he could.

The sheriff shouted from outside. "Alright, folks, what's goin' on here?" The people parted for him to enter the store. "What's the ruckus about?"

Jason smoothed his jacket before facing the sheriff. "Sir, Reverend Winford is interfering with official business. I came here peacefully to collect Miss Pierce for her work in the saloon. Tell this man to step aside."

McGee cast a tired look at Rowe. "We spoke about this before. I'm afraid you have no argument against Mr. Garth. You're gonna have to let the woman go or face arrest."

The sheriff would have to pry Rowe away before he allowed an injustice to occur. "These people will see how you allowed a woman to be taken into a saloon against her will. How will that look on your election ticket for the next campaign, Sheriff?"

The flesh around McGee's face moved and all but concealed a narrow portion of his small eyes. "You really think your high-falutin' learnin' and fancy talk puts you above the law, don't you, son?"

"Please, Sheriff. No, he doesn't." Marissa's plea carried across the store. "He's speaking on my behalf." She gazed up at Rowe with fear and a glimmer of hope in the depths of her brown eyes. "As my fiancé."

Rowe couldn't decide if he should breathe a sigh of relief,

kiss Marissa in front of everybody, or wonder aloud what he had done. He could save her from a terrible fate, even if it cost him his position and his ministerial license.

Jason pointed a finger at Marissa's hand. "It's a sham proposal. He didn't ask her to marry him. There's no ring."

"You heard him say that she would become his wife," Zachary shouted as he made an arcing motion at the door with his cane. "The folks outside heard him. That's at least fifteen witnesses, countin' Rebecca and myself."

"There was no proposal," Pete countered. "He didn't ask the question."

As Jason and Zachary got into a shouting match over the sheriff's call for order, Rowe dropped to one knee. "Marissa, will you marry me?"

It was hardly the proposal he thought he would make, inside a shoe shop of all places, under the threat of law enforcement and a corrupt business owner. The sheriff, Jason, Pete, and all others standing by grew silent as they awaited Marissa's answer. He saw her eyes well with tears, and he knew they were from anything but joy.

"I will." She placed her hand in his.

Zachary stamped his cane on the floor. "There you have it. Husband and wife-to-be. Call Tom to put it in the paper."

"There ain't no ring." Jason's voice was ice cold.

Sheriff McGee shook his head. "A ring's not necessary to a marriage proposal. I heard her say yes."

"She'll have a ring soon," Rowe promised.

The sheriff waved Jason and Pete away. "Everybody get out. Go on back to tendin' your business. You folks outside, move on over yonder."

"This isn't over." Jason looked squarely at the Arthurs. "I'm leaving for Coffeyville today to have my lawyer draw up the papers for your lawsuit. I'll get my money one way or the other. *And* my woman."

Rowe put Marissa behind him. "She's spoken for now, Jason."

The saloon proprietor edged in close. "You had better be gone by the time I get back. And if you take her with you, I'll hunt you down and shoot you both."

"Garth, did you hear what I said, or do you want to be jailed for trespassing?" The sheriff called to him from the doorway.

Jason left the premises. McGee stood guard until he and Pete were safely down the street.

"Thank you," Rowe said to him.

The sheriff made a hacking sound and spat in the dirt outside. "Don't thank me. Boy, you've got to be the dumbest educated fool this side of the Missoura. You have no idea of the kind of trouble you just heaped upon yourself."

Chapter 21

E's RIGHT," MARISSA voiced as McGee tended to the people out in the streets. "We have time to retain Mr. Boyd before Jason gets back from Coffeyville." Her newly minted fiancé took her hand. It was a strange and foreign thing, to have someone as a betrothed. If anything, she had imagined leaving the saloon and living a decent life somewhere as a spinster with a cloaked past. Never in her wildest imaginings had she thought she would marry a minister.

Rowe said, "I didn't do this to buy time. Is that why you agreed to marry me?"

"I thought you were only saying those things in front of Jason to get rid of him." She didn't really think that, but at the same time she couldn't believe what he had done either.

"This town can call me many things after today, but they can't call me a liar. As soon as I make my wages, I'll get you a ring."

Rebecca clapped. "Such a relief to have this dilemma resolved."

Zachary affirmed her statement. "You're going to be a wife, Mari. Your problems with Jason are over for good."

Marissa's heart cried out for her to embrace what they said, but her mind drew caution. She retreated from Rowe, wanting the space between them for safety, to distance herself from his magnetic pull and her own heart's longing. She broke off the courtship to protect him, and here he ran right back into courting trouble. She didn't know whether to rejoice or weep.

"You two have much to plan in a short time. Zachary, we should let them talk." Rebecca put a hand on her husband's shoulder and directed him to the stockroom of the store. "You know where to find us."

Marissa stared mutely at the couple as they retreated from view. Left with Rowe, she could either face him or go outside among the townsfolk, where news of the proposal was spreading far as dust from a good gust of prairie wind. The latter choice was akin to slapping herself across the face. "We have a scandal."

"We have a wedding." His voice resounded with more life than hers, but it did contain trepidation. Rowe was not completely oblivious to the consequences. "It will take Jason at least two days to ride to Coffeyville and back, and that's if he doesn't stop to rest. That leaves forty-eight hours to obtain a marriage license and find a clergy in Claywalk to perform the ceremony." He crossed her boundary of space.

Marissa folded her arms in front of her, one last physical barrier that Rowe could not penetrate without force. "I can't marry you in two days."

"I'll respect any decision or idea you come up with, but this is the best I know to do. If you're still worried about my reputation, the damage is done, as far as the town sees it."

Already he began to accept his changed fate. Marissa sighed heavily and chewed on her lip. "We are so different. I don't think of God the way you do."

"But you believe in Him."

"I believe He exists, but that's different from how happy you become when you preach about Him. We'd be unequally yoked, as Abel said."

Rowe paused, looking out the store window at the people walking through the open door of Tom Euell's newspaper office. "Joy in the Lord can't be taught or forced. In time I hope you see things differently."

"It's not only that."

"Then tell me what it is that you're afraid of."

That odd voice spoke in her mind's ear. *He will do to you as Jason has done. All men use women for one purpose or another.*

What could she possibly offer Rowe? Marissa listened to the voice as though it were an actual person standing before her.

You're his pawn to regain the church. Some would think it good that he redeemed you through marriage.

Marissa coughed at an irritation that caught in her throat. Rowe moved his hand to her, but she stopped him with a swift shake of her head. "Give me the weekend to think." She swallowed, and the irritation was gone.

"Think about what? You just accepted my proposal."

"Give me some time. Please, just wait till Monday to get the marriage license." Seeing how he looked far from pleased with the dismissal, she added, "I didn't say I wouldn't marry you. I just need to be left with my thoughts."

His face darkened with an emotion that he contained. Marissa was sure he had plenty to say, but he remained respectful of her boundaries.

"The weekend then. But I want to know by Monday morning if you've truly accepted my proposal."

The screen door clattered against the frame as he exited. His leaving strides were brisk as his heels dug hard into the gritty dirt road.

Marissa second-guessed herself, wondering if her success in delaying her decision was a failure at a second chance at life.

Zachary and Rebecca turned anxiously when she opened the door to the stockroom.

"What was said out there?" asked Rebecca. "Where's Rowe?"

"I suppose he went home." There was no other respectable

establishment he could go to, especially in the mood she sent him away in. "I told him that I would give him an answer on Monday."

"Why, Mari? He offered the best solution any of us could think of. He wants to marry you, even if you didn't need his help."

"I need time. Marriage is forever, and I can't just go from one...situation to another. He knows that."

How could she explain her reasoning to them when they agreed with Rowe's idea? The shame of having to tell Rowe of the liberties Jason took with her made her cringe inside.

Rebecca's face settled into a frown, and she tossed her head. "Marriage is not a 'situation.' It's a perfectly normal life event."

"When it naturally progresses. Rowe's proposal would not have come today but for Jason's contract." Marissa heard the saloon keeper's mocking voice in her head. *He won't have you as his wife. You're far from the gentle, sheltered woman he'll pick to marry.*

"And how do you know if Rowe's proposal today isn't part of God's timing for you? He is a good man who'll help anyone, but he wouldn't offer marriage if he didn't want to be your husband."

Zachary touched Rebecca's hand. "What she's trying to say, Mari, is that she thinks you should accept Rowe's proposal. She believes he'll be a good husband for you, and so do I."

"I haven't told him no." Marissa felt cornered, as if they thought her a fool for not jumping at such a perfect offer. If only they knew the mixed feelings tumbling through her. "Once I'm married to him, how will the town treat us? Will they run us out? I don't know if he can live with the possibility of never having a congregation because of my past."

"We can't answer those questions any better than you, Mari," Zachary said softly.

An ache quickened from her hands to the soles of her feet as she envisioned Rowe's inevitable disappointment in her—and in their life together.

Rowe didn't sleep well that night. He tossed and turned, his mind concocting unwelcome scenarios in which Marissa refused to marry him and ran back into Jason's arms. Finally he managed to drift off in a dreadful doze and dreamed of Marissa behind bars, calling his name while Jason steadily approached with a sharp knife. His feet were sealed into the ground like lead. He awoke to her scream reverberating in his ears.

Rowe lay still until the reality of the silent bedchamber took over his dream-addled senses. "I have to stop this."

Arising from the bed, his nightshirt dampened with sweat, he poured himself a glass of water from the pitcher. As the cool liquid ran down his dry throat, he steadied his mind against the disturbing dreams.

Moonlight streamed through the upstairs window to provide a natural light in the dark, allowing him to focus toward the rumpled bed and one nightstand. He imagined Marissa as his wife, with all its implications. Her aversion to matrimony ran deeper than her fears of being judged. He understood why she distrusted men. She needed someone willing to show her the love that God intended for men and women to share. Something happened to close her from receiving that love. Marissa desired it, that Rowe could tell every time they were in each other's presence, but she always stopped short of accepting it.

He never imagined that he could love another woman again after Josephine. Yet God sent Marissa when he least expected, where he wasn't looking. Would she accept him on Monday? In a few agonizingly slow hours he would be betrothed to Marissa, or left behind with yet another memory of a woman he had loved and lost.

As the sun continued to rise in the midmorning sky, Rowe made his way to the post office. The mundane errand would occupy his time for the rest of the Saturday morning, and then he would need something to do in the afternoon.

Citizens lined up in front of the counter for letters from back home or mail-order packages. Rowe stood in the tiny, two-window structure as he waited his turn. The post office clerk peered at him above thick bifocals when he came up to the counter. "Haven't seen you here in a while, Reverend." Mercifully he didn't go into a conversation about what happened the day before.

"I neglected to see if I received any mail in the past two weeks."

"Mail's been delayed since that twister touched down in Fort Leavenworth. You had quite a bit last time I checked, though." The clerk swiveled in his chair to the section of mail boxes behind him on the wall. He pulled out one drawer and combed through it, withdrawing a tidy stack of envelopes tied up with string. "Most of these are from Virginia."

"They're from my family." Rowe checked Nathaniel's dark, heavily etched handwriting on the top envelope. Ever the consistent one, his younger sibling wrote to him every week. He read the most recent on the way out of the building.

I haven't heard much from you since your move, older brother. Am I to believe that your usual enthusiasm for the pen has waned, or that you have been eaten by wolves?

Rowe chuckled. Nathaniel always leaned towards the sardonic side, even if it was to say that he missed his older brother. Rowe sidestepped manure left by a horse and read onward.

I hope you have been getting your mail, because by the time you get this letter, I shall be on the train headed for your new neck of the woods. If all goes well with my travels, I should arrive in Claywalk on August 27. Hopefully my arrival won't be a surprise to you.

A black cloud may as well have formed in the clear blue sky and rained silver-dollar-sized hail on his head. Was this Nathaniel's idea of a joke? If indeed his travels had gone well, then Nathaniel was scheduled to arrive in Claywalk today!

Rowe tore open the oldest letter of the bunch and could box his own ears for not having the sense to pick up his mail on time.

Well, brother, I was going to walk off the train and surprise you, but the wife persuaded me otherwise. So here is your advanced warning. I am coming to see you. I've already bought my passage west and will be leaving the state tomorrow.

This was the last thing he needed before Marissa's answer to his proposal.

Rowe tucked the mail bundle under his arm and dashed to the livery. Nathaniel's train would be arriving this afternoon if it hadn't already come and dropped him at the station in the early morning hours. He fervently hoped that it was the former so his little brother wouldn't think, however correct in a sense, that he had been abandoned.

"I need a wagon and horse team for the day." Rowe addressed Timothy from the front of the stables. The carrot-haired youth ambled toward him, carrying two full buckets of murky water used for cleaning the stalls. He set them down at his feet with a loud grunt.

"I got a small schooner I can rent out to you for five dollars." Timothy wiped his sweaty face on his shirt collar.

Rowe opened his billfold to see if he had enough money for the rental. He just scraped by with an extra twenty cents. Nathaniel better had eaten something aboard the train, else he'd have to wait until they got to Rowe's cabin for stewed beans and canned meat.

In a few minutes Timothy drove the wagon and horse team out of the stables. He handed Rowe the reins as Rowe climbed atop the bench. "I need it back by eight o'clock this evening, or I'll have to charge you for an extra day. We appreciate your business, Reverend, sir."

Rowe drove the team of horses out of town, running beneath the hot sun. The wagon jostled and bumped along the road.

Unseen buzzing insects swarmed noisily in the ancient grass. Rowe flicked a giant green grasshopper from his arm. More of the creature's friends leapt aboard the wagon for the ride into Claywalk.

He arrived at the first set of tracks to the sound of an oncoming engine's piercing whistle. He stayed the horses and waited for the locomotive to pass. The hulking brown beast shot a plume of black soot in the air as it churned steadily for its station. The air simmered with the combined heat and smell of burning coal. Rowe crossed the tracks after it passed.

The streets were sparse as he drove the wagon through them, following the signs to the passenger entrance of the station. The heat kept most people on their shaded porches or indoors. Rowe figured that his brother also would want to find a place to get out of the sun. A tobacco farmer worked all day in the Virginia humidity, but the plains' dry heat and relentless hot breath of driving wind seized a man's lungs in an instant.

He left the wagon near the platform where Dusty had waited to take him to Assurance. Wiping the stinging sweat out of his eyes, he stepped up onto the platform to the ticket booth. "Excuse me, have any trains arrived into the station today, besides the one here now?"

The miserable-looking attendant dabbed his neck with a damp handkerchief. "One train came in this mornin', about seven. It was mostly freight, with two passenger cars."

"Do you know if any passengers were headed for Assurance?"

The attendant glanced at the schedule and freight inventory. "All I could tell you was how many tickets sold today at this station. No one came up here to me askin' 'bout the next town. Who you lookin' for?"

"My brother. His name is Nathaniel Winford."

"Ask the boys down at the end of the platform. They've been unloading and stacking freight. They may have seen 'im."

The day wasn't going to swing by breezily. Rowe thanked the man and strode to the brown locomotive resting alongside the platform. He watched the passengers get off the train, studying them to see if one may be Nathaniel. He waited until the last person emerged from the car, an old man with a walking stick.

Rowe wiped the sweat from his face again and began his trudge to the end of the platform to speak to the freight handlers. Weary travelers rested on benches shaded beneath the extended roof of the station house.

"Forgot my face already, Rowe Andrew?"

Rowe searched the benches for the owner of that voice. Nathaniel smirked at him from beneath a straw hat.

"Get up, you scalawag. I've been combing this station all over for you."

Nathaniel tossed his head back in a hearty, loud guffaw. Then he took his feet off the travel trunk they were resting on. "That's why I didn't say anything. You had the unmistakable look of guilt as you pleaded with the station attendant for news of your brother. You forgot I was coming today, didn't you?" he chided in his quick, melodic delivery. The family always thought he'd join a choir or become a university lecturer one day.

"I didn't forget. I just found out this morning." Rowe embraced his little brother with a clap on the back. Nathaniel hugged in return and then pushed Rowe back at arm's length to examine him.

"Look what the prairie has done to you. You're as tanned as if you worked on the farm all summer."

"Speaking of which, how did you manage to leave during the tobacco harvest and curing?"

"We hired three new hands in July. You would have known that if you'd read your mail. How far is your town from here? I'm famished."

"It's about an hour's drive, but the horses need to rest and be watered."

"So do I. I've had nothing but a hardtack biscuit and coffee this morning. Why don't we take your horses to the local livery and then we find a good chophouse?"

"How good? I have exactly twenty cents left over from my wagon rental." Rowe felt how lightweight the billfold was in his pocket.

Nathaniel rolled his eyes. "What do they pay ministers out here with, barley and chickens? I'll feed us, not to worry." He reached into his own pocket and produced a money clip thick with bills. "It's been a very good year for us, in spite of the recession."

They completed the return trip to Assurance by the start of suppertime, using the wagon to take Nathaniel's travel trunk to the cabin before returning it to the livery. Despite Rowe's guided tour of the town, his brother was unimpressed.

"For a burgeoning rail town, it hasn't made much progress, has it?" he remarked as they walked back to the cabin.

"Give it time, Nate. They've only just started on the plans. They'll have the tracks laid by next year."

"What train would stop in the middle of nowhere?"

"You would want your goods transported across the country. Assurance has many tobacco enthusiasts."

"Perhaps."

Rowe unlocked the cabin door. What was he going to do with Nathaniel during his visit? The man had a knack for finding fault with everything.

He entered before his brother and lit the lamps and stove. Nathaniel straddled a chair as he said, "You have no woman to help around the house or put supper on for you?"

Rowe's mouth watered at the memory of Marissa's slow roasted chicken. "You're going to have to make do with Rowe Winford's Prairie Specialty tonight. Stewed beans and canned beef."

"Is that what you've been living on the whole time? Your mother will be upset."

"You never explained the purpose of your visit."

Nathaniel wiped his mouth. "That's easy. I came to see how you live and to bring you back to Virginia."

Chapter 22

SATURDAY EVENING MARISSA went home early with the Arthurs after Zachary decided to close the shop for the day. Her head ached from lack of sleep the night before, making her patience all the more short. People came in to ask questions about her accepting Rowe's proposal. She declined to answer, choosing instead to tidy up the stockroom.

Rebecca talked about wedding preparations on the wagon ride home. "You'll have to have a reception. I can bake a layer cake."

Mrs. Arthur wasn't considering that most of the town would be in attendance only to ogle at the union, not to celebrate it. Marissa made a suggestion. "Maybe a small dinner in Claywalk instead. Just the four of us."

"Nonsense. There will be more than that. Zachary and I have friends in the church."

Zachary tugged on the reins to make the horse turn left. "I told them they have to watch me give you away."

Marissa's heart grew heavy at how the Arthurs considered her their daughter. She had done nothing to earn their kindness, or Rowe's, but it appeared as though she was doing everything possible to damage their lives. "Even if Rowe and I marry, you still have to contend with Jason's lawsuit. What will you do?"

"We'll handle it when the time comes. Don't you worry about that." Rebecca patted her hand.

"How can you be so calm when you know what's coming?"

Zachary's face had the lines and wrinkles of an old man,

but an inner warmth shone in his eyes. "God won't let anything get to us without it first going through Him."

Marissa shook her head in disbelief. "You can't just leave things to chance."

"Marissa, sometimes faith really is that simple. When we're at the end of our rope, that's when the Lord takes hold."

Their absolute trust in God made little sense, especially in light of the wedding pressing into her thoughts.

Marissa helped Zachary unhitch the horse and went into her room to be alone. She closed the shutters on the window, pitching the room into a murky gray.

In mere hours she would be sharing her life with Rowe, living in the same house, and sleeping in the same bed. He would have to be told that Jason took her virginity. What if he were as disgusted by it as she was?

Marissa glanced at the Bible Rowe gave her on the dresser. A woman whose virtue was stolen was ruined. Even the Bible said so. She read it in a chapter of the Old Testament whose name slipped her memory.

Maybe Rowe thought she participated in the usual saloon girl activities in a prior place and time. It would be easier to let him assume that was how she lost her innocence, but a marriage couldn't be entered into with secrets, even a marriage formed out of desperation. The truth of her life had to be disclosed, but how?

Will God hear me if I pray? The last time she asked for help, it didn't go so well.

Sleep eluded her again that night, and the morning found her staring listlessly out the window at the new sun that climbed its way past the fading moon. Through the dark hours she wrestled with whether to let Sunday go by without giving Rowe an answer. Her circumstances would be no better if she lost another night of sleep waiting for Monday.

Marissa washed and dressed. Rebecca was in the kitchen

boiling oatmeal when she emerged from the bedroom, still buttoning the sleeves of her lilac dress.

"Mari, have something to eat. Zachary's still asleep, but he'll get to the food once he smells it."

"Thank you, but I can't. There's something I must tend to this morning."

"Are you going to church with us?"

"Not exactly."

Rebecca ceased from stirring the oatmeal and let it bubble and gurgle on the stove. "You're going to tell Rowe now, aren't you?"

"It needs to be done."

Rebecca wanted to know more, that Marissa could see. But Rowe had a right to hear first. "I should be going."

Rebecca caught her hand before she turned. "Make sure you've squared your decision away."

Marissa gave a mere nod. If Rowe was so willing to throw away everything to keep her from being imprisoned, the least she could do was give him an answer to his offer.

Rowe's horse still grazed beside the cabin. She smelled cooked bacon and coffee brewing from inside. He hadn't left for church yet.

Marissa's legs trembled as she climbed down from the sidesaddle. The mare nuzzled her arm as she tethered its reins to the newly constructed fence post. *When I cross this fence, my life will change.* She petted the horse's velvety nose before lifting the gate latch. Her legs suddenly needed help to walk.

She drew all the fresh air she could into her lungs as she tapped her knuckles upon the old wooden door and awaited an answer. A lock of her hair blew across her eyes. Great stars, she forgot to pin it up that morning. Too late. Footsteps came.

The door opened. Marissa got all her words together in one breath and blurted them out before her tongue could freeze. "I thought about it, and my answer's the same. I'll marry you."

"Well, I didn't think anyone in town would be this friendly."

"Oh!" Marissa put a hand over her mouth. A tall, dark-haired man very much like Rowe stood in the doorway with an amused grin on his face. She thought it was him at first, with the same broad-shouldered frame and square jaw, but then she noticed the differences. This man was leaner. His face was longer, with small blue eyes and sharp creases in the folds of his mouth. His skin was tanned darker than a well-used saddle and weathered worse than a plainsman's hat. He persisted in smirking down at her.

"I thought you were—"

"My brother? Of course, unless you have the wrong house. I see now why Rowe doesn't wish to leave Assurance."

She crossed her arms in front of her, against his scrutiny. What was Rowe's brother doing all the way from Virginia, and how come he never said anything about a visit? "I'm very sorry. Is Rowe available at this hour?"

"Should be. The poor fellow couldn't sleep last night. I heard him wearing out the upper floor. You wouldn't be the cause of all his trouble, would you?" He let her inside the cabin.

"I'm afraid I am, sir." Marissa got the distinct impression that he was eyeing her from behind. She faced him and saw that she had been correct. Slowly he raised his eyes again to head-level.

"Let me call him down here, then." Rowe's brother went to the foot of the stairs and hollered up. "You have a visitor here to see you. I think she has something important to tell you."

Marissa's heart raced again. Rowe could be upstairs getting ready for church. He may not take kindly to her unannounced visit, especially when he had company. She willed herself to stop fretting like a little girl. Rowe was not some bear ready to roar because she happened upon his cave. He was, in fact, one of the most patient and compassionate men she had ever come across in her life.

"I thought I heard you talking to someone, Nate. Who's here to see me?" Rowe came to the top of the steps, his stark white dress shirt buttoned halfway with a shaving towel draped around his neck. Seeing Marissa, he stopped in mid-gait.

A white cloud of shaving cream covered the lower half of his face. Rowe's brother cleared his throat, motioning with a finger over his mouth. Rowe swiped at the shaving cream with the towel as he loped down the stairs. She had never seen him look so embarrassed.

"Marissa, what brings you here? Have you, uh, met my brother Nathaniel? He'll be staying in town for a few days." He fumbled with the buttons on his shirt as he talked. The wet towel left a growing watermark on the fabric. He blotted it with the dry end to no avail.

"I'm going to fix myself some coffee. Would anyone else care for some?" Nathaniel asked casually.

"We'll take some in just a moment. In the study." Rowe addressed him without his eyes leaving Marissa's.

"That would be my polite and courteous dismissal. Excuse me, Miss." Nathaniel pulled the coffeepot from the stove. The door to the study closed behind him.

"You have my attention." Rowe's voice was quiet, vulnerable, even, as he edged closer. The clean scent of verbena soap and washed linen came from him. "I think I know why you're here."

All of Marissa's insides were shaking. Fresh from

humiliating herself before Rowe's brother, she felt awkward saying the words all over again. It took several moments before she could regain use of her voice. It came out low and warbling. "I haven't slept in days. I couldn't wait until tomorrow to give you my answer."

The room wasn't large. She wondered if Nathaniel was able to hear everything from the study. The only way to prevent him from eavesdropping was to position herself right under Rowe's ear and whisper. She wasn't so bold today as to attempt that.

"It would seem I haven't any control over how I think or feel about you. In the times I've asked God to take me away from this town and let me live elsewhere, He's brought me closer to you. Even with all my troubles, from Jason's beating to his horrible contract, God has allowed you to share in them all. You haven't abandoned me."

"And I never will."

"You don't have to do this. No one would blame you."

"Then I'd be like those who make sport of you. It's the same as locking you in jail myself."

Marissa heard Nathaniel shuffling around. If he was listening, he had to be burning with curiosity as to what it meant. "Our marriage would be based on a sense of duty." She said it as a statement, but she was testing him.

He shoved the towel in his pants pocket. "You are what I want, contract or not. I've been falling in love with you since we met. I hope you feel the same way in time."

She was reluctant to admit that she felt that way at present, believing that the love she had for him would not be strong enough to counter the ruin sure to follow in his life's work. If Marissa had to deal with another person's rejection, his was the one that would be her undoing, no matter how she tried to convince herself differently. Still, loving him as she did, she was willing to take a chance.

"The answer is yes. I will marry you." Saying the words made it real for her. Marissa went into his arms. He held her against the solidarity of his chest.

"Marissa, I almost thought this day wouldn't occur. I am so blessed to have you." He pushed his fingers through her loose hair and tilted her head for a kiss. She sputtered, getting a taste of the bitter tang of shaving cream.

"Pardon me." He wiped his mouth a second time. "I thought I got it all. Let's tell Nate the good news."

Rowe took her by the hand and led her to the study. Nathaniel sat at Rowe's desk, tin mug in hand, reading last week's newspaper.

"Nathaniel, you asked me yesterday if I had a woman to help me around the house. Well, I will soon. Marissa has just agreed to marry me."

Nathaniel finished the article he was reading before he looked at them over the top page. He speculatively settled on Marissa and then his brother. "Congratulations."

"You don't sound too excited." Rowe walked Marissa to the settee and poured her a mug of coffee. "Aren't you glad that someone here will be looking after me so the rest of our family won't have to worry?"

"I am glad. Does she know what she's gotten herself into?" Nathaniel gave her a wink that wasn't at all playful.

Rowe's younger brother couldn't fool her with his false pleasantry or the melodic cadence of his voice. She sipped her coffee. It was a tad acidic, not unlike her new acquaintance.

"You'll have to get her a ring."

"I'll look at wedding bands tomorrow. Do you want to help me choose, Marissa, or do you want to be surprised?"

"I'm interested in seeing what you'll choose." Her stomach rumbled now that the initial excitement and anxiety were over. The hickory-smoked bacon sitting on the stove smelled good.

"I need to get to church, even if it is with the makings of a beard." Rowe scraped his fingers along the dark shadow of stubble on his chin. "I'll see you there later, Marissa, if you choose to come. Are you coming, Nate?"

"After I finish breakfast."

Rowe kissed Marissa's cheek. "Good-bye, dear. Don't frighten her with your stories about me, Nate." He lifted the newspaper that Nathaniel folded haphazardly and uncovered his Bible. A definite jaunt peppered his gait as he left them.

"Well, you've made my brother happy. Have you eaten yet this morning?" Nathaniel stood to go back to the stove.

"No, I haven't."

"I'll bring you some food as well, then."

Marissa drank coffee at the kitchen table until he returned with two plates of bacon, biscuits, and a jar of molasses. "I'm not going to waste time. I just need to know. My brother says he likes it here, but is he telling the truth or trying to convince me?"

"I see no reason for Rowe to lie to you, Mr. Winford. He's done well for himself. He makes a good, steady living." *That is, until the people at church find out he'll be marrying me after all.*

"He looks miserable, as though a hundred things weigh upon his mind."

Marissa bit into a thick strip of bacon, chewing quickly so she could talk. "It takes some adjusting to live in Assurance. He's been getting to know people and learning how to minister to them."

"Is he liked?"

"For the most part. But there are people who don't take kindly to his decisions."

"I can imagine. When we were young, he was very spur-of-the-moment. I don't believe any of that has changed."

"Why?"

Nathaniel positioned the molasses jar atop a biscuit and let the contents drizzle over the bread. "How shall I put this? He's been in your town for how many weeks—six, seven? That's hardly enough time to establish himself, let alone choose a wife. Don't you find your courtship to have been a bit brief?"

"I haven't had too many courtships to tell you what would be the ideal length of time, Mr. Winford." She drained the remaining half of her coffee.

"Good answer." Nathaniel laughed.

His toying manner made her shift uncomfortably. Marissa watched him down the biscuit and catch the molasses drippings with his thumbs.

"Has he told you about Josephine?"

"Of course."

"And how guilt-ridden he was over her death?"

"Yes, it's terrible to lose both wife and child at once."

"She was quite a lady. She would teach Sunday school, host dinner parties, play piano, and sing. You will have big slippers to fill."

Marissa grew speechless as a sense of inadequacy swept over her, but she would not return to that old, useless way of thinking. She had a strong premonition about Rowe's brother when he first opened the cabin door. Whatever his reasons for being harsh, she wasn't about to let him get the better of her.

"I have no intention of filling anyone's shoes. Your brother loved his wife dearly. I wouldn't think of trying to remove her from his heart, nor is there a need to. He..." She didn't want to say *love*. "...accepts me for who I am."

"Just who are you? Has Rowe learned all there is to know about you in the span of a few weeks?"

"Mr. Winford, I have the very distinct impression that you don't like me very much."

The creases around his mouth deepened as he poured himself another mug of coffee. When she declined more, he shut the lid on the coffeepot. "It's not that I dislike you. I want to know if you are all that compels my brother to stay out west. You see, the rest of us Winfords think he should return home and work on the farm."

"Rowe didn't work on your tobacco farm when he was in Virginia. What makes you think he would leave the ministry now for it?"

"Our tobacco crop has stabilized. The revenues have increased while many of the country's industries suffered through the recession. He could be a rich man as a farmer."

"He's not concerned with money."

"Every man is, especially if he hopes to marry and have a family."

"Have you considered that work for him may not involve the family farm? That there's some other task that he was meant to fulfill?"

"You won't convince me because I see nothing here to support your statement. Weren't you going to church?"

Marissa was going to be a preacher's wife. She could no longer stay away from the church on account of not wanting to be ridiculed by its members. Dusting crumbs from her lap, she left the biscuits untouched. Whether it was from the strong, bitter coffee or Nathaniel's conversation, she couldn't swallow another thing. "Are you coming?"

He closed his eyes. "I may be behind you."

"You told Rowe you were going to church. You don't want to hear him preach?"

"I've heard him many times before. He won't miss me. Good morning, Miss." Nathaniel never called her by her name.

Rowe didn't see his brother in church. Not many people attended that day, whether because they disapproved of his engagement to Marissa or because Mr. Charlton may have repeated their conversation from the other day, he did not know. The front pew was empty where the Charlton clan normally sat. This did not bode well for his future as pastor.

He did get a view of Marissa from the crowd, and she wore a troubled face throughout the service. The first day of their engagement, and she appeared more like it was her first day sailing at sea. He told Nathaniel not to frighten her. What inconsiderate, crass remarks did that tobacco hound make once he was alone with her?

It was a mistake to leave Marissa in the cabin with Nathaniel. Rowe thought it would be good for the two of them to become acquainted, but he should have told her to come to church with him instead.

He came home after service to change his clothes before going to the Arthurs' for dinner. Nathaniel sat outside in front of the door, writing a letter to his wife back home.

"What happened to your coming to church after breakfast?"

"Come now. Our mother rustled us up to get to Sunday school when we were boys. I don't need you doing it." Nathaniel didn't look up from his letter.

"What did you say to upset Marissa?"

"Did she say anything?"

"Her face did. She was smiling when I left her. At church her mouth was frozen in a straight line."

Nathaniel stopped writing. "I asked her about you. She implied that you have your heart set on being tied down to Assurance."

"I told you already, Nate. I'm not going back to Virginia to be a tobacco baron. My place is here."

"Our mother begged me to bring home her oldest son."

"I love her, but she'll just have to accept that I live halfway across the country. Our mother knows this is God's calling for my life. All of you do, so why try to persuade me to leave it?"

"Is it God's calling, or that of your new lady?"

"Leave her out of a subject that we've been arguing over since the war ended."

"You're the one that asked me if I upset her."

"See that you don't do it again." Rowe stepped over Nathaniel to get inside the cabin. Nathaniel twisted his neck to look up at him.

"When is the wedding?"

"Sometime this week before Thursday. I'm going to her home now to discuss the details."

Nathaniel hopped to his feet. "Thursday? Why are you flying down the aisle?"

Rowe turned his back. "It doesn't concern you."

"Did you get her with child?"

"No! I said it doesn't concern you." He climbed the stairs two at a time to get away from his brother's persistent prying. "You don't need to know every detail of my life. You're not my keeper."

Nathaniel barged into the house after him, shouting as though that would give greater effect to what he was saying. "There's a reason you're in a hurry to get married. I'm going to find out why. Be assured of that."

Chapter 23

ONDAY MORNING ROWE left the general store, proudly patting the space over his chest where his newest purchase resided. He chose the best he could afford among the limited selection of jewelry: a thin, gold band containing three small garnet stones, their color a deep and rich red. Marissa would be elated.

He left his fiancée home with the Arthurs after the two of them returned from Claywalk with the marriage license. No word of Jason arriving back in town yet, which left Rowe time to consider an elegant way to present the ring to Marissa. He would put it on her finger tonight, when he took her out to the open prairie in a schooner to watch the sunset. It could be a surprise, if the general store owner could keep from bragging to the town about the biggest sale of the day.

Rowe rented a schooner for the evening from Timothy, packing it with a blanket in case Marissa got cold or if they wanted to sit on the ground. He also ordered a basket of sweets from McIntyre's and placed it behind the cushioned bench. At half past six he drove the schooner to the Arthur home and knocked upon the door.

Marissa answered, to his delight.

"Have you had supper?"

"We're about to say grace," she told him.

"Go back and pray over the food, but come outside again when you're done. I have an evening picnic for two planned."

Her lovely eyes twinkled. "But it's nearly sunset."

"I know. I thought you might want to enjoy one last pleasant evening before the autumn chill sets in."

"I'll tell them where I'm going." She went indoors and came right back outside. "Uh, where am I going?"

"To the hill just outside town. I'll have you back by half past eight."

Marissa disappeared into the house again and emerged with her shawl. "Mr. Arthur warns against improper behavior toward me, else he will give you a rapping with his walking cane that he never uses."

"Were those his exact words?" Rowe walked her to the other side of the schooner and helped her up. He vaulted up beside her and assisted with draping her shawl around her shoulders.

She held the front of the garment closed. "I edited them for propriety."

Rowe turned the horses for their destination. They took the schooner just outside the edge of town and off the worn, dirt road path toward the grassy hill overlooking the rolling sea of land. Marissa laughed and cooed over the mischievous prairie dogs that scampered in and out of their many holes. The animals communicated in a series of pips and chirps.

"I've always wondered why they are called dogs," Rowe said, as the bravest one of the colony emerged from its burrow near the horses' hooves to see who disturbed his underground home. "They look like giant rodents."

"They are part of the rodent family. Sometimes they do make barking sounds."

As if to illustrate for Marissa, one of the animals produced a squeaky bark and sniffed the air before disappearing beneath the grass.

Rowe and Marissa ate their meal while the prairie dogs entertained them with their antics. As the sky turned orange and the sun began its slow descent, Rowe took the ring box from his waistcoat.

"You said you'll marry me, but will you wear this ring?" He opened the box, and she gasped.

"Oh, it's beautiful. Yes, I will be proud to wear it."

His hand shaking, Rowe took it from the box. Marissa held out her left hand and he slid it on her finger.

"I worried that it might not fit, but it looks like it was made for you." He studied the glittering gems. The garnets twinkled and winked, catching the brilliant red fire of the remaining sun's light. It couldn't compare with half of the luminous joy that radiated from Marissa's face.

She touched his cheek and gave him a long kiss beneath the watercolor sky.

He encircled her until she was in his arms completely. Her breath on his face was warm and sweet. He felt her rapid flutter heartbeat against his chest. By all accounts it was per-missible and expected to say he loved her, but Marissa still didn't seem ready to hear it. As much as he wanted to get the three words out that evening, he decided to wait until their wedding day. She couldn't balk at him then.

Rowe kissed the satin skin of her brow. She buried her face against his neck. Her neatly pinned hair was soft and sleek as it brushed his lips. "Will I get a cane rapping for this?"

"Only if it's considered to be improper behavior." She made no effort to remove herself.

He found her mouth and kissed it hard. "What of that?"

Marissa opened her eyes slowly. "Most improper." She returned his kiss with equal boldness and duration.

He uttered some form of agreement, but his words were muffled. At that point Rowe didn't know what he was trying to say anyhow. Nor did he care. Their closeness was won-derful. The exhilaration of it sang through his veins.

Marissa broke away, breathless. "But it isn't right. I mean, it is in a way, when we're married. Now, though, we–I–I don't know how to describe this."

"I know what you're saying. We must get a hold of ourselves." He released her, reluctantly. "We should go back to town. In a few days you'll be my wife, and we can kiss all we want."

"In the sunset."

"In the sunset, in the moonlight, wherever it pleases you."

She hid her face. "I thought about what it would be like to be your wife. The women at the saloon sometimes talked to me about their...times with men. But it won't be cold or impersonal like that, will it?"

Her question seemed naïve to him, especially with the saloon position she once held, where she was surrounded by men. "No. It's a cold and impersonal act to them because they're not honoring God with what they choose to do with their bodies. It's different between husbands and wives who love each other."

She moved her hands about restlessly. "I can't imagine such a union to be enjoyable."

Marissa had to know about relations. Didn't she?

"I really don't know how to put it into words, Marissa. It's something wonderful and indescribable that can only be experienced fully with the person God chooses for you."

Her face blushed. "I can believe that." Tightly she drew her shawl about her shoulders and neck until only her head could be seen above the downy buttercream fabric. "I can't wait to show Rebecca and Zachary the ring."

The evening dissolved of its passionate headiness and took on a much welcomed lighter tone. They ate the basket of sweets from McIntyre's as the schooner's wheels grated along the clear main streets of the town.

"Rowe, what's that?" Marissa pointed with a half-bitten

pastry to a moving figure in the middle of the road. Rowe stopped the horses.

The animals snorted in irritation at having their gait interrupted. The figure came closer.

"How did your evening tryst go with the lady, brother?" Nathaniel stumbled into view. "I watched you prepare for it all day long."

Rowe scowled hard at him. "What's that you're holding?" Nathaniel extended his arm to showcase a bottle of Wild Rogue. "I got it from a fellow who came into town an hour ago. Courtesy of your friend, Mr. Garth, saloon keeper. Or should I say, friend of your fiancée?" Nathaniel uncorked the bottle and took a swig.

"It's illegal to drink spirits in the streets," Marissa said.

"She would know, wouldn't she?" Nathaniel crossed over to Rowe's side of the schooner, weaving slightly. "But I didn't know until an hour ago that she's little more than a common dancing girl, still under contract of employment. How did you convince Garth to let her have the evening off?"

Rowe was furious to see his brother inebriated and walking the streets like an addle-pated vagabond, and even more outraged at his words. "She won't be under contract when we're married. It's Jason's one last ploy to get her to come back to him."

"Let him have her," he slurred. "What would our family think of you chasing after common whores?"

"That's enough. You're going to pack your trunk and stay at an inn until the next train arrives to take you back East. I won't have you living under the same roof with me anymore." Rowe signaled to the horses.

Nathaniel jumped in front of the wagon. "Why?"

Rowe had to yank hard on the reins. The schooner jerked back and bounced on its axles. Marissa fell against him. "Because you have no respect for my future wife. Get out of my way, Nathaniel. I'm not going to shout at you in the middle of the street."

His brother carried on, ignoring him. "Respect for her? I don't have any respect for you anymore. You call yourself a minister, but you yoke yourself with the worst kind of woman."

"I'm being patient with you. Don't provoke me."

"You would choose a slattern over your own blood?"

"Nathaniel, look." Marissa interjected, rising from her seat. She held out her hand with the ring. "Rowe gave me this tonight. I'll cherish it and him forever. Tell me what to do to make you see that."

"Marissa, sit down." Rowe didn't need her to get involved, even if she was the main topic.

But she continued to try to assuage Nathaniel's contempt. "You are so very wrong about me. Jason should have told you about my position. I was not a prostitute."

"If he didn't tell me, I'll surely not hear it from you."

Rowe saw the look of despair upon Marissa's face as she sank down. He could stand it no longer. "Nathaniel, pick up your things at the cabin when you're sober, and leave."

He thrashed the reins and the horses dashed forward. Nathaniel jumped out of the way in the nick of time.

Rowe pulled the wagon up to the Arthurs' house, pausing before he climbed out. "Marissa, I'm sorry for my brother's drunken outburst. You'll never have to deal with him again."

Marissa willed herself not to cry. It wasn't the first time she had been called names, and it certainly wouldn't be the last. She was determined that Rowe not see how much Nathaniel's hateful words upset her. Rowe had worked hard to surprise her with the ring. The least she could do was put on a brave face.

He kissed her good night. She felt too empty inside to enjoy it.

Inside the house, while Zachary and Rebecca admired her ring, her mind was on Nathaniel's stinging appraisal of her station and the renewed threat of Jason in town. Everything he told Nathaniel was indication that he schemed to get her back.

Rebecca grasped Marissa's hand and moved it under the light. "I was going to let you borrow my gloves for the wedding, but it would be a shame to hide such a pretty ring."

Despite herself, Marissa smiled as the garnets cast little dots of red light across the table surface.

"Goodness, only one more full day to prepare." Rebecca tapped on the table. "I have so much to do."

Zachary chuckled. "You're not the one getting hitched."

"That is beside the point, Zachary Arthur. I'm still making sure Mari's the prettiest bride in Kansas. We'll practice dressing your hair tomorrow, Mari, alright?"

"Mm-hmm."

"See, Rebecca? Even she's not as fidgety as you." Zachary pulled himself to his feet by grabbing the edge of the table. "You are feeling better about getting married to the reverend, aren't you?"

"Yes." Marissa preferred not to mention what Nathaniel said. In two days the point would be moot.

The next day she sat for Rebecca while the older woman contemplated hairstyles.

"What if we interlace pearls instead of an ornament?"

She combed and gathered Marissa's hair in an array of beautiful, complicated twists. The Arthurs' bedroom was turned into a bridal dress chamber, with open trinket cases laid out containing Rebecca's decorative hair combs and jewelry. A powder blue gown newly purchased from the general store covered the quilt on the bed. Stockings, gloves, bustle, corset, and underskirt surrounded the two women.

"I think I can weave my pearl necklace at the crown and thread it through the top knot." Rebecca demonstrated by taking a section of hair and pinning it into a high bun. "What do you think?"

"It's going to look stunning, whatever you do with it." Marissa picked up a hand mirror so she could view her profile.

"Of course, I'll have to set your hair once we get to the hotel in Claywalk tomorrow morning. The wind between here and there will make a rat's nest of my work."

"I can't believe I'm getting married tomorrow. We were fortunate to find a preacher to officiate the ceremony on short notice."

Rebecca held the comb poised above Marissa's head. She stared, reminiscent, into the larger vanity mirror. "How I wish that Elizabeth were here to see you. You look so much like her."

Marissa inspected her own features closely and, for an instant, caught a glimpse of her mother's bright eyes staring back at her. She turned the hand mirror over in her lap. "What did she look like on the day of her wedding, Mrs. Arthur?"

"Lovely, dressed all in white."

She noted her light blue gown draped across the bed. "I'm unable to wear that color."

Rebecca caught her meaning. "Mari, you could have chosen a white dress from the store. You shouldn't focus on what happened with Jason years ago."

Marissa grimaced. "I haven't told Rowe about what Jason did to me. I was going to last night on the way home from the schooner ride, but his brother interrupted before I could get the chance."

"That man is terribly rude. He hasn't bothered to introduce himself to me or Zachary yet." Rebecca set her hands upon her hips.

"Last night Nathaniel had too much to drink and confronted Rowe with everything he heard from Jason. There's no convincing Nathaniel that I'm not a trollop."

"He's not the one who needs to be convinced. Rowe knows who you are and respects you for breaking free of that saloon."

Marissa touched the garnet stones on her ring. "He's heard so much already that's not true, but it's impossible to prove the claims false. Do you think he'll believe me when I tell him today?" She read the older woman's face for a positive sign but got a neutral reaction instead.

"I don't have an answer for you, " Rebecca said calmly. "I can only go by what I've seen in Rowe's character. Regardless of his response, you must tell him if you want to start your marriage on a clean slate."

"No secrets between us." Marissa remained at the vanity until Rebecca finished pinning her hair.

She helped Rebecca finish packing the trunk for the wedding before she left to find Rowe. Marissa located him where she thought he would be, at his cabin, still attempting to repair that broken fence. He was so busy concentrating on his unsuccessful tries at nailing two wood rails together that he didn't hear her approach.

"You corroded piece of iron rust." He hurled insults at the nail. "Do as I tell you!"

Marissa walked the path to him. His shirt clung to his broad back with sweat as he bent over in the sun. Thick muscles honed from military combat rippled beneath.

"I am not going to waste the whole day on you." He drove the nail into the wood and brought his hammer down upon it. Missed by a fraction, he split the wood in two. The nail remained upright in one portion of the ruined rail on the ground.

Rowe made some animalistic sound and tossed the hammer in the dirt. He sent the wood flying with the toe of his boot.

"Is this why you're so calm on Sundays, Reverend? Because you take your frustrations out on our limited supply of timber during the week?"

He spun around. Marissa could hardly keep from giggling. His face was angry, flustered, shocked at the sight of her, and near sunburned all in one. She produced a handkerchief from her dress and wiped his brow.

"You really shouldn't do this kind of work during the midday if you're not used to the heat. It doesn't get cool here sometimes until well into November."

"This is calming for me." He picked up the hammer and held it above the broken rail. "Good vent of frustration."

"Well, I need to have a word with you."

He paused in mid-swing. "I thought you'd be busy with wedding preparations today."

"I am, but there's something that's been on my mind for a long time. You ought to know about it."

"Are you getting the jitters?"

Marissa drummed her foot in the dirt. "Somewhat. But it's not about the wedding itself. It's about me. Perhaps you should sit down."

He grinned and let the hammer drop in the grass. "I'm not going to faint, Marissa. I'm fine standing, unless you intend to keep me waiting for what you have to say."

"I hope you retain your good humor after I'm finished."

Rowe laid an encouraging hand on her arm. "Something is obviously weighing on you. What is it?"

It was now or never. "You know precisely what goes on under the tables of many frontier saloons, don't you?"

"Yes. Ill and tawdry practices are everywhere. I'm not the sheltered preacher boy people think I am."

"There are things I've done as a saloon girl that I'm not proud of."

He said nothing, but his eyes showed clear understanding. Marissa took a deep breath and went on. "You know this, and you still want me as a proper wife?"

"I don't want you for anything less."

"Then you must know that I never sold myself, despite what you have been hearing from certain people. But Jason forced himself on me once."

She searched Rowe's face to see if he believed her. Unable to read his expression, she continued. "He told me that I owed him something for taking me in. I didn't have money. The one valuable thing I did possess, he claimed for himself."

"When was this?"

"Two years ago."

He was still and immobile as a granite statue. Only his eyes showed signs of life as they darkened and smoldered to deep cobalt.

"Rowe, what's wrong? Say something."

His gaze latched onto her like a roiling, stormy sea. "Why didn't you tell me this before?"

He put his back to her and trampled through the fence opening. The horse whinnied in anticipation as he placed a saddle pad in front of its withers and laid the saddle across its back in rapid succession.

"I did want to tell you." Marissa picked up her skirts to run after him. "I didn't expect any of this to happen so fast. Not our courtship. Not falling in love. I would have told you eventually if things had progressed at a slower pace."

Rowe gathered up the reins and swung onto the horse.

"That man. It would have been better if had been anyone but that man." It was almost as if he were talking to himself.

The wind picked up speed, blowing through Rowe's shirt and tearing Marissa's hair from its pins. His face dark, he rode the horse past her. "You should go home. Now I need time to think."

She grew fearful that all was lost. "Where are you going?" The wind howled and whistled about them like accursed laughter as he took the path to town. His horse broke into a gallop.

Marissa called after him, but he didn't stop. Rowe raced steadily onward, leaving her mind in confusion and her heart shattered in a thousand pieces.

Chapter 24

SICKENING FILTH. THAT'S what Jason Garth was to take an unmarried, frightened young girl against her will. Rancid, vile filth.

Rowe had to leave Marissa before she saw the extent of how angry the disclosure made him. The more he thought about it on the way into town, the more it stirred his already boiling blood.

That explained why Marissa was hesitant to accept his proposal at first. She was afraid that he would control her as Jason did. It made sense now why she would have sooner gone to jail than risk the possibility of another man's domination.

It was also why she shied away from revealing her true self. In fact, Marissa exhibited the same skittishness as widows and young women taken advantage of by soldiers during the War Between the States. Of course he had suspected the abuse, but the truth of the abuser's identity hurt more than he dared admit. Jason Garth. Would his evil face haunt them the rest of their lives?

Rowe dismounted in front of the general store and went in for an extra box of nails. He had plenty of them in his tool chest, but he needed to do something to cool his head before he confronted Jason.

The pain may as well have been stones that crushed her body and spirit, so terrible its effect upon her.

Marissa trudged the path to town with all the anguish and

fear she experienced prior to the past several days returning in full force.

Jason's prediction came true. Men did not want soiled saloon girls as permanent fixtures in their lives. Rowe's rejection proved it.

How foolish was she to think that a preacher would be different from any other man? It was a must, in fact, that his standards for choosing a wife be infinitely higher.

He lied to me when he said my past didn't matter, she thought bitterly. *I did learn to trust him with my secret, and see where it went. He could accept my past in the abstract, but not in its naked reality.*

The pit of her stomach turned even more at who she spotted upon arrival at the town square.

Nathaniel sat on the wooden sidewalk in front of Zachary's shop, reading an almanac with a degree of distraction. He acknowledged her with a nod as he looked up and tucked the book under his arm.

"Miss Pierce, allow me to apologize for my rude manner last night. I had a bit too much to drink, and it got to my better judgment."

Marissa got out of the street so that a coach could stop parallel in front of the store. "You've had an ill opinion of me ever since you met me."

Nathaniel gave a remorseful inclination of the head. "Yes, I jumped to conclusions."

"I should say so."

"Miss Pierce, I only wanted the best for my brother, you understand. He's had a nasty time since Josephine's passing."

Marissa grew rigid at the mention of Rowe's first wife. Rowe said he didn't measure her against Josephine, but that did not stop his brother, Jason, or anyone else who knew about Rowe's past from doing so.

"Perhaps Rowe would move on if you'd only let him."

Nathaniel nodded complacently. "He is a grown man. If he can abide here, then he has fortitude. I'll let him live his own life."

She was stunned by his change of face. "You will?"

"Will you accompany me to McIntyre's for a flavored soda? We can finish talking there."

"I don't know, Mr. Winford."

"I'm trying to make amends, as your future brother-in-law."

Marissa shook her head and gazed downward. "I'm not sure if there's going to be any wedding. Rowe and I have had a...disagreement. He's stormed off somewhere."

"But why?"

"I'd rather not state the cause, if you don't mind. I came here to inform the Arthurs before I go home to unpack my trunk."

"Don't say anything to them yet until we get this straightened out with Rowe." Nathaniel took her by the arm and led her away from the shop. "I'm sure this is a misunderstanding. You know how hasty he can be sometimes."

"I have never seen him that way."

"We'll find him. I'll set him straight. Come on."

He pulled her along, up the street and around the corner. Marissa didn't see Rowe in any of the stores or outside. They passed the hotel and McIntyre's.

"Didn't you say you wanted a flavored soda?"

"In a moment, as soon as we find my brother."

They walked to the next street. Nathaniel still held her by the arm. Marissa withdrew slightly, believing that the subtle gesture would cause him to release her, but he retained his grasp. She caught sight of the saloon's red and white letters ahead.

"I really don't think Rowe would be in this area of town. Let's turn back."

"No, we're right where *you* need to be." Nathaniel's hand

clamped down on her arm as he quickened his pace. The direction of his steps became clear, heading straight for the saloon.

"Nathaniel, stop! Let me go!"

His strength and broad frame were similar to his brother. Marissa strained herself as she tugged against the force he exerted. He dragged her down the middle of the road. She dug her boot heels in the dirt. Nathaniel yanked her forward, the might of his pull sending her stumbling to her knees.

Two men passed, and she cried out to them for help.

"Get up." Nathaniel hauled her to her feet in front of the onlookers and continued walking. Marissa raised her fist and hit him hard on the temple. He seized her arm and wrenched it painfully across her back. "Jason! Jason Garth, get out here!"

The saloon proprietor heard his shouts and rose from the wooden chair on the establishment's sidewalk. Taking his time, as though savoring the moment, he stepped into the middle of the street. Jason showcased his yellowing teeth in admiration of Nathaniel's efforts.

"Looks like you did it after all."

"As promised. My work here is finished." Nathaniel shoved Marissa into Jason's arms. "I've delivered your strumpet."

Rowe dug into his apple pie as Dusty talked shop over beef tips and mashed potatoes. He discovered the farmhand in the general store fifteen minutes before, purchasing shovels to muck the Charlton horse stalls. The two of them agreed to have a quick stop at McIntyre's for some lunch. Rowe needed some more distraction and time to think before he confronted Jason, and Dusty offered pleasant company while he wrestled with what to do next.

His dessert polished off but with no plan in mind, Rowe

pushed his chair back and rose from the table. Turning, he spotted his brother for the first time, sitting by himself in a corner. Nathaniel should be in the hotel, recovering from last night's drunken debacle or making arrangements to leave Kansas on the next rail. Instead he tore heartily into a drumstick and swallowed the foam off a mug of sassafras.

Two men came into the restaurant and approached him while he ate, their faces insistent and firm.

"It looks like Nathaniel's got himself in trouble again. Excuse me, Dusty."

"Need some help?"

"Not right now, I don't think." As Rowe advanced upon the three men, he heard their heated discussion.

"You're crazy for takin' her back to the saloon. You didn't have to drag her like a dog in the streets," the male in a leather-fringed coat admonished.

His compatriot, a middle-aged railroad surveyor, agreed. "Whore or not, she's still a woman."

"I did what was necessary to protect my brother," Nathaniel snapped. "You didn't stop me when it happened, so don't bother me while I'm eating."

A sick feeling of dread poured over Rowe. "What's going on here?" He drew their attention.

The rail surveyor faltered. "That man who says he's your brother got hold of Miss Pierce, Reverend. He took her down this here road and gave her back to Jason."

Rowe glared at his brother. "How dare you?"

The restaurant patrons paused from their own conversations to see what the commotion was about. Nathaniel swallowed more sassafras soda.

"You didn't need her. She'd only bring trouble to you and hurt your ministry."

"You don't know that." Rowe slammed his fists on the

table. The sassafras crashed to the floor. "That's not for you to decide."

The owner rushed to them, ready to clean up the mess and throw all four of the men out. Dusty came up alongside Rowe, his fists balled, ready to stand by a friend.

"These gents tryin' to pick a fight?"

"Nathaniel's taken Marissa back to the saloon. We have to get her."

"It's too late." Nathaniel jumped to his feet, pushing past the owner. "Her contract's renewed once she sets foot in the saloon again. She's bound to it because she's still without a husband."

It took every ounce of Rowe's willpower to refrain from driving his knuckles into his brother's smug face. "You put a sentence on her that wasn't your right. You're no brother of mine." He stomped to the restaurant's open door. "Go back to Virginia, Nathaniel. I'd better never see you in these parts again."

Rowe ran down the street toward the saloon. His body grew hot. Rage swelled within, quickening his legs and sending blood pumping through his chest. His breath came out in deep growls.

Dusty called behind him. "Don't go yet. Let me get the sheriff."

"Get him, then. Contract or no contract, Marissa isn't going to work for Jason. It ends today."

Marissa talked steel into her spine as Jason pulled her through the saloon. All her years of protecting herself, all her training in survival returned as she passed the familiar faces of Simone and Nellie, who watched in sympathetic stunned silence as Jason pushed her up the stairs.

"Whatever you hear, keep the patrons from asking

questions," Jason warned Pete from the head of the stairs. The clerk nodded, his nervous gaze barely scraping Marissa's face.

Jason pressed the barrel of a gun into the small of Marissa's back. "Just in case your displeasure at being delivered to me makes you want to run again." He shoved her down the hall and into his office.

Jason pulled the chair out from his desk and pushed her into the seat. "Sorry I had to do it this way, darlin'. That's what hardheadedness will get you when you violate a contract."

Marissa rolled her eyes at Jason's meaningless apology. "I assume you'll use another term for 'coerced at gunpoint' when you draft future retention policies."

"You always liked to get those big words out of your books," he chuckled dryly. "See if there's any you recognize in this document."

He slid a new contract across the desk to her, pen on top. He indicated to the inkwell on her end.

"Sign it, and we'll pretend that nothing happened. No charges, no suits against the Arthurs. You can go back to being Arrow Missy. I'll even let you have your old room again, but no locks on the door this time. You'll have to earn that privilege."

"You may have arranged for me to be dragged here kicking and screaming, but I'll never put my name on anything that concerns you. Are we clear?"

Jason snickered. "I'm callin' the shots, and you'll get one in the gut if you don't follow directions."

Her eyes never left his. "You wouldn't have gone to the trouble to bring me back here if you only wanted to shoot me dead. You could have done that in the streets or when you visited Zachary's shop. Instead you enlisted Rowe's brother to get me, because you believe I can revive this crooked, run-down hole in the wall."

"You grew a bigger spine since you've been away." Jason sounded impressed, although his annoyance at her boldness colored his face.

"This isn't going anywhere. I won't sign."

"Do you think this gun can only be used to kill? It can injure too. I can make you a cripple with a bullet to the leg. You won't be able to dance anymore, but those boys downstairs'll be real glad you have to make a living off your feet."

Marissa's realization of her former employer's cruelty reached new heights. Jason was a hustler, a scavenger, and he would always scratch and scrabble in the dirt to get what he thought was rightfully his. Nothing that he ever gained was acquired honorably. Making her unable to walk would allow him complete access to her body without a fight.

Jason lowered the gun to the ball-and-joint socket at her knee. With the other hand he dipped the pen in the inkwell and flung it at her, splattering black droplets all over the front of her dress.

"Sign the contract."

Rowe ran straight through the swinging saloon doors and headed for the back bar counter. "Bring Jason out here now!"

"You're crazed, Reverend." The barkeep threw down a washrag and reached under the counter.

Rowe seized the man by the collar and hauled him over the counter. Pete dropped the Smith & Wesson revolver as he hit the floor. Rowe scooped it up before he could reach for it again.

The two serving girls shrieked. The handful of saloon patrons got to their feet, shouting, laughing, or cursing at the uproar. Rowe scanned the crowd for any signs of more gun brandishing.

"I won't say it again." He called out at them, "Where's Jason?"

"He's upstairs." A serving girl came forward. "In his office with Missy."

Still holding the revolver, Rowe charged up the stairs. Several doors closed off to him. A man came out of one, buckling his belt. A saloon girl followed, screaming when she saw the gun in Rowe's hand.

"Jason's office. Where is it?" He rested the gun at his side, pointing it toward the floor so they wouldn't think he'd fire on them. He couldn't afford to dispose of the firearm.

The girl pointed to a closed door at the end of the hallway. "Get downstairs. Now." Rowe crept past her and the man. Jason could very well be waiting with a gun of his own, since all the noise and screaming gave the proprietor ample warning.

What a mess he made for barging in, outnumbered by employees and patrons. He could get shot any minute. Still, Marissa needed help, in spite of his rashness.

I'm sorry, he prayed. Please don't allow Marissa to be in danger because of me. Just get her out of this place safe and sound.

Rowe put his free hand on the door knob. It was unlocked. He turned it promptly and kicked it open the rest of the way.

Jason whirled around, gun in hand. Marissa stared up at him.

"Your brother said you might come up here, startin' trouble." Jason's fingers remained on the trigger of the gun. "That's why I gave Pete a firearm."

"Your clerk wasn't quick enough."

"Obviously, since you're holding it."

Rowe kept the revolver barrel on him. "I don't want to use this. Just let Marissa leave."

"Ha! A preacher man with a gun? You couldn't use it, anyway."

Rowe stood at a point where he could see Jason, Marissa, and the stairs, in case anyone climbed up to the second floor. "I was a soldier before I was a minister. If need be, I'll defend my fiancée."

"Maybe, but you wouldn't risk losing your ministry over a whore. You shoot me, and the town will see you as a jealous client who doesn't want her to have other customers."

"You're the jealous one, Jason. Marissa told me you raped her. You may have blighted her past, but you will not steal her future."

Marissa released a soft gasp. Her eyes shone moist. "You still want me?"

Rowe kept his sights on both her and Jason. "Marissa, I'm sorry for leaving you the way I did. I didn't want you to see how furious I got at Jason for what he did."

Jason snickered. "You believe that, Marissa? The preacher's tellin' you lies. He left you alone because he finally came to his senses. He couldn't change you. Tell her, Winford. You wanted to prove yourself to the town by makin' an example of her. You wouldn't have courted her if she hadn't left the saloon, now, would you?"

"She was on her way out before she met me. That's irrelevant."

"Is it? Zachary Arthur's been trying to get her to live with him and his wife for years. How is it now that you came to town, she works in his store and lives in their house?"

"Because I took her to them on the night you came close to killing her."

"You hear that, Missy?" Jason's voice escalated into a shout. "He and Zachary planned it. A changed life, a bigger church."

"You're a liar, Jason," Marissa declared but gazed at Rowe

in disbelief. "Tell him, Rowe. Tell him you didn't use me to try to gain a bigger congregation."

"Don't believe a twisted word that comes out of Jason's mouth." Rowe squeezed hard on the gun handle. "I never thought of using you."

The saloon proprietor leered. "I must be onto somethin', by the way you're holdin' that gun. Ask him, Marissa. Ask him if he didn't want to use you to build his church."

Her lovely, expression-filled face lifted, sending knots through Rowe's chest. "Is it true? Did you plan to use me?"

How could she listen to Jason, a man whose very presence threatened her life, as he tried to get her to reject everything beyond the saloon as a venomous lie? Rowe didn't disguise the aggravation in his tone of voice as he faced a moment of truth.

"I saw how sad and trapped you were. Zachary and I agreed that we would help you leave the saloon for the life you wanted. We also thought you could help the town by giving your testimony in church, but no one can make you a Christian, Marissa. As much as I wanted you to become one, I couldn't decide for you."

"That didn't stop him from seizing the opportunity to influence you and make an example of you for the church. Did it, Reverend?" Jason demanded.

"You're full of lies." Rowe spoke to him, but his words were directed at Marissa. He wanted to lift her and carry her away from Jason's warped manipulations, but a gun stood in his path. "I had goals for the church to improve, but Marissa wasn't a pawn. She had the Arthurs as examples of good people who treated her with respect."

"Those old idiots always coddled her." Jason threw snide remarks instead of any significant counterpoints.

"She chose an alternative to what little you had to offer. I started to fall in love with her from the beginning, yes, but I didn't steal her from you."

"You interfered with how I conduct my business. You shouldn't mess with another man's property."

"No person is anyone's property. Release her."

Jason moved, whipping the pistol around to aim for him. Rowe ducked into the hallway as the first bullet pierced the door's wood frame. He reappeared in the doorway, pointing his gun at Jason. He pulled the trigger. The pistol flew out of Jason's hand as Rowe's bullet struck the barrel.

Marissa jumped from her chair and ran to the door. Rowe shielded her as they raced down the stairs and through the swinging entry doors.

"Rev'ren!"

Dusty approached, pistol in one hand. "I heard a shot. Where's Garth?"

Rowe glanced at the flood of patrons and servers pouring out of the saloon. He pushed Marissa to Dusty. "Get her out of here before Jason tries for her again."

"What about you?" Marissa grabbed his arm.

"I'll stay behind to explain to Sheriff McGee what happened. Go to the safest place you know, Dusty, and don't stop."

Rowe shielded their backs as they fled down an alley. Seconds later Jason stumbled from the saloon, laughing and cursing. "You! Lookie here." He halted at arm's length before Rowe and waved a document in his face. "Arrow Missy's new contract, signed and completely valid. I got the best ladies this side of Kansas, Reverend. You sure I can't offer you one of them to compensate your loss?"

"You have nothing to offer anyone. All of your employees have left you."

"They'll come back, especially the girls. I pay the most.

They're not as warm and firm as Marissa was, but they get my approval."

Rowe's back muscles tensed as his natural male instinct to protect rose in white-hot fury. "You're worth less than the ground a man spits on."

Jason gave him a heavy shove. "Fight me for her, then."

"No." Rowe recovered his stance.

"What's wrong, preacher? Scared you'll lose your witness?" Jason shoved him again. "Fight for your woman."

Rowe's last vestige of composure exploded in a cloud of crimson. Images of a teenaged Marissa, struggling beneath Jason in a fight to escape the assault upon her body, filled his mind. The scars that it left her with, the pain, bitterness, and feelings of shame she bore daily made him lose control. This loathsome swine was responsible for everything wrong in Marissa's life, nearly every teardrop she shed.

Jason spit out a string of curse words. "You gonna fight or turn the other cheek for me?" He charged forward and delivered a backhand across Rowe's face.

Rowe countered, rearing his fist back and letting it fly. Jason stumbled back, taking the punch. He launched forward a third time. Rowe blocked his hits. Jason's hard knuckles pummeled him as he struck again and again.

"Reverend Winford, stop!" Sheriff McGee's voice resonated in his ears, but it sounded far away.

Rowe heard the crowd, both men and women now, shouting. Jason's arms closed around him in a vice grip. He fought the leaner man off, refusing to be held back.

Rowe drove Jason to the ground to subdue him. The saloonkeeper swung his fist alongside Rowe's jaw, sending pain shooting up into his temples, following with a sharp kick delivered to his knees. Rowe fell on top of Jason's chest.

"You fight almost like a man, preacher." He spat blood and phlegm on Rowe's shirt before he pushed him off.

Rowe jabbed him in the stomach. "You beat upon women. How would you know about being a man?"

They grappled in the dirt. Dust flew in their eyes and in their mouths. Jason raised the toe of his boot and kicked Rowe in the rib cage.

Lancing pain formed in his side. Rowe staggered on his knees, drawing ragged breaths. He caught the snide glint in Jason's eyes as the man moved for another hit. He rolled out of the way of the attack and reared his elbow upside Jason's head.

Gunfire rang in the air.

The crowd silenced.

Jason slumped to the ground.

Two pairs of hands seized Rowe. He grunted as a large, meaty arm dug into his stinging side.

"Reverend Winford." Sheriff McGee jerked him to his feet. "You're under arrest."

Chapter 25

MARISSA JUMPED AT the crackle of gunfire. Women screamed, and the crowd swarmed in all directions, blocking her view of the saloon. She pulled on Dusty's arm for him to stop.

"We have to go back. Rowe's in trouble."

"I'm sorry, ma'am, but he told me to see to your safety. That's what I'm gonna do." With strength uncommon in men of his wiry, lean frame, he wrapped his arm around her waist and hoisted her atop his horse.

"Dusty, he could be hurt. Please." Marissa used the height advantage of the horse to see over the crowd sixty paces behind them. It was so thick that she couldn't tell whether the people were still watching a fight or crowding around a fallen man. She lost sight of the sheriff.

Dusty swung into the saddle behind her and sent the horse galloping for the lake path. They passed by the church and Rowe's cabin. He didn't speak until they were well on the other side of the path leading to the Charlton farm.

"I'll go back to see about him, Miss Marissa. Soon as I get you squared away."

"He could be hurt," she protested again. Misery gnawed in her chest. "The crowd could have shot at or trampled him as they were running."

It was noble of Rowe to stay behind to talk to Sheriff McGee, but why did doing the right thing come with a price? The world was filled with men like Jason and Nathaniel whose selfish greed caused so much trouble for others.

Horses' hooves clomped behind them, followed by a pair

of bickering young voices. Marissa peered around Dusty's arm to see Sophie and her brother David riding up the road as well. David was trying to make a point to his older sister, who held her chin high, refusing to turn her head in his direction..

"I'm tellin' you, Sophie, Reverend Winford fought Jason because of Miss Pierce. There ain't any other reason why a preacher would go and do something like that."

"Don't say ain't, David. I'm not disputing your point, redundant as it is." Her voice retained its practiced, ladylike softness above the acidic undertone. "I find it inexplicable why he would engage in violence for that—that overgrown, underdressed Jezebel. Taken away by the sheriff, no less."

"Rowe didn't get shot?" Marissa didn't care that she blurted into their conversation. The fact that Rowe was alive was all that mattered.

"Sheriff McGee carried him off to jail for sluggin' in the streets," David answered. Marissa heard Dusty exhale in relief behind her.

Sophie's eyes flashed. "Gracious, what is Marissa doing near our house? Dusty Sterling, what are you up to, bringing her out here?"

"Sophie, ma'am, the Rev'ren requested that I take her to a safe place. Other than the church, this is about the safest place you can get to in Assurance."

Every feature scrunched up on her face. "She's the cause of all that trouble today. How can you even want to protect her? You should have left her on the streets."

To Marissa's amusement Dusty remained cool and detached from Sophie's hard criticism. He adjusted his Stetson so that it sat at an angle above his brow. "With all due respect, Miss Sophie, your bad mouthin' ain't ladylike. I'm gonna pretend I didn't hear none of it."

"And I'm gonna tell my father you brought a hussy onto

his farm. You remember his rules. Workers wanting to associate with women of ill repute must do so in town and keep it off our property."

"Go tell your father. Ride on ahead of me, in fact, 'cause that's where I'm goin' anyhow. I'll see what Mr. Charlton has to say."

Marissa knew Mr. Charlton by his accomplishments listed in the town newspaper: generosity in the funding of the church, ample investments in the railroad, and collaboration with farmers and rail tycoons for plans of the future train station in Assurance. He was a dedicated and prosperous man whose demands for temperance in the town drew both admiration and scorn. Seeing her on his property might make him oust her on her bustle.

"Will he receive me well, Dusty?" Marissa whispered. He chewed his jaw in unspoken irritation at Sophie's constant haggling behind him.

"Should. He trusts me with his crops and cattle, and look where I come from."

"You're the best cattle rustler and farmhand from Texas there is."

"I'm mighty proud of the compliment, but that ain't all there is to me. Ain't fittin' to tell a lady where my boots have been."

Sophie spurred her horse ahead of them. "I'm telling Daddy so he can put a stop to this tomfoolery. Come with me, David."

Her brother didn't move from the rear of the riding party. "Go by yourself. You're jealous because Miss Pierce can hold Reverend Winford's attention while you throw yourself at him and still don't manage so much as a 'hello, ma'am.'"

She snapped her head to look at him. "See here. I don't throw myself at any man. I showed myself to be a friend for him when he's so far away from home. We're both from the South."

"That's about all you have in common."

"What do you mean?"

Though Marissa had heard it all from Sophie over the years, she maintained interest as David responded to his sister's tired indignations. "The reverend will be polite and obligin' to you, but that's about it. He doesn't see you as a woman to court, Sophie. I'm sorry if the truth hurts your feelings."

Marissa put her fingers over her mouth to disguise a giggle. Sophie disguised her wounded pride with an imperious perch of the nose. "Well, he won't be doing much courting in jail." She took off on her horse, riding it at a brisk trot to the stable.

Marissa and Dusty arrived at the homestead shortly after. "Pa's out back tendin' to the chicken coop with Bernard." David cocked his head in the direction Sophie was going. She had already put her horse in the stable and picked up her skirts to walk around the mud puddles left by slop buckets and feeding troughs. "I'll take your horse for you, Dusty."

"Much obliged, Junior. I appreciate it."

Marissa sensed David didn't want to get involved with the business about to unfold. The boy jumped to his tasks, seemingly relieved to be occupied with a job less demanding than that of contending with his sister.

Marissa followed Dusty around the corner, where the littlest Charlton child, Rosemarie, pulled weeds from her own small vegetable patch, waving as they all went by. They went after Sophie as she stepped through the dim entrance of the coop.

The hens squawked and fussed as their home was being invaded for eggs and a good cleaning by the head of the

Charlton household. Sophie's father swept the floor of the henhouse, swiping at feathers that strayed into his face.

"What's all this?" He looked up when his daughter, Dusty, and Marissa crowded the space at the front of the coop and blocked the filtering sunlight.

Dusty moved for some light to enter. "Sir, I have a need to call upon your courtesy. Miss Pierce needs a safe place to stay for a few hours until she can go back to town."

Sophie barely let him get the second sentence out of his mouth before she swished down the linear walkway of the coop, upsetting the already agitated chickens with her rustling gait. She didn't bother to wait for her father to acknowledge her presence. "Daddy, you'll never believe what happened in town today. Rowe Winford was taken to jail."

Mr. Charlton sneezed. "The reverend?"

"Yes, Daddy. He and Mr. Garth were fighting in the street outside the saloon. David and I saw it all on our way from the locksmith. It was about this here troubling Marissa Pierce."

"Rev'ren Winford's brother tried to force Marissa into the saloon to sign another contract," Dusty supplied. "The rev'ren went in to get her, and the place got plum crazy. He and Jason were near to killin' each other over her. Rowe told me to take her to the safest place I know until things cooled down."

Mr. Charlton's eyes fell upon Marissa. "Are you alright, Miss Pierce?"

She nodded twice. "Yes, sir. I'm worried more for the reverend than I am for myself."

"It's too late for you to fret now," Sophie fired.

"Hush up, Sophie." Her father wiped his sweaty brow, leaving a feather stuck to his forehead. "Your comments aren't helping any. The reverend in jail...great scot, how'd that happen?"

"I just told you, Daddy." Sophie raised her hands,

exasperated. A hen, in its misfortune, walked into it and got a surprising swat on the backside. "Rowe and Mr. Garth started to fighting." Her voice grew shrill as she yelled over the infuriated hen squawks. "Fists, legs, and everything. I knew the reverend looked mighty and all, but I didn't know he could do what we witnessed. You would think Rowe's in love with that woman." Her face wrinkled at the statement, as though declaring it left the combined taste of pickles and turnips in her mouth.

The feather fell from Mr. Charlton's forehead. He gave his daughter an iron-sided, stern look. "There's nothing to be done about it. He is in love with her, and it's none of your business because he doesn't want you."

Sophie gasped. "Daddy..."

"Don't 'Daddy' me. Did you hear nothing of Reverend Winford's sermons on deceitfulness or idle gossip? I suspect they had everything to do with how you behaved so undignified when you invited him to supper and how you go about town taunting other young ladies. I never thought the daughter I raised would grow to be a cruel gossip and rumor monger."

Tears pooled in Sophie's wide blue eyes and collected in tiny droplets on her long lashes.

Mr. Charlton disregarded the performance. "I admonished the reverend last week about his courtship to Miss Pierce, but now I see his determination to have her as his wife." He nodded to Marissa.

She expressed her gratitude with a small smile. Begrudging as his statement was, it was better than outright rejection.

Mr. Charlton's forehead creased with hard lines as he frowned upon his daughter again. "Sophie, perhaps I've waited too long to say this to you. Your mother and I let you become vain and spoiled because we thought you deserved to feel pampered after we came up from working on other people's lands in Louisiana. We did you a disservice. You have become a child that's grown too big for her bloomers." He handed her the broom. "From now on you do your fair share of work on this farm. That will keep you from meddling into the affairs of others until you can learn to occupy your time with more worthwhile pursuits."

He left her to the henhouse and the flying feathers. "Dusty."

"Yes, sir?" Dusty slipped past Marissa out of the chicken coop.

Marissa remained inside the structure, watching Sophie cry silently, still marveling over what her ears had just heard.

Dusty returned. "Mr. Charlton says to take you into the house and get you some tea to drink. He'll take you back to town when things have calmed down. I'm gonna go see about Rev'ren Winford."

"I need to see Rowe too if he's in jail. He can't stay there. You know how long it can take for a circuit judge to make his rounds."

Dusty shook his head woefully. "Don't know what to tell you, Miss Marissa. We sure got into a mess with this one, didn't we?"

The tea Mrs. Charlton served proved refreshing to Marissa's exhausted body and parched throat, but it was ineffective against her anxiety for Rowe. She felt so useless, unable to do anything for him while he was in jail.

You don't have to be alone. A gentle voice whispered in her mind. The tone was a far cry from the harsh, mocking one that had taken residence in her thoughts over the past weeks. On the wagon ride to the Arthurs' home that evening she thought of Rebecca and how the woman asked her if she knew about Jesus Christ. Rebecca told her that God would never leave her. *You must believe that*, she had said.

Marissa wanted to believe that God cared for her and that He was waiting to help. The Arthurs and Rowe experienced part of her troubles, but they had a peace about them. It was their faith that held them together when she was close to losing her mind.

"Here we are." Mr. Charlton stopped the wagon in front of the Arthurs' porch. "Do you need me to speak with Zachary and Rebecca about where you've been today?"

Marissa saw Zachary from the house's open window. Upon seeing her, he hopped from his chair. "No, I can tell them. Thank you, Mr. Charlton. For everything."

The brawny man nodded with a grunt. "I'm not in favor of this union between you and the reverend, but I still think he has potential to be a good preacher. I'll try to put in a good word for him in town and at church. People might listen still."

"I'd appreciate that, and I know he would too."

As Mr. Charlton drove the wagon back in the direction they came, Marissa went up to the house. Zachary and Rebecca had the door open before she could knock. "Did Jason hurt you again?" Zachary asked.

Marissa worried she was going to give the poor man a new set of wrinkles. "No, other than an ink-spattered dress. Mrs. Arthur, may I speak to you alone?"

Zachary glanced at his wife, perplexed. "You don't want me to hear?"

"It's nothing bad." Marissa stepped inside the house and closed the door on the afternoon heat. "Just something that she and I talked about before."

Rebecca shooed her husband to his chair. "It's alright. We'll be in the kitchen."

Marissa followed after Rebecca. They gathered around the cold stove. "What is it? Did something happen that you couldn't say in front of Zachary?"

She ran her hands over the mussed twists in her hair that

Rebecca had so meticulously dressed that morning. "No. I just remember what you told me about God, how He never leaves us. I was mad at you when you said that because I thought you were forcing me to believe as you do. I thought you were trying to control me."

"You were angry about many things at the time. I understood."

"Yes, but now I see what you've been trying to tell me. I'm tired of struggling."

Rebecca touched her hand. "You realize that accepting Christ into your life doesn't make your problems go away. Your fiancé is in jail as we speak."

Marissa grimaced. "I know life won't ever be free from trouble. I just can't do this on my own anymore. If God loves me, I want to see it. I want to know Him."

"Then ask Him to reveal more of Himself to you. Tell Him these terrible hurts you've suffered, how you felt He abandoned you. He'll listen."

"Will you help me?"

"I can pray with you, but you have to ask Him yourself. You have to invite Jesus into your own heart, and you have to do it willingly."

The woman's conviction was sound. Was that why Marissa did not have peace in her own life, because she had not personally invited Jesus to be her Savior? Could He, *would* He, come and take control if she asked? *Let Me help you, Marissa.* The voice was so small, so calm and sweetly beckoning.

In front of her friend she bowed her head and prayed for the Lord and Savior Jesus Christ to come into her heart. Warmth swept inside her where the bitterness had taken root. Her hands stopped aching.

Problems would still come, but she no longer had to face them alone. She had a Protector.

Rowe heard the town abuzz outside. Men, women, barking dogs. They produced an unintelligible clamor as they gathered outside the small jail, waiting for news of the duration of his confinement.

He crossed the floor of the miniscule cell to peer beyond the iron bars at the sheriff. Julian McGee sat at a dark wooden table, his feet propped on top. McGee amused himself with a game of Solitaire that he had spent all afternoon playing. "Yes, sir, you are some preacher." He stacked a red queen in front of a king. "If it weren't for all those witnesses outside, I would think I had been hallucinatin'."

"I didn't intend for this to happen, Sheriff."

Sheriff McGee shrugged. "Most people don't intend to wind up in jail. Folks here think I should just go around and arrest whoever they don't like, but I can't do that without hard proof, you understand me?" He put his feet on the floor and stood. "And I've been lookin' for an indisputable reason to catch that feller over yonder for months."

Rowe looked across the room to the opposite cell. Jason sat in the back corner, most of his slumped form lost in shadow.

"You knocked him out cold when I got to the saloon," McGee said with a touch of admiration. "He'll be nursin' that head for a few days."

"I shouldn't have hit him so hard."

"A woman can make a man do many things, even a man like you. I didn't think much of you at first, what with your holier-than-thou preachin' and all. I thought you were just a soft-headed city boy with no real experience. "

"And now?" Rowe braced himself to hear how far he had fallen from grace.

"Now I think you stand by what you say and defend the

people that need you. That's a real man. You stuck up for that woman when other folk would see her out of town."

"A man with better self-control wouldn't have allowed things to progress to this point."

Rowe still hadn't made full amends with Marissa to let her know that he wished to go forward with the wedding. With this latest fright from Jason, she could be fed up with his half rescues and good intentions. And for all his efforts to be a minister, he surmised that his work was rendered useless that afternoon. Who wanted to go to church to hear a law-breaker preach?

McGee produced a set of keys from his belt. "Jason was bound to get on somebody's bad side. He was lucky it wasn't someone who would've killed him. Well, don't look so surprised." He laughed at Rowe's expression when he approached the cell padlock. "You didn't think I was keepin' our preacher in jail, did you?"

He unlocked the cell door and pulled it open. Rowe was bemused. "I don't want special treatment because I'm a minister."

"You're not getting it. The law in Assurance requires you serve four hours for disturbing the peace within an establishment and for fighting in the streets without weapons. You served that time."

Rowe stepped out, grateful to be able to stretch his legs. His body ached from the fight. His rib cage suffered a bruise and still smarted from Jason's well-placed kick. "What about him?" He gestured to the other cell.

"I'm keepin' Garth. He has to go before a judge for other charges." McGee counted them off. "I found unpaid taxes in his office today. I may also be able to get him for keepin' business after hours and prostitution."

"You didn't know Jason had prostitutes?"

"Yeah, but I could never prove it until his ladies admitted it today. One gal named Simone told me she was headed back to her family in Springfield. Guess when he passed out in front of 'em, they got scared."

Rowe looked at Jason again. With those charges being racked up, the saloon would have to close. The judge in all likelihood would sentence him for maintaining a brothel. "So Jason's contract with Marissa is null and void now?"

"That's right. Don't mean a thing now that he ain't got a business to run."

A blessed flood of relief poured over Rowe. *Thank You.* He exhaled gratefully. "Thank you, Sheriff."

"Say, you need to get goin' unless you want to stay in here longer."

"No, four hours will do just fine."

Rowe made haste for the door. Outside Dusty jumped up from the steps when he saw him. "'Bout time McGee let you out of that iron can he calls a jail. I've been here for hours."

"Thanks for waiting." He clapped the man on the shoulder. "Let's get out of here before this day becomes even more eventful. Where did you take Marissa?"

"To the Charltons. Mr. Charlton said he would drive her back to the Arthurs' later. Did McGee let Jason out too?"

"No, Jason has some dealings to tend before a judge. I'll tell you while I look for my horse."

They departed from the jail building. Part of the crowd had begun to disperse. Those who saw Rowe gave a wave or a loud cheer, to his chagrin.

"Good job, Reverend!" a boy shouted. "That'll teach Jason to pick a fight with you!"

A man whooped. "You're out here with the best of 'em now."

For those who displayed glee at the brawl's outcome, several others showed disapproval.

"Unseemly for a preacher," a red-haired man huffed. "Just outrageous, fighting for a saloon gal."

"I never saw the like from Reverend Thomas," a steel-haired, middle-aged matron provided.

Rowe agreed with the latter comments. He proceeded to walk amongst the crowd without stopping to discuss the happenings of the day. He wished it never occurred. More town approval, more adoration or contempt, when all he really wanted was Marissa's forgiveness and acceptance.

"I want to marry her if she'll still have me, Dusty. I don't care if the threat of contract is gone. This town will either accept us or they won't. She and I can't live for them."

"I'll agree. What are you going to tell the church this Sunday?"

"I'll publicly make my apologies for today's ruckus."

"Yeah, and maybe they'll also stop being so hardheaded about ya'll this time."

But the downward tilt of Dusty's head told of his unspoken doubts.

Chapter 26

WHAT A BRIGHT and timely young man Timothy Lyle was. During the fight at the saloon, the livery worker had found Rowe's horse tethered outside of McIntyre's where he left it. He brought the animal to the stables to prevent anyone from becoming a horse thief. Rowe promised the youth two Seated Liberty Dollars from his next set of wages for the gesture.

Now Rowe rode his horse beside Dusty's stallion to the Arthurs' house. Despite his stiff jaw from Jason's quick fist and the growing ache in his side, his mood remained buoyant now that all but one impediment stood between him and Marissa.

"You still getting married tomorrow?" Dusty flicked the reins for his stallion to turn up the offshoot road to the Charlton farm.

"As much as I want to, I think I need to wait until after this Sunday."

Dusty's mouth dropped to his chin. "You ain't thinking about not getting hitched to her, are you? You just moved a herd of no-good bum steers for Miss Marissa."

"No, but I want to make my apology to the town in church. It's necessary that they understand."

"Can't you do that after the wedding?"

"Not if I want to extend an invitation to everyone as guests."

"Oh." Dusty calmed down and nodded. "Makes sense. Well, guess I'll be seeing you. Can't say I'm not looking forward to watching Miss Sophie clean the stalls."

"What?"

"It's a long story. Maybe your fiancée will tell you." Dusty waved good-bye.

Rowe had no idea what the cowboy was talking about, but it wasn't as important as seeing about Marissa.

He and the animal were getting to the point of exhaustion, but the Arthur home was the last place he needed to go before he could put something in his stomach and see how bad off his fight badges were. He patted his bruised ribs gingerly, grateful to not have anything broken.

Marissa answered the door when he knocked. Seeing her face light up made Rowe's pain diminish. She was safe and unharmed.

"I thought McGee wouldn't release you," she said, throwing her arms around him. "I thought he was going to have a trial for you and everything."

She squeezed too hard on his ribs. With a grunt he took her by the shoulders and held her at arm's length. He regretted not being able to take her in his arms the way he preferred, but it was so much better than never being able to hold her again. "I'm a little sore."

"Do you need Dr. Gillings?"

"No. Between me and Jason, that man's business has increased one way or another since I came here."

She clucked her tongue at his dark humor. "There you go again, trying to take all the blame. I was so worried about you. I heard a gunshot just as we were leaving town."

"There were many gunshots. You probably heard the sheriff firing into the air to clear the crowd."

"That's when he arrested you?"

"Yes, but I don't remember much more than fighting Jason, then getting hauled off to jail with him. Marissa, about the wedding tomorrow."

"I know. I can't expect you to travel if you're too sore to sit and stand very long. Maybe the day after?"

"Later than that."

He heard her breath catch in her throat. "You do still want to get married, don't you?" Her face changed and became somber.

"Of course, but after this Sunday. I must address the town about what happened this afternoon. I'm going to do it at church." Rowe brought her to him in an instinctive gesture of comfort, forgetting his new bruises. The aches and pains promptly reminded him.

She rested her head on his good shoulder, and her delicate floral scent reached his nose, soothing him. "I don't like that you got into a scuffle with Jason, but I understand how it happened and how it affects your position in the town."

"Some people will think I lost my senses and fought him over a saloon girl. Not because of what he did to you *when* you were a saloon girl."

Marissa smoothed down his hair near his ear. "What can be said? Even with Jason locked up and charged, they'll think it anyway. That's just the way it goes."

"I know, but I want to reach the ones willing to hear the truth and to hear my regret for giving in to violence."

She leaned her hand on the doorframe. The soft lantern behind her warmed the tones in her skin, so that she appeared to be lit from the inside. "Will you meet me at the shop tomorrow morning before opening hour? There is one more thing I need to do before we marry. It'll bring me much comfort to put it behind me. I'll tell you more when you arrive."

"I'll be there. What is it you're doing?"

"I'm going to see Jason at the jail." Marissa paused, anticipating an interruption. She spoke again when Rowe remained silent. "He and I have never truly discussed his act of rape.

He must know that he cannot use it to scare me and control me anymore. I'm free now. I gave my life to Christ."

While the news of her conversion was something to celebrate, Rowe's stomach drew tight in knots at the idea of Marissa facing Jason again. Life had the two of them weaving in and out of each other's lives with hardly any rest in between. The lines blurred between abusive father figure, guardian, and swindling employer. He knew that Marissa needed to settle her view of Jason if she wanted to move forward for good.

If it were up to Rowe, and for reasons dealing with Marissa's physical security, he'd tell her to keep her distance from Jason as far as the sun got to the moon by night. However, it wasn't his choice to make. Marissa had to do this for her own peace of mind, or she'd always risk feeling as though she were running away from her problems.

"Do you need me to come to the jail with you?" Lightly holding her, he felt all the tension leave her body in response to his question.

"Yes, if you wish. I would like to have your support."

He was going to bed early tonight, then. "Let me go home to take a bath and sleep. Let's hope the sheriff is in a good enough mood when he sees me there again. I didn't turn out to be the preacher Assurance was expecting, did I?"

"No, you didn't." The edges of a smile crept about her mouth. "But that's not such a terrible thing. You helped the town by exposing a dishonest businessman."

He cupped her face and planted a kiss on her lips. "Goodnight, Marissa. I love you."

She didn't retreat at his words. "I love you too."

Marissa spent the time before breakfast the next morning praying for strength and wisdom in her words. Today would have been the day she married Rowe, but once again, plans had been altered. She put her faith in the fact that God knew what He was doing by delaying them. They both had important matters to settle. Rowe had to speak to the church and she had to break from Jason's hold for good.

Rowe deserved the best she had to offer him as a wife—companionship, tenderness, a mind free of fear, and a heart free from bitterness. The past would always be in her memory, but she couldn't afford to carry it as a burden for the rest of her life.

After dressing and eating, she rode to Zachary's shop. Rowe was already waiting for her in the chair outside the door. He arose stiffly, favoring his leg and his ribs. His heartening smile quelled part of her anxiety.

"I thought we might say a prayer before going to the sheriff's office," he said.

They joined hands and gave thanks to the Lord, asking for guidance and peace for the morning ahead. The chill in the early morning wind calmed as their prayer ended. The sun warmed their backs as they went to the jail housed within the sheriff's office.

Marissa stuck her hand through the iron bars on the door and knocked three times. "Hopefully the sheriff is inside."

"Doesn't someone always have to be present in the building when you have a person jailed?" A look from her, and Rowe remembered where he was in the country. "Right. I forgot how things are done here."

"Elections will be held next year. Maybe Assurance will get a deputy sheriff to help McGee."

The door knob jiggled, and the sheriff stood before them, separated by the iron bars. He pursed his lips to one side. "Well, the reverend's back, eh? I got a letter from your brother to give you. He told me when he left to make sure you receive it." He produced an envelope folded in half from inside his shirt pocket.

Rowe took the letter. "Where is Nathaniel? I haven't seen him since I ran out of McIntyre's."

"I had the blacksmith watch the jail while I escorted the feller to Claywalk last night. I promised I wouldn't put any charges on him if he left town and got on the next train."

Marissa craned her neck to see the letter. "What does it say?"

"It reads, 'Dear brother, I am on my way back to Virginia where I belong. I was wrong for manhandling your betrothed and getting into your affairs. I don't approve of your choices, but you are your own man. I should think our family won't see you again. Live well. Signed, Nathaniel.'" Rowe put the letter back into the envelope. His shoulders heaved. "Well, I can't do anything about that."

"I'm sorry." Marissa's spirits sank at the depressing news. It shook her how Rowe's family was stubborn enough to cast him out for living a life different from theirs.

Rowe put his hand on the small of her back. "I'll be alright, Marissa. They were this way long before I came to Kansas."

Sheriff McGee cut through the thick air of disappointment with a loud cough. "What are you two doin' back here, anyhow? You find another contract to dispute, or another fight you got into?"

"No, Sheriff." Marissa almost laughed at his sleepy-eyed expression and the rumpled hair that was flattened against one side of his head. "I wanted to speak to your prisoner this morning, if it's alright with you. I will be very brief."

"What you need to speak to ol' Jason about? Once the judge gets here and tries him, he's gonna be headed on the train to Missoura to be put in a county jail."

Marissa was satisfied that distance was going to separate them. "I wanted to have some parting words with him.

I promise after that you will never have to bother with me again."

McGee's eyes went to Rowe. "What about the reverend? I can't have Garth cuttin' up when he sees him. You'll have to wait just inside the door."

Rowe touched Marissa on the arm. "Will you be alright?" She nodded. "I will. It's probably best you waited here. Jason might shut his mouth if you stood at my side."

"Time's tickin'." McGee unlocked the iron bars and pushed them open.

Marissa stepped into the stale, dim jailhouse. Her skirts fluttered as a breeze came in behind her, making the lamps flicker and casting her long shadow about the small interior. Daylight trickled in through a tiny window near the ceiling, barely large enough to stick her arm through. The farther she went into the room, the more it smelled of leftover food, cigars, and a neglected chamber pot whose contents had not been emptied in several hours. The floor was permanently stained near a dented spittoon.

Her boots made suction sounds as she moved across the sticky floor to Jason's cell. She saw his long, rangy frame reclining atop the narrow straw pallet toward the back. His coat had been removed and tossed in a pile on the floor beside him, next to a half-eaten bowl of porridge that congealed overnight. "Jason."

His face was toward the wall. She saw movement in his shoulders.

"What?" he replied, muffled, but gruff.

"It's Marissa."

"I know who it is. What do you want? I thought you'd be married by now, or on your way to a justice of the peace."

"I will be, but I needed to speak to you first."

Jason groaned as he sat up on the pallet. Even in the dim

lighting, a large purple knot could be seen rising out of his forehead. "You come to see if I was really in jail?"

"No, I knew of that yesterday."

He stared at the brick wall of his cell and then stood on his feet. Marissa backed away from the bars as he crossed the little space between them. Large-knuckled hands wrapped around the bars. "Again, what do you want?"

Beneath the purple lump she saw who he really was. Jason was more than the violent, quick-tempered, deceitful saloon-keeper she regarded him as for the past three years. He was a darkly troubled and broken man whose ways and means brought him to this point. Something or someone in his past made him turn out harsh and embittered, causing him to believe he had to be mercenary to get what he wanted from life. Marissa got chills as she realized how close she came to becoming like him, had it not been for her newfound faith.

"I want to thank you. Thank you for taking me in after my mother died and for making sure I had food to eat and a place to lay my head. I likely would have succumbed to cholera myself or lived on the street as an orphan if you hadn't intervened."

He continued to grip the bars as he read her face. "You're welcome," he voiced with a hesitating pause, uncertain of where the dialogue was going.

"With that being said, everything else you did to me was wrong. The beatings, forced labor, raping me when I was younger. You tried to train me to become a prostitute. Thank God you failed." A tear gathered in her eye and fell onto her bodice, splotching it. She wiped her cheek with a gloved hand. "I can never in my life undo what you did to me, but I'm choosing to forgive you. It doesn't erase the pain and it doesn't clear you of your crimes, but I won't let your venom poison me for the rest of my life."

Jason kept his mouth shut, looking in her general direction

but never in her face. His knuckles were white around the bars.

"I hope one day you see how wrong you were and ask God for forgiveness. I'll be praying for you. Good-bye."

Marissa turned her back and left him standing at the front of his cell. Rowe awaited her with outstretched arms. It didn't matter if the sheriff witnessed her air all of her unspoken grievances against Jason. The worst for her was over.

Chapter 27

O N SUNDAY MARISSA sat on the end of the middle church pew. She looked to the day with expectation of a better life, with God's promises of mercy and goodness. She no longer felt tethered to the past but was made a new woman of hope and strength. Whatever came upon her now or in the future, she was equipped to persevere.

Marissa knew Rowe possessed the same fortitude. No matter what became of his address to the church today, God would take care of him. He would see to both of their needs.

Zachary and Rebecca came back from talking to their friends and sat in Marissa's pew. The service commenced. Marissa clutched the hymnal in anticipation of her fiancé's address.

Rowe stood after the hymns were sung. He approached the pulpit slowly, almost limping. Marissa saw him lay a hand on his side for one quick moment. A faint shadow ringed around the right side of his jaw.

His injuries looked worse healing than they did when they were fresh. Townsfolk who didn't see him earlier in the week gasped.

"Before I begin the sermon, I would like to make an apology to the town." His voice was raw, tired.

Marissa could practically hear the sound of backs leaning forward from the pews.

"Most of you know what happened five days ago at the saloon. I engaged in a fight with the owner, Jason Garth, over a provocation he made concerning someone close to my heart, Miss Marissa Pierce."

Rowe looked out to the congregation where she was seated. Finding her, he visibly relaxed before returning to his delivery. "It's no secret now that I am in love with Miss Pierce. The wisest thing to do would have been to not give in to the temptation to fight Jason for her, but I'm only a man, and I'm far from perfect. I also happen to be the pastor of this church. That position heightens the extent of my imperfections. I am aware of them, as I am sure you are. I hope that you'll forgive me and allow me to continue ministering to the town. And Miss Pierce and I both hope that you will accept our decision to become husband and wife."

The sanctuary was quiet before seasoned farmer Elmer Hudson stood up. "Well, I'll be, Reverend. I can't speak for everyone else, but I forgive you. You did us all a favor with that Jason."

The congregation reacted first to the interruption. Then a few added their assent, one by one. The farmer, encouraged, went on.

"It's good to have a preacher that falls short like we do but still tries to make his wrongs right. That lets us know that he's one of us."

Mr. Charlton joined him while Sophie remained silent in the pew, her face turned down in a sulk. "And I know Miss Pierce is a changed woman, given her actions of leaving the saloon. I also remember what the reverend said about shunning people. Most of us came to this town to start over. We can hardly fault others for trying to do the same."

A number of the congregation members expressed surprise at the approval shown Marissa from a previous detractor. Marissa herself didn't expect him to make a visible stance in church.

People spoke their approval, while others clapped theirs. It went on for a full minute. Marissa stood when people began to rise on their feet. Rowe had his church. He established himself.

He caught her eye as she broke into a wide smile. His mouth moved, but she couldn't hear over the applause. He stepped down from the pulpit. "Would you come to the front of the church, Marissa?"

She stalled, meeting the sea of faces as the townsfolk swerved around to look at her. Rebecca gave her skirt bustle a push. "Go on. Go to your groom."

She slipped out of the pew and came down the left side of the aisle. On her way she passed people she had known throughout her life, and some she met in recent years, those who were friendly and those who didn't care much for her. All of them witnessed her take Rowe's extended hand.

"I love you," he said. "Do you think they believe I'm sincere?"

She mouthed the words beneath a round of applause. "I think so."

Epilogue

B Y THE POWER invested in me, I now pronounce you husband and wife. Rowe, you may kiss your bride."

Marissa's heart radiated with joy at the Claywalk minister's words. She gazed into Rowe's smiling face before her eyes closed for his kiss.

The guests applauded. Zachary and Rebecca Arthur, the Charltons, and a good portion of the church congregation were all there to congratulate them.

The church was decorated in white and dark rose, Marissa's favorite color. Handmade silk roses, a wedding gift from Linda, draped the first several rows of pews and the bridal bouquet. Marissa looked radiant in her gown of white, with square neck edged in lace. The skirt fanned out and trailed behind her.

Dusty came up to Marissa during the reception and swept her into an unexpected squeeze, planting a big kiss on her mouth. "Tradition, Reverend," he joked to Rowe before he could protest.

"Just as long as you keep that tradition to one." He clapped the cowboy on the back heartily.

Dusty sputtered from the force of the contact. He grinned as he regained his merry composure. "Well, Mrs. Winford, how does it feel to trade your garters in for lace?"

Marissa glanced up at Rowe admiringly, proud to carry his name. "I won't know until my husband takes one from my leg and you catch it, Dusty."

Dusty frantically waved both hands in front of him.

"Nope, that's alright. I have no intentions of gettin' hitched anytime soon."

"It's really not up to you," Rowe teased. "Besides, if you keep pestering Miss Charlton for a dance, you may find yourself at the aisle soon."

Dusty ran a hand through his sandy-colored, careless hair. "I wouldn't practice reading the marital rites if I were you."

When the time came for the bridal toss, Timothy Lyle caught Marissa's garter and Linda Walsh the bridal bouquet.

Marissa watched Dusty stroll over to Sophie as she returned to her table. She heard him speak to the girl. "Looks like you and I won't be getting hitched until after the liveryman and the dressmaker."

Sophie cast him a proud look with her wide eyes. "I'm sure it didn't take a flower toss to tell you that."

"For all your changed ways, Miss Sophie, you still turn those pretty thorns up at me."

"I should say, Mr. Sterling, I am on my best behavior toward you because of this auspicious occasion. I'll ask you to do the same."

He gave her a wink. "One day you'll see, Miss Sophie. One day."

Marissa chuckled and turned away. One day, indeed. She had a feeling that her dear friend Dusty had turned prophet.

The reception went on into the evening, when the newly married couple thanked their guests and said their goodbyes. Rowe took Marissa to her new home by the lake. The moon shone on the calm water that night, illuminating it like a mirror of highly polished lustrous silver.

"Welcome home, Mrs. Winford." Rowe carried her across the threshold of the cabin and up the stairs to their bedroom.

"Look at this." Marissa was pleasantly surprised when

she saw the room furnished with polished, gleaming woods, plush blankets, and a scattering of rose buds upon the bed. He set her down upon the thick mattress.

"My heart," he whispered, running his hands through her pinned hair until it spilled over her shoulders and down her back. "I've waited for this."

She brought his fingers to her lips. "I can stay in your house forever now."

He kissed her mouth. "As far as I'm concerned, you will never leave."

He dimmed the oil lamp on the table.

COMING IN FALL 2014 FROM
BRANDI BODDIE

BOOK 2, BRIDES OF ASSURANCE

A WINDSWEPT PROMISE

Chapter 1

Assurance, Kansas, April 1871

"Sophie, your jambalaya's burning!"

As her younger brother David called, Sophie Charlton dashed out of her bedroom and ran down the stairs into the kitchen. A pot gurgled on the stove, brown bubbles spilling out from under the lid. She grabbed a towel from the table and hoisted the pot by its side handles away from the hot surface. Her brother simply stood by the stove and watched.

"David, why did you let the flame get too hot underneath?" She opened the firebox door and inspected the kindling as it burned to ash.

"Ma said not to touch the food. It's for the Founders' Day Festival."

"It wouldn't have been for anything if you had let it burn. This is supposed to go into my prize-winning food basket."

"I called you to come downstairs, didn't I?" He gave her a matter-of-fact look.

"At the very last moment." Sophie shut the door to the stove and went to the pot of jambalaya. Stock trickled down into the grooves of the table. Steam rushed out as she lifted the lid.

"Is it bad?" David craned his neck to see.

"No, the stock boiled a bit too high, but I think it'll still be alright." She grabbed a long-handled spoon and prodded the mixture of sausage, peppers, and tomatoes. "Next time you see it boiling over, take it off the stove. Don't call me all the way from upstairs."

"Well, it's your dish. I ain't the one trying to enter some silly town belle contest."

"It's not silly." Sophie glanced at her freshly laundered and starched yellow-striped dress to make sure no stock had spilled on it. A lady's garments should always be pristine. "And 'ain't' isn't a word, David. You're sixteen years old. How often must I tell you that?"

"That I'm sixteen years old?"

"No, that your grammar is—oh, never mind. I don't have time for this. I have to get ready. Go outside and help Dusty with the wagon." She left the pot to cool on the table's surface next to the pie she baked earlier.

"Dusty's already done hitchin' the horses up. See out the window."

Sophie viewed the family's wagon and the team of horses waiting in front of the walkway on the warm April Saturday. The pair of bay geldings stared past the fence at the main road into town, black blinders strapped on their heads. Her father's hired worker was nowhere to be seen. "Where is Dusty?"

"Probably getting cleaned up. You should finish dressing too."

Stating the obvious. She hated how her brother thought that made him sound clever. "Do not touch that pot. I'll be back down in a moment."

Sophie returned upstairs and passed her parents' room, where she could hear her mother and father talking as they got ready for the festival. She grinned to hold back a squeal. Finally she was allowed to compete for the chance to be crowned Assurance's town belle. Her mother thought she had been too young to compete in prior years, and last year her family wasn't in town for the festival at all. This was Sophie's chance.

She walked into her bedroom where Linda, her best friend, waited to help with her hair and dress. "Did it burn?"

"The jambalaya? No, but I hope it'll still taste good. Men will bid on that basket."

Linda rolled her eyes. "Sophie, you know most of those men are coming out to see you. They don't care if you stick a brick in that basket with a saucer of hay."

"But the contestants' names won't be on the baskets to let them know which is which."

"I don't think you have anything to worry about. Now, what ribbon do you want to lace your bonnet with, the yellow or the light blue?"

Sophie chose the ribbon in Linda's left hand. "The blue. We need to hurry. The judging starts in less than two hours."

Linda had her hair dressed and assembled with a bonnet within fifteen minutes. Sophie checked her reflection with the mirror on the vanity table and pinched her cheeks hard until her efforts were rewarded with two pink marks. "I have to pack the food."

"It can't be cool already." Linda fluffed Sophie's bangs out from beneath her bonnet with a comb.

"It'll just have to cool on the way to town, then. Go get in the wagon. Mother and Daddy should already be out there. I'm coming." Sophie picked up her skirt and ran on the tiptoes of her cream side-button boots.

She followed mud prints from a pair of larger boots into the kitchen. "Dusty!"

The cowhand stood over her pot of jambalaya, holding the lid in a dirt-stained hand. Bits of grass fell from his canvas shirt to land dangerously close to the rim. "Howdy, Miss Sophie."

"Dustin Sterling, you get your filthy face out of my

jambalaya." She marched up to him and snatched the lid from his hand. "What do you think you're doing?"

"The smell was real good drifting outside. I just wanted to know what you were makin'." His Texas drawl remained calm and unhurried as he stood to his full six feet. Sophie gripped the lid tighter. How would it look on top of his head in place of that ever-present tan Stetson? If only she could reach that high.

"You're worse than David. I'm making this for the festival. And why aren't you cleaned up? We have to leave in minutes."

"It won't take long for me to scrub my face and change shirts. Is that food for lunch or supper?"

"Neither. I'm entering my basket for bid as part of the town belle contest."

He looked over her with hazel eyes. "You sure make a pretty picture with that bonnet."

"Why, thank you." The urge to put the lid on his head receded. "Hopefully the judges will think so too."

"Can anyone make a bid on the baskets?"

Sophie pulled two bowls from the cupboard and a large porcelain jar. "Any man. Every lady in the contest will have one, but the baskets are unmarked. The winner gets the basket to take on a picnic with the lady who prepared it."

"So the winner won't know who he gets to take on the picnic?"

"That's right." Sophie scooped the still-steaming jambalaya out of the pot and ladled it into the jar, careful not to spill any of it on her dress. Dusty should know she didn't have time to sit and visit with him. Why did he persist in trying his luck? Cowboys. So brash and overconfident. She sealed the jar with a cork.

"I just might enter a bid, seein' as how I know what will be in your basket."

She paused. "You wouldn't."

His teeth shone white in his tanned face as he grinned. "Dusty, no. It's my first time entering the contest. Don't spoil it for me."

"How am I spoiling it for you? You should be happy you got at least one guaranteed bid on that—what did you say that rice and sausage was called?"

"Jambalaya."

"Jambalaya," he repeated in sing-song. "Smells almost like what the Chili Queens sell on the river down in San Antonio."

"Hmph." Sophie hunted for a basket on a lower pantry shelf. The more nondescript a container, the less chance he'd have of distinguishing it from the others. "I'll have you know this is a Creole recipe passed down in my family, not some street fare to peddle around on a cart. You wouldn't like it anyway. I made it spicy."

"I'm gonna place a bid on that basket, anyhow."

She huffed. "Why? Picnic or no picnic, I don't want you trying to court me. I told you before."

His dirt-caked boot heels made dull clicks on the floor as he went through the side entrance of the kitchen that led to the bunkhouse out back. "And I told you before. One day, Miss Sophie. You'll come around."

"Not today or any day that my feet touch the green earth," she called after him.

He whistled a tune that carried across the field.

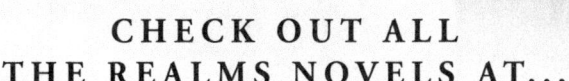

FREE NEWSLETTERS
TO HELP EMPOWER YOUR LIFE

Why subscribe today?

- ❑ **DELIVERED DIRECTLY TO YOU.** All you have to do is open your inbox and read.

- ❑ **EXCLUSIVE CONTENT.** We cover the news overlooked by the mainstream press.

- ❑ **STAY CURRENT.** Find the latest court rulings, revivals, and cultural trends.

- ❑ **UPDATE OTHERS.** Easy to forward to friends and family with the click of your mouse.

CHOOSE THE E-NEWSLETTER THAT INTERESTS YOU MOST:

- Christian news
- Daily devotionals
- Spiritual empowerment
- And much, much more

SIGN UP AT: **http://freenewsletters.charismamag.com**

8178